Alongside his accidental career in finance, TIM EWINS performed stand-up comedy for eight years. He also had a very brief acting stint (he's in the film *Bronson*, somewhere in the background) before turning to writing fiction. His first novel, *We Are Animals*, was published by Lightning Books in 2021. He lives with his wife, son, dog and cat near Bristol.

Praise for *Tiny Pieces of Enid*

'A powerful and poignant story about love and loss, frailty and courage. Beautifully imagined and peopled with strong, endearing characters, this book both gripped me and touched my heart'
Hazel Prior

'A poignant, poetically fractured tale of two women trapped by circumstance, the bittersweet circle of life and love. I found it strangely hypnotic and very moving'
Beth Morrey

'One of the most beautiful portrayals of love I've ever read. I will always remember Enid and Roy'
A.J. West

'A wonderful, poignant and powerful read. I absolutely loved it. There's such tenderness there, and great clarity too'
Matson Taylor

'Incredibly moving. The pages are filled with characters you can't help but fall in love with. A heartfelt tale focusing on the realities of life with dementia'
Louise Hare

'Beautiful. Quietly devastating and utterly believable. I loved every second of it'
Ericka Waller

'Compelling and sad and hopeful, but never sentimental. A warm hug of a book, as comforting as chicken soup and just as nourishing'
Polly Crosby

'A poignant, warm and thought-provoking story'
Susan A. King

‘Like a bird layering twigs to build a nest, Ewins has woven together past and present, memory and reality to create a startlingly beautiful novel with complex characters walking the fine line between fragility and strength. An absolute delight’
Laura Besley

‘He’s done it again. *Tiny Pieces of Enid* is warm and moving and full of heart. If it doesn’t make you cry more than once, I don’t know what’s wrong with you’
Frances Quinn

‘A moving and thoughtful examination of memory and ageing, with a central character you can’t help but root for. A wonderful story about love, friendship and the “tiny pieces” that make us who we are’
Rebecca Ley

‘A beautiful, sensitive, lyrical portrait of the reality of living with dementia, and the twists and turns our lives take, up to the very end’
Victoria Scott

‘I was deeply moved by this delicate, beautiful book. A sensitive and poignant story’
Victoria Dowd

‘A powerful and moving story about dementia and love that lasts a lifetime. Unflinching and heartbreaking. I love it’
Nicola Gill

‘Moving and timely. Brilliantly evokes the drama of the everyday that may go unnoticed by others but, for those involved, takes on Titanic proportions. Superb’
Tom Benjamin

‘A beautiful book, its pages suffused with warmth and humanity. It truly moved me and will stay with me for a long, long time’
Louise Fein

'This lovely book reminds us that character and love both outlast our lifetimes and these are the things we remember in the end'
Jacqueline Sutherland

'Tim Ewins brings his own brand of quirky to something very different. If you don't love Enid like a member of your own family after reading this book, then you have no soul!'
Cat Walker

'Enid is a delight. Her story tells of a love that defies everything, while the rendition of her mental decline is drawn with sensitivity and compassion. I couldn't put this down'
Paula Greenlees

TINY PIECES OF ENID

TIM EWINS

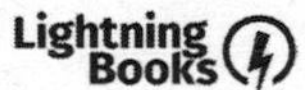

Published in 2023
by Lightning Books
Imprint of Eye Books Ltd
29A Barrow Street
Much Wenlock
Shropshire
TF13 6EN

www.lightning-books.com

ISBN: 9781785633102

Cover by Nell Wood

Typeset in Dante MT Std and Zona Pro

British Library Cataloguing in Publication Data
A catalogue record for this book is available from the British Library.

For my mum,
and for her mum:
Nanny Enid

PART ONE

TWIGS AND WEEDS

1

ENID LAY MOTIONLESS on the hospital bed with her eyes closed. She wasn't sure if she could move; she hadn't tried, and she didn't want to.

'Your mother hasn't responded for over twenty-four hours.' The voice was short but not unfriendly, not addressing her. Male and important. Enid couldn't guess the voice's age though. In fact, she found she couldn't recall any numbers at all. 'We'll keep her where she is. We can monitor her through the night, and then do a few more tests in the morning.'

Enid hadn't understood any of the words that the voice had said, but she had the distinct feeling that they had been about her, rather than to her. She wanted to know where she was, but her eyelids didn't even flicker when she attempted to open them. Some parts of her body felt numb, and the other parts ached. She felt sure that she was positioned flat on her back with her arms by her sides, arranged like a corpse. It was not comfortable.

'Alright, thank you. I'll come back tomorrow. What time's best?'

Enid knew that voice. It was her daughter's. Always busy. She had such a fast-paced life. Enid didn't recognise any of her daughter's words though. It was like she was talking a foreign language. Enid wanted to say her daughter's name, to ask for comfort, to ask for her husband, Roy, but her mouth didn't move. What was her daughter's name? She began to doubt that it could be her daughter at all. Or even that she had a daughter.

'Visiting hours are 5.30 to 6.30.'

'Ugh,' Enid's daughter exhaled, short and busy. The abruptness frightened Enid. Where was she? Where was Roy? She seemed to be paralysed, but her mind was restless. Other noises came into focus; a squeaking wheel, a repetitive beep, stifled, distant chatter. Then, her daughter again.

'I can move some things around.'

Enid felt someone lift her hand, squeeze her palm softly, and then lower her fingers back to the bed, but it wasn't Roy.

'Alright Mum, I'll be back tomorrow. I love you.'

A few winters ago, Roy woke up at three in the morning to an empty bed. Where was Enid? She'd always been a good sleeper. She was fiercely proud of it in fact. She'd never sleepwalked as a child, and unlike many of her friends, she hadn't suffered from insomnia as an adult. Unless they had over-indulged in some homemade wine and lost track of time, Enid was rarely up between the hours of 10.30 pm and 6.00 am. It was almost a source of frustration for Roy, who had always been a very light sleeper.

So, to wake up and find her gone was worrying. He sat up in bed, though it hurt to do so. His back ached. Slowly, he pushed his legs out from beneath the warmth of the duvet and fumbled his feet into the fluffy slippers Barb had given him the previous Christmas. When he stood, his legs shook under his body weight. He was already wearing his pyjamas, but he put on his dressing gown for added warmth and made his way downstairs.

Enid wasn't in the kitchen, as he'd hoped she would be. The lounge was empty too.

'Enid,' he whispered, though he hadn't meant to whisper, so he cleared his throat and tried again. 'Enid.' There wasn't any reply. He walked through the kitchen and into the lounge-diner. Enid wasn't there either. Roy quite often sat in the lounge by himself with a cup of tea at 3.00 am, but now the house felt even more still than usual. Quieter, although he knew it couldn't be. The knowledge that Enid was not asleep upstairs was unsettling. He became agitated and scared for his wife, and for himself. He shuffled to the phone in the hall.

They had an old rotary dial phone which they'd purchased just a few decades ago. Who should he call? He couldn't dial 999, although that seemed like the obvious choice. Both Enid and Roy had reached an age where any call to the emergency services might result in them never returning to their own home again.

Of course, Barb would be over in a flash if he rang her. She only lived down the road and it would be reassuring to see her, but she would insist on ringing the police. Barb thought that Enid and Roy's concern about having to leave their home was unfounded, but she was young. She was young and she was wrong.

Enid had Sellotaped a piece of notepaper listing the contact numbers of their family and friends on the wall above the phone; some had been crossed out and replaced over the years, some were faded, and some had been traced over again and again with an ink-deprived pen. Roy ran his finger down the page.

The number at the bottom wasn't in Enid's handwriting. It read: *Neil (neighbour) – 07800231340 – call if you need me.*

Roy started to dial. The number didn't lend itself to a rotary dial phone, and as the dial returned back to its starting position, Roy heard a noise upstairs.

He froze.

'Enid?' Silence. After a few seconds the dial tone sounded from the phone to indicate that it had timed out. Roy replaced the receiver and slowly shuffled upstairs. He could hear someone sniffing sadly. It was his wife.

He found her in the spare room sitting on the bed. She was looking down into her hands and quietly crying.

'Enid,' Roy said softly, and she looked up at him.

'I'm lost,' Enid said.

'You're at home. This is the spare bedroom.' Roy shuffled over to the bed and held Enid's hands in his hands. It was worth the ache in his back when he bent down. 'You sleep in the next room, with me.'

Enid allowed him to guide her out of the spare bedroom and back into their shared room.

'How silly,' Enid said when they were back in bed. 'Lost. Dear me.'

'Indeed,' Roy agreed, 'whatever next?'

Time dragged at the hospital. Barb scrolled through Facebook on her phone, reading aloud any posts innocuous enough to be overheard by nearby patients on the ward.

'Vicki's having another baby,' she said. 'You wouldn't know her, Mum. She used to work with Calvin.' Barb looked up at Enid, and then back at her phone. 'Claire says she's bored. I don't know why she posts that stuff.' Barb sighed. She could really do with Calvin now. He was better at this kind of thing than she was, and he'd always got on so well with Enid. Calvin wouldn't be reading other people's posts to his mother-in-law; he'd be soothing her properly. Except he wasn't Enid's son-in-law any more, and Barb's pride wouldn't allow her to just ring him and ask him to come to the hospital. He lived in a different house now, with a different woman.

'Oh, Mum,' Barb said, leaning her elbows on the hospital bed and feeling deflated. 'What are we going to do with you?' She sighed, before widening her eyes.

Enid's lips had moved, ever so slightly.

'Mum, can you hear me?'

Enid let out a small whimper.

'Mum?'

Another noise escaped Enid's lips, a fragment of a distinguishable word. Both her eyes twitched, and then one of them opened, wide and full of panic.

Barb had never seen her mum stare like this. Her whole face was strained, one eye open, tight-lipped and intense.

'Mum,' she said again, 'it's Barb.' Enid looked at her desperately. 'You're awake.' Then, maintaining eye contact, Barb called back into the ward for help.

Enid's mouth opened, and with stiff, visible cramp in her

jaw, she groaned loudly.

'Are you OK?' Barb asked her mum, again wishing for Calvin. It was a stupid question, but she felt so helpless. Enid breathed in deeply, as if trying to suck back saliva that wasn't there. Barb could hear footsteps rushing down the ward towards them.

'It's alright Mum. You don't have to talk. Try to relax.' Enid's one open eye appeared even more intense for a moment, before it calmed, and then shut.

As the months had gone by, Roy had grown used to Enid's night-time walks. Sometimes he would wake up at the same time as she did, just from the movement of the duvet. Enid never made much sense when she woke, but a gentle hand on her arm and another on her back would normally calm her down. Occasionally, she would become violent, which wasn't ideal because Roy's body wasn't quite what it used to be, but it was nothing he couldn't handle. Once, she had hit him on the leg and a bruise had formed but it could be hidden under his trousers, and it hadn't hurt. Watching his wife deteriorate though, and watching her grow scared at the loss of her own identity; that hurt.

What worried both Roy and Enid most, were the nights that she left the bedroom without him noticing. When it started, Roy would normally find her in the spare bedroom, just as he had on that first night. After a while, Enid ventured further. A few times Roy had found her in the lounge arranging the placemats on the coffee table, and once she'd been in the kitchen hiding the kettle. The day after the kettle incident had been the first time they'd discussed the night-time walks in the waking hours.

'We wouldn't have been able to have a cup of tea,' Roy said as he flicked on the kettle. Enid looked at him with a questioning face, and he smiled at her. 'I found you trying to hide the kettle last night.'

'You didn't,' Enid replied with a hint of surprise in her voice. 'Oh.' She put her hand to her mouth and Roy chuckled kindly.

'I did,' he said, and they didn't discuss it any further.

Enid could smell hospital food. Some kind of cooked meat. Stew maybe? The smell was warm and surprisingly comforting. She was sitting upright, looking forward. She could see Roy, hunched in a foam chair on the other side of the bed. He looked anxious. Next to Roy sat Barb. The height of her chair made her appear shorter than she was. Enid had no idea how long they'd been there. Perhaps just a few seconds, perhaps a week.

No one except Barb had really said anything for quite a while. Enid had tried but found that she could only produce confused staccato sounds without any meaning, so she'd given up. Occasionally, Barb would look down at her phone and Roy would study the ward, inspecting his wife's new temporary home. It wasn't an uncomfortable silence, and Enid was happy to have her family with her.

Like Roy, Enid was finding it hard to understand the institution in which she had become a prisoner. The woman in the bed next to her kept jolting her head backwards before letting it roll forwards again. On the opposite side of the ward, a tall, gaunt, bald man sat in his bed, raising his hand and opening his mouth as if he were about to say something, but then he'd close his mouth and lower his arm again.

Enid enjoyed the repetition.

A woman in a navy-blue uniform walked over, greeted Barb and Roy, and then turned to Enid.

'I'm going to ask you to drink some water again, Enid.' Enid flinched. This kept happening; people in navy blue would turn up, asking her to drink water, and then they'd stare at her neck, heads tilted. Enid eyeballed her, letting her know that she was onto her.

'Mum,' Barb said, 'Eleanor is a speech therapist. She wants to help you talk again.'

So, the woman was called Eleanor. Knowing that she couldn't warn her daughter about the woman in navy blue, and that she couldn't ask for help from Roy, Enid turned away from all three of them. The tall, gaunt, bald man in the bed opposite was asleep now. He slept on his back with his mouth open and his arms by his sides. Enid focused hard on his breathing, evident from the repetitive movement of his top lip.

'Mum,' Barb said, and then again, 'Mum.'

Eleanor interjected in a voice full of compassion, hiding her true agenda, whatever it was.

'Enid, we've been through this. That's Malcolm, and he is a nice man.' Enid ignored her and focused harder on Malcolm's lip, frowning.

'She's been doing this quite a lot,' Eleanor said to Barb. Not to Enid, and not to Roy. 'She gets very agitated, very quickly. She's safe while she remains here on the ward, but it's worth remembering that when you start making decisions about her future.' There was a pause and Enid lost focus. She sighed, looking at the man across the ward, wondering who he was.

Barb put her hand on her mum's forehead. Enid couldn't remember her daughter ever having done that before.

'Can we…?' the woman in navy blue asked, pointing away from the bed and looking at Barb.

'I'll give you two a bit of alone time,' Barb said eventually. 'I'll be back in a few minutes, Dad,' and then louder, 'Mum, I'll be back in a few minutes.' Enid looked at her, expressionless and without moving her head. Both Enid and Roy watched as Barb and the woman in navy blue walked to the desk at the other end of the ward. When they stopped, Roy turned back to Enid.

'They keep telling me you've had a succession of small strokes love. Now, I don't know what that means exactly, but it's why you're finding it difficult to talk. Hopefully, what with all they're doing now, you should be right as rain soon. You can come home.'

Enid didn't understand everything that Roy said, but she enjoyed the intimacy of being alone with him.

'And don't worry, love,' Roy pressed his forefinger and thumb together and drew a line in front of his mouth. 'I've not told them anything.'

One afternoon, the doorbell rang. Roy had just put the kettle on. He called through to Enid, who had settled herself on the couch, ready for *Countdown*.

'I'll get it, love.'

He opened the door as far as the chain would allow and peered out.

'Hello?' he asked. 'Can I help you?' It was Neil, their neighbour. Roy and Enid liked Neil, but they didn't socialise much, probably due to the age difference. In his mid-thirties, Neil was just a kid.

'Hi, Roy.' Neil tilted his head to see through the gap and gave a small wave.

'Hang on.' Roy shut the door, undid the chain, and opened it fully. 'What can I do for you?'

'Well,' Neil said, rubbing the palm of his left hand with his right uncomfortably. 'It might be something of a sensitive subject, but it wouldn't sit right with me if I didn't ask. Is Enid alright?'

'Yes, of course she is,' Roy said a little defensively, and then, as if to qualify that Enid was indeed alright, he continued, 'She's just been to the shops.' He didn't know why he said it. It wasn't true.

'Right, well, maybe you'll know about this anyway, but it's just that, last night, when I came home, I heard someone round by your garage. I thought I should check – you know – Neighbourhood Watch and all.' Roy frowned with interest. 'The thing is, Roy, there wasn't anyone there, but when I turned to leave, I saw Enid in your caravan looking through the window at me.' Neil shuffled uncomfortably. 'I'm pretty sure she was crying.'

Roy felt his stomach drop. He'd found Enid himself that night. She'd been in the caravan, even more distressed than normal. The memory hit him hard and he felt his eyes sag with emotion. Catching himself in front of Neil, he stiffened his expression, and became resolute.

'Yes,' he said. 'That's right, she was in the caravan for a while last night.' He paused, thinking. 'She was sorting it for our holiday.'

'Oh, so is everything alright then? Like I say, she seemed pretty upset and it was very late.'

Roy forced a laugh. 'No, she wasn't upset, and she certainly wasn't crying,' he chuckled again. 'Whatever next?' Neil stared at Roy, and Roy's face straightened. 'She's fine, Neil.'

'Who was that?' Enid asked when Roy came back into the lounge.

'Oh,' he sighed before sitting down. 'Neil from next door. Cup of tea?'

'I'll get it, love, you've just sat down.'

Roy watched *Countdown*'s Nick Hewer start the timer on the big white clock, but he didn't look at the letters.

How hadn't he noticed Enid getting out of bed last night? Neil would never have seen her if he had. She must have used the side door to get to the caravan. A string of bells and birds made out of cotton hung on the back of that door. The bells tinkled every time the door was opened. Roy was surprised he hadn't been woken by the sound of the bells. Or maybe that was what had woken him. Maybe Neil had seen Enid mere minutes before he had found her. Perhaps the fault here lay in the deterioration of Roy's own body, and the slowing of his joints.

Roy knew their house so well. He and Enid had lived in it since before they were married, yet somehow, now it felt like the rooms were getting smaller. The walls were closing in and he felt suffocated. Even bloody Neil was checking up on them.

Roy had noticed that Enid had become more emotional as she grew older too. Sometimes, when Barb and her daughter Alex went home after their weekly visit to Enid and Roy's house, Enid would become so consumed by love that she'd cry.

'Why are you crying?' Roy would mumble, without making eye contact.

'Oh, we're just so lucky, aren't we, to have them, and to

have each other? I love you all so much,' Enid would reply, and then she'd tense her whole body with her arms held up in front of her face, fists clenched, eyes scrunched, mouth and cheeks smiling.

Then Roy would do what he always did when he felt uncomfortable: he'd make two cups of tea. It wasn't much, but he did his best.

Enid walked in with two cups of tea on a tray, and she handed him his.

'Thanks, love,' he said. 'I think we deserve a holiday. How about we dust off the old caravan?'

2

Barb watched as the paramedics manhandled her mother into a wheelchair. 'It's alright, Mum,' she cooed, hoping that the sweet tone would hide her guilt. 'You don't need to worry.'

Decisions had been made, all of them by Barb, most of them against Roy's wishes and none of them in front of Enid. Roy had fought to have his wife back at home with him, which Barb had found touching but unrealistic. Instead, encouraged by healthcare professionals and her ex-husband, she had found a care home specialising in dementia, not far from Enid and Roy's house. Today, her mum would have to move into it.

'You always used to tell me about the time I had to go in an ambulance,' Barb said as her mum was raised, chair and all, into the back of the vehicle. 'Do you remember? I was six and I'd twisted my ankle.' A look of recognition passed across Enid's face. Perhaps she did remember.

Half an hour later, the ambulance pulled up outside the old Victorian building which Barb had picked for her mum to live in, and, ultimately, to die in. As the paramedics hauled Enid out of the back of the vehicle, Barb looked out towards the shore. She could see the pier from here, the distinct shape of the bay below and a few scattered boats which were always seemingly motionless in the estuary. On a clear day, her mum would be able to see Wales.

'It's nice here Mum – I promise – and you'll have lots of visitors.' Barb touched her mum's shoulder. She wasn't used to going against her dad's wishes and it felt wrong.

'Can you see the sea?' she asked her mum, holding back tears. Enid didn't move. 'It's Clevedon Sea, Mum. It's really close to home. Dad lives just over there.' She pointed out of the window in a general westerly direction. If her mum were to walk for fifteen minutes and take several correct turnings, she could, theoretically, end up at Barb's childhood home, where she had once lived, and where Roy still lived. The proximity suddenly felt meaningless.

'Hopefully you'll be able to move back one day,' Barb said, knowing that this wasn't true and feeling guiltier with each word. 'Earlier,' she continued, unable to stop herself, 'when we were getting into the ambulance, you remembered me twisting my ankle when I was six. That's a really good sign, Mum. That's your memory coming back.' But Barb could see the blank expression on her mum's face. Even if Enid had remembered Barb injuring her ankle earlier, she clearly couldn't remember having had the conversation now.

Once the wheelchair was clear of the ambulance, Enid found

herself perched on a steep hill overlooking the sea. It was picturesque, and there was something familiar about the line of trees that stretched along the road, before the sea's horizon, but it was not home, and Roy was not there.

'Remember what we said, Mum: this is going to be your home, at least for a bit.' Barb had bent down in front of her, continually forcing eye contact. 'Your room is that one,' Barb pointed behind Enid, so she couldn't look even if she wanted to. 'You'll be able to see the sea from your window.' Enid curled her top lip. She wanted to knock her daughter over with the wheelchair, but it was being held by a man she didn't recognise, and she wasn't sure she'd be able to move it herself anyway. Instead, she held her head back for a fraction of a second, then lurched forward and spat.

'Mum? Are you OK? You're dribbling.' Enid narrowed her eyes, shooting Barb a venomous look. It must have worked, as Barb stood up and took a step back. She frowned at Enid, then walked away from the ambulance. With a jolt, Enid found herself being pushed, against her will, towards the building. As Barb reached the entrance, the thick wooden door swung open and a balding man in glasses forced his way out in one large and hurried step. He looked at both Enid and Barb for the briefest of seconds, and then turned to see the door closing behind him.

'For fuck's sake,' he muttered under his breath, just loud enough for Enid to disapprove. The door opened again and a man in a knitted jumper and dark tinted glasses held it open from inside.

'Thank you.' A short, dark-haired woman walked through, nodding gratefully. She was holding a toddler in one arm, and the hand of a young boy in the other. Blonde curls bounced across the toddler's blotched but pale face as the woman walked.

'Come on,' the bald man snapped at her as the door closed again. 'Quickly.'

Enid flinched. Had the woman flinched too? No. Maybe. She gave Enid a weak smile as she moved to the side to let the wheelchair pass.

'Stop fucking dawdling,' the man spat at her, ignoring Enid completely, 'and get in the car.'

That was the first night that Enid saw the parrot.

The curtains were shut, and the lights were off, but the room remained light. Other people, younger people, would still be outside. The bed felt comfortable enough, but it wasn't Enid's. The covers were all wrong; the duvet was thin and there was a blanket across the bottom. Enid could feel its weight on her feet. Her usual duvet cover had a collage of woodpeckers, and this one had patchwork print, though it was still rather pleasant. Her hands were by her side, tucked in unnaturally tight by the bedsheets. She shrank her head lower, so that her neck was fully covered by the sheet folded over the top of the duvet.

Had she taken herself to bed? She couldn't remember having done so. Perhaps she had drifted off and just woken up now. Things always seemed to come to her slower when she'd already been asleep. She heard an unfamiliar scratching sound outside, several scratches in quick succession. A broom against gravel? Roy's fingertips on his unshaven stubble? Then a scream, short but natural-sounding, before silence again. Enid lay motionless, waiting.

She looked around the room. The ceiling wasn't hers: it was the wrong shape. Rather than the usual four corners, Enid could see five, and the walls looked flat, not textured with the wallpaper she had chosen, that Roy had hung all those years ago. Near the door hung a watercolour of a pier which Enid recognised as Clevedon Pier, though she didn't recognise the picture itself. A white wooden structure concealed the radiator and the walls looked freshly painted.

There was that scratching sound again.

Perhaps she was at Weston General. She had grown used to sleeping in hospital beds from time to time. Here though, she had the room to herself, and it was more homely than the shared wards in the hospital. No, this couldn't be a hospital. It wasn't as homely as an actual home though – not any home Enid knew anyway.

On the bedside table, she could see a plastic cup of water and a book. Enid recognised the cover of the book, and the creases down the side. It was hers; it belonged in her house, and she must have read it, or be reading it still, but she didn't know what it was about, and the words on the spine meant nothing. Still, the very presence of the book had a somewhat relaxing effect. Maybe Roy had put it there. Another scream, a click, and then the rustling of leaves. The sound of the sea. Then silence.

One of the curtains blew into the room, and for a moment the walls grew even lighter. Enid tutted to herself quietly. She must have left the window open. It couldn't be bedtime yet; she could see the pink of the sky outside. Again, she heard scratching outside the window. This time it continued, over and over. She closed her eyes tightly and waited for it to stop. Her knuckles clicked in an attempt at forming a fist, but the scratching grew louder and louder. The clicking started up again. The scream, when it came, was in Enid's room.

She opened her eyes and froze. Her body felt even stiffer than usual. The curtain was back by the window and the scratching had stopped. The clicking had stopped and so had the screaming.

She turned her head and saw the parrot for the first time. Its feathers were in stunning shades of red, blue and yellow. The bird tilted its head, watching Enid, taking her in. Enid looked at its thick black toe, white markings down to the claw, tapping the edge of the dresser. The bird opened its beak, and Enid listened to the caw, to the scream, short and natural.

She listened to the large blue wings scratching against the bird's body as it moved along the dresser, closer to her bed. She kept her focus on the one eye that she could see, the white iris camouflaged in the bird's markings, the pupil dark and expressionless.

As the bird cawed again, the sound pierced through Enid. She clutched at the sheets but her fingers only pressed against them, unable to bend at the knuckles.

Click. Click. A softer caw. One wing rose upwards. The tip of it touched the birds head, gave a quick scratch, and then lowered back down again. The bird craned its head forward, and then, for just a few moments, it was completely still.

Enid looked at the parrot and saw herself; the red on the inside of her own drooping eyelids, the wisps of grey through her dyed ash-blonde hair, the blue of her veins showing through the skin on her cheeks.

I know you, she thought.

3

'Can I go outside yet?' A six-year-old Barb was sitting in front of an only half-eaten bowl of porridge. Her mum walked out of the kitchen into the lounge-diner with a saucepan and a tea towel in her hands.

'Absolutely not, Barbara,' she said, pointing the saucepan at Barb. 'Not until you've eaten your porridge.' Barb let out a long moan.

'But I don't want to eat my porridge,' she said.

'It's nice,' her mum replied. She didn't really seem cross, but Barb could tell that she wasn't going to give up until she'd eaten at least some of the stupid porridge. 'Why don't you want it anyway?'

'I want to see if my birds are in their nest.'

Her mum turned and walked back into the kitchen. 'Those birds,' she said, despairingly. 'It's nice. Eat it.'

Barb had noticed the nest around a week ago, when it had consisted of only a clump of twigs and weeds. It hadn't been woven then, and it didn't resemble a place where anyone could raise a family. When she'd tried to touch it with a stick, by way of investigation, her dad had stopped her.

'It's a nest,' he had told her. 'Some birds will lay their eggs there, and then we'll have baby birds in the garden, but only if you leave it alone.' Since then, Barb had watched eagerly, from the other end of the patio, as a small brown blackbird had worked hard to shape her home.

'Mum,' Barb called from the table, and she heard a vague acknowledgement from the kitchen. 'I don't want to eat my porridge because I love you.'

Her mum came out again, this time laughing. 'Eat your porridge,' she said.

The nest was positioned low down, close to some yellow paving, covered only by the same weeds that propped it up and some faded white guttering. The small brown blackbird felt safe. Some of the twigs were touching the house wall, leaving only one exposed side to protect from predators. She snuggled into the soft fine grass that she'd placed inside, on top of the mud which she'd laid for stability. For the third time this year, she prepared to lay.

Across the lawn, near the bushes at the end of the garden, she could see the orange of her partner's beak pointing skyward. His black body looked striking against the green of the morning grass. His beak dipped down to the ground, and then quickly rose back up again, dripping with moisture from the morning dew. It glistened, and from the nest, she sang to him.

His beak dipped again, back up, back down, and back up again. He turned his head, then dipped back down again, this time emerging with an earthworm in his mouth. From the nest, she watched her partner's dark-brown eyes blink, and she blinked back twice. The markings on her chest, clearer than his dark feathers, moved rhythmically as she did.

He didn't fly back. Instead, he hopped through the grass, creating a gentle spray of dew behind him.

As he reached the nest, she watched him drop the lifeless earthworm close to her chest in the straggle of grass in front of her. They both looked at it for a few seconds before she pecked hard into the worm's middle. She was going to need the energy. They had done this twice already this year and it was about to start again.

Roy walked into the lounge wearing a buttoned-up white shirt with dark-red braces, and grey pinstriped trousers. It was the weekend, so he wasn't wearing his suit jacket. He was a proud man, and he liked to dress well.

'Dad,' said Barb, elongating the word into a whine, 'I don't want to eat my porridge.' Roy looked in the bowl and kissed his daughter on the back of her head.

'It looks nice,' he said. 'Whyever not?'

'Because I love you,' Barb smiled, showing her top and bottom teeth.

A few moments later, Roy walked into the kitchen to find the kettle already at boiling point.

'Tea?' Enid offered, and Roy nodded, seeing that the bag was already in his mug on the kitchen worktop. Enid bent low to the fridge, pulled out four carrots and then stood to drop them in the sink by the window.

'What…' Enid started, slowly turning her head to look at her husband, 'is Barb doing in the garden?'

'She didn't want to eat her porridge,' Roy said, 'because she loves me.' He grinned knowingly at Enid, before pulling her into a tight embrace next to the sink. 'And may she never eat porridge again,' he said.

4

Olivia closed the door behind her and placed Oona, her just-mobile toddler, onto the hall floor. She could hear David, already in the kitchen, opening the fridge, the clink of a glass as he grabbed a beer. Dillon, Oona's brother, barged in behind her.

'Wait,' Olivia instructed both kids, as she took her own shoes off and threw them in the rack. Then, as Dillon wriggled in her grasp, she pulled off his trainers, seconds before he managed to reach the living-room carpet. Finally, she kissed both of Oona's legs as she undid the Velcro on her daughter's tiny boots. She stood and smiled, watching her littlest toddle into the lounge after her brother.

'David,' Olivia called, walking purposefully into the kitchen. David was standing by the table, necking his beer. Soon, he'd be in the pub and she would be left to sort the children.

'David,' she said again, full of confidence, 'can you please not raise your voice to me like that in public?'

'Like what?' David asked, seemingly genuinely unaware of how he'd sounded outside the dementia home. 'I didn't raise my voice, I didn't shout at you. What are you talking about?' It was true, Olivia thought, he hadn't shouted at her – not exactly. He would never shout at her with the children present; it was more the tone. It was the tone he took when he actually did shout at her, at home, when the children were out or asleep.

'You know what I mean,' she replied, confidence already fading, 'just, please not in public. One of the carers saw you, and the lady in the wheelchair too.'

'The guy who opened the door for you, you mean? Why do you care so much about what *he* thinks?' David placed his beer on the worktop, still three-quarters full. 'And the lady in the wheelchair has dementia, Liv. She barely thinks at all.' He picked the bottle back up just seconds after putting it down, and took a short, quick swig, all pent-up energy. 'You're so melodramatic.' He strode past her and upstairs. Olivia looked at her watch. It was still early evening; he wouldn't normally leave for the quiz for another hour.

The children would have sausages, waffles and beans that night. A quick dinner. She needed to get them bathed and into bed. Olivia liked seeing David's dad at the dementia home, even though David did dominate the conversation, but it always meant a late night for the kids. She turned the oven on and slammed the pan down on the hob. Calm, she told herself. Calm.

The thing was, when David became angry with her at home, Olivia was never sure whether it had been as bad as she always thought. He never did it in front of the children and he always downplayed it afterwards. Olivia doubted herself. She'd always scared easily and was a bit of a wallflower. David was right; she was melodramatic. But although he hadn't shouted, this time she felt sure that his tone had been out of order, because they hadn't been alone. The old woman in the wheelchair had flinched.

Olivia heard David walk back downstairs and through the hall into the lounge. She heard him tickle Oona, and then say something in a goofy voice to Dillon. Both children laughed. Olivia smiled; he was such a good father. She heard the footsteps approach the kitchen, and felt her husband stand behind her, rest his head on her shoulder and wrap his arms around her waist.

'I'm off to the quiz,' he said. He smelt of aftershave and beer.

'You OK?' Olivia asked, and she felt his body deflate against her back.

'I'm a little hurt,' David replied, 'you make me out to be a monster. I'm not a monster.' He paused. 'But I don't think you mean to do that, do you?'

'No,' Olivia said. 'I don't. I'm sorry.'

5

Enid was sitting on a bed that she didn't know, in a room which she just couldn't quite put her finger on. She was sure that Barb had told her why she was there, but Enid had either misunderstood, or couldn't remember.

Two large wardrobes and a chest of drawers with an oval mirror stood against the wall. On top of the chest sat a picture of Roy. Enid recognised the frame, but it didn't live there; not on the drawers; not those drawers anyway.

The frame, the picture of Roy, and her handbag, which Enid had placed by her side on the bed, were, in fact, the only familiar items in the room. There were two doors; the one through which Enid had entered the day before, and another, mysterious door. Who had been with Enid when she'd first arrived? She couldn't picture a face. Possibly male. Pale skin? Maybe. A beard? Possibly stubble. Trustworthy? Absolutely not.

Enid grimaced. It still hurt to stand, but now, after what felt like a lifetime of practice in the hospital, she could just about manage it without help. Slowly, she walked over to the picture of Roy and tried to talk to him. The words came unformed and short, breathy. Even if Roy could hear her, he wouldn't be able to understand.

Picking up the frame, Enid looked hard at the picture and said everything she needed to say, but this time without words. Then she put Roy, along with his frame, in her handbag on the bed.

Back at the mirror, Enid looked at herself. Her hair was greyer than she expected, with only hints of blonde dye here and there, and her skin was older. How old was she? Enid tried to think but she couldn't come up with any numbers, let alone her age. She understood the general concept of counting, but numbers themselves were devoid of meaning. If Enid could remember the word depicting her age, she wasn't sure it would mean anything.

The big glasses surrounding her eyes were familiar – they must be hers – but she wasn't sure about her earrings. Where had they come from? She took her glasses off and put them in her bag.

She picked up her handbag from the bed, opened the bottom drawer and pushed the bag to the very back. She closed the drawer, re-opened it, and stood thinking for a moment. Was the bag well hidden? She picked up the pillow from her bed and squashed that into the drawer too, in front of the bag. The drawer didn't shut properly any more.

Now satisfied that no one would find her belongings, Enid planned her escape. There were two doors; the one through which she had entered the day before, and another, mysterious door. Who had been with Enid when she'd first arrived? She couldn't picture a face. Possibly male. Pale skin? Maybe. A beard? Possibly stubble. Trustworthy? Absolutely not.

They had come through one of these doors, but Enid couldn't remember which one. Whichever it had been, she didn't want to go back through it now. It was full of old, sick people. Enid walked cautiously to the door on the other side of her bed.

Her hands, thick with arthritis, fumbled around the handle and eventually pushed through to a bathroom, although not a bathroom that Enid recognised. She was trapped.

Back in the room, Enid looked at herself again in the mirror. She wasn't sure about her earrings. Where had they come from? She decided that she would hide them just in case. She took the earrings out of her ears and looked for her handbag. Where was it? Not on the bed where she'd left it. Where was Roy? His picture wasn't on the chest of drawers any more. There was no way that she could live in this room. The bed didn't even have a pillow.

6

Sometimes Roy visited and, less often, or potentially even more often, Barb visited. Sometimes Barb brought Enid's teenage granddaughter, Alex, with her, and sometimes she didn't. Alex never visited by herself.

Everyone talked so much, and although Enid could understand most of what was being said, she found it hard to respond. Once a thought had formed in her mind, she'd have to put it into words, which inevitably led to stammering. Stammering prompted other people to suggest what Enid might be trying to say, and this would cause her to lose her trail of thought altogether. She was always being told that her speech was getting better, but she felt as good as mute.

She knew that she was losing periods of the day too. Barb sometimes told her that Roy had visited that morning, but Enid wouldn't always remember seeing him. Sometimes the carers talked about Barb as if they'd only just seen her, but Enid would have no recollection. She wanted to remember time spent with both.

What made her feel even more lonely were the vivid memories she had of her more distant past. She remembered the excitement she had felt in the waiting room when Barb had been about to give birth to Alex, her first and only grandchild. She remembered the summer nights she had spent drinking wine with Roy in their garden. Enid remembered her home, where, presumably, Roy still was.

There were no recent memories though, nothing of that day, or of that week. As time went on, Enid's surroundings became more familiar, but as far as she could tell, nothing ever happened in them, not any more. Enid didn't know how long she had lived in her new room, but she was certain that only one event of any interest had ever happened there.

It was an event that only ever came to Enid in the early evenings when she was in bed, when the curtains were shut, the lights were off, and the room remained light. When other people, younger people, would still be outside, lighting bonfires on the beach, or walking their dogs along the front. A memory of scratching and of clicking, of bright reds, tropical blues and blazing yellows; of a head tilting, a scream; a caw; a warning.

Olivia sighed inwardly. As usual, David was dominating the conversation. His dad, Martin, had always been a quiet, gentle man, and Olivia had always found the contrast between him and his confident and outgoing son rather stark. She and Martin used to have quite a close relationship, but since he'd moved into the care home she always visited with David and neither she nor Martin managed to get a word in edgeways. She found her gaze drifting. Besides Olivia, David and his father, there were three other people in the conservatory.

The first was an elderly woman with purple-rinsed hair. She was pushing a toy pram and intermittently talking to the baby doll inside. David had asked her to be quiet when they'd first arrived, much to Olivia's shame. Olivia recognised the other two. The faded blonde-dyed grey-haired resident sitting just opposite and to the left of them was the poor soul who had witnessed David snapping at Olivia outside the home just two weeks ago. The woman's visitor, presumably her daughter, had also been there. Olivia wanted to hide. The younger woman opposite stood up and pulled her bag onto her shoulder.

'I've got to go, Mum.' Olivia had been right: mother and daughter. She kept her face down, but listened in.

The elderly woman found it hard to speak, but when she eventually managed to force her sentence out, Olivia heard her ask when Donald would visit next. The younger woman laughed.

'Don't let Dad hear you say that,' she said, still laughing, though kindly. 'You're not married to Donald any more, Mum. You mean Roy.' After a pause, the younger woman continued. 'Look, I've got to go. I love you, Mum.'

Olivia listened to the sound of the woman's flat boots leaving the conservatory. When she glanced up, back to her own family, she caught a glimpse of the elderly woman looking puzzled and touching her forehead, just above her right eyebrow.

'I've got my quiz tonight,' David was telling his dad. 'We lost to "The Know it Ales" last week, but we're going to thrash them tonight. I can feel it.' He clenched both fists and gritted his teeth with excitement. Olivia watched Martin smile at his son. It was a smile that gave away his complete disconnect from the conversation, but also conveyed the unquestionable love he had for his son. Not that David noticed.

There was a loud groan from one of the other rooms behind them and Olivia turned. It wasn't an uncommon noise in the home, but it always unsettled her. No one else seemed to worry much though. There was another groan and the woman with the purple hair looked up from her pram and stared hard at Olivia, placing her index finger up to her lips.

'Shh,' she spat angrily. 'The baby's sleeping.'

'A friend of yours, Dad?' David scoffed, and Martin frowned at him. David turned to the woman. 'Sorry, can you leave? We're trying to talk.' The woman hardened her stare at Olivia, and then left the room, leaving the pram behind her. 'Some parent she is,' David said, with clear spite in his laughter.

'Oh,' the remaining woman opposite said, seemingly unintentionally. Thankfully, David ignored her. Olivia noticed that she was now looking at them. Maybe she'd been eavesdropping, Olivia thought. Or maybe she was just staring. Who knows how ill she is?

'How about you, Olivia?' Martin asked, finally finding a turn to speak. 'Are you going to the quiz?' Olivia opened her mouth.

'Olivia doesn't do quizzes, Dad,' David answered. 'It's not her thing.' Olivia gave Martin a little smile.

'Oh, no, it's not my thing,' she said. It was true; it wasn't. 'And we've got the kids to think about.' There was a brief silence and Olivia felt the need to plug it. 'Anything to keep him out of the house,' she said, forcing a laugh. Martin nodded at her, kindly.

'She likes to wait up for me, though,' David continued, 'so we can talk about my evening when I get in.' And then he snorted.

'Ha.' The elderly woman opposite burst out one sarcastic, staccato laugh. Again, it was seemingly accidental, but it was enough to make Olivia, David and Martin look at her. The woman tried to say something but couldn't seem to find the words.

'Uh…um…'

Olivia wondered if the woman remembered her from the other week, or whether she had created the incident in her own head. Maybe there wasn't anything to remember. Olivia knew she could be a little melodramatic sometimes.

Eventually, David and Martin turned away and David resumed talking. One of the carers – dark tinted glasses and a woollen jumper – came into the conservatory and knelt on the floor by the woman opposite. She was, again, Olivia noticed, touching the skin above her right eyebrow.

'Would you like me to take you back to your room, Enid?' the carer asked in a low, soft, Scottish accent. The woman looked at him, lowering her hand as she did, and Olivia could see a faint white scar on her forehead, partially hidden in the creases of the woman's skin.

'Ready? Up we go.' Enid felt the strength of the carer as he held onto her arm to help her to her feet. Duncan was a muscular lad through that jumper, but Enid could stand up by herself now and always felt a little irked that people insisted on helping her.

She looked down at the floor as she shuffled past David, but gave a private smile to Olivia, and was happy to see Olivia return it quickly, before looking away.

As Enid walked past the abandoned pram, she peered inside. The doll didn't have arms, or a mouth, or the smooth plastic skin that she had expected. Instead, she found herself looking at a dark shiny beak, folded blue wings and a bright red, feathered head.

Click.

Click.

Click.

'Come on, Enid,' Duncan broke in, gently, still ushering her by the arm. 'Leave the doll.'

They were only a few metres away from Enid's room when she forgot who Duncan was. She stopped shuffling forward and started to shake.

'Enid,' the stranger said gently, in his low, soft, but unfamiliar accent, 'just a few more steps now.' Lightly, he pulled at her arm. Enid scrunched her eyes tight. Using her free hand, she hit the stranger across his chest. She felt him let go of her and she opened her eyes.

'Oh,' she said, and immediately regretted what she'd done. How could she have hit someone who was helping her? The man smiled kindly and held back onto her arm.

'Just a few more steps, Enid.'

'Awful,' Enid managed to say, the fully formed word taking her by surprise.

'I seem awful, Enid, I know. But I'm Duncan. You know me.' Enid couldn't think of any other words.

She couldn't find the right words to say that she had been talking about herself.

7

Like most, Enid's first marriage had started happily. She'd met Donald when she was twenty, having only had one previous boyfriend. He had been older than Enid; tall, well-dressed, slicked-back hair and confident. They had gone to the same school. All of Enid's friends had fancied him, and Enid had fancied him too, though neither she nor any of her friends had ever talked to him. She'd always felt sure that a man who dressed as well as he did would be a gentleman.

She was still living with her parents when Donald approached her four years after she'd left school. She had been on her way home from the printers where she worked as a secretary, and he had sidled up to her and asked to meet her one Saturday. She hadn't thought about him for years, and the proposition had felt completely out of the blue, but still, she had practically swooned.

'Me?' she had asked, taken aback.

'Yes, you,' Donald had laughed. 'I don't know if you remember me – we went to the same school.'

Enid hadn't been able to stop herself from giggling. 'I remember,' she said, and Donald's face told her that he knew she did.

'I see you walking this way every day, and I just thought…'

'Oh, what a fool I am,' Enid interrupted. 'Yes, yes of course I'll meet with you.' Then, just to make sure she had fully understood the implications of the question, she said, 'Just me, alone?'

Donald had laughed again. 'You're adorable,' he said.

That Saturday, they had met by the pier, walked along a windy, pebble-dashed sea wall and sat outside one of the cafés that lined the front. No. 5 The Beach. Enid ordered a cup of tea and a water. Donald ordered a cup of tea, joking that he'd prefer a bitter.

Donald told Enid about his family: Mum, no Dad, a little sister whom he was extremely protective over, and about his friends: a group of four, including Donald, who were all interested in old motorbikes. Donald worked with cars, but his heart was with bikes. Enid rested her chin on her hand, elbow on the table, and took it all in. Donald made jokes and Enid laughed. Donald touched her hand over the table and she felt weak. Donald asked to meet her again and Enid giggled and nodded.

The second date was just as good as the first. Donald told Enid what he remembered about his dad, and how his absence had affected him. His dad had walked out on his mum when Donald was nine. That was why he was so protective over his little sister, who must have been five at the time, Donald mused.

He told Enid about how he and his friends had pulled together their savings – small by their own merits but collectively sizable – and purchased an old motor to tinker with during the evenings. A few of them worked at the mechanics with him, so they could plan what they wanted to do when they were at work. Enid was impressed, Donald was so smart.

By the end of their first year together, Enid and Donald were spending at least one day a week in each other's company. Enid would spend the other days looking forward to their next date. After knowing each other for just thirteen months, they had their first fight. It was over nothing big; Enid had walked home from work a different way two days on the trot, and Donald had wondered why. It had been settled pretty quickly, and after fourteen months, Donald had insisted on taking Enid to retrace their first date.

They met at the pier and walked along the seafront. They normally walked hand in hand now, but today Donald insisted that they didn't, recreating the magic of the previous year. Even with the explanation, Enid had assumed that something was wrong. Donald told her stories about his week and gave her updates on the motor he and his friends had been working on. He was in good spirits, and that calmed Enid's worries. Eventually, they came to No. 5 The Beach, the same café that they had visited on their first date. Donald didn't ask her what she wanted.

'Two cups of tea please, and a water.' He looked at Enid and smiled. 'Though I'd prefer a bitter.'

The café was practically empty, so they sat on the same table that they had done fourteen months before. Donald reached across it and touched Enid's hand just as she picked up her cup of tea. The tea spilt, just a little. She put the cup down and looked up at Donald, apologetically.

'Enid,' Donald said. He was looking directly into her eyes, and she noticed this as being different somehow, though she couldn't put her finger on why. 'There's a reason why I wanted to retrace our first date,' he continued nervously. 'You're so beautiful, I could look at you all day, every day.' He looked hard into Enid's eyes, and there was a happy silence between them. 'I should have asked you this on our first date, as soon as I met you. But hopefully now,' he paused as he fumbled in his pocket, 'isn't too late.' And then he produced a ring.

Enid looked at him. She wanted to hear the words, to live the moment that she'd dreamed of.

'Will you marry me?' Donald asked with casual confidence.

'Of course,' Enid replied holding out her hand, wedding finger raised. 'Yes, of course I will. I can't wait to tell my family.'

Donald knelt on one knee, put the ring on Enid's finger and then they both stood up and kissed. When they had sat down again, Donald cleared his throat, a show of clearing the nerves that evidently hadn't been present.

'So, tell me, what am I marrying in to?' he laughed. 'Tell me about your family, your childhood.' And it occurred to Enid that up to now, he hadn't asked anything about them.

Enid knew that her mum had wanted her to marry. There had been pressure to find a man ever since she'd left school at fifteen, but when Enid had brought Donald home, she'd found her mum quiet and stand-offish. She knew that this was no reflection on Donald himself. Since she'd left school, Enid had started working and found her own way in the world, without a man. She assumed that her mum's attitude had changed simply because she didn't want Enid to forfeit her independence.

'Stay together,' her mum had told her after Donald had left the house one afternoon. 'Court each other by all means, but don't get married; not now.' It was a strange thing to say, Enid thought, but when had she ever done what her mother had told her? If she had, she'd be married already, probably to Bill, her first boyfriend, and he had children now.

'Your mother just worries about you,' Enid's dad had reasoned later that night. 'Donald seems like a nice young man, but you're her little girl; that's all.' Enid's dad had been wrong. In the run-up to the wedding, her mum continued to fall quiet when Donald came to visit, and she often retreated into the kitchen, muttering under her breath when Donald took a seat in the lounge.

Luckily, Donald's mum was more welcoming to Enid, and after the wedding the couple had lived in her spare room – Donald's childhood bedroom. After a year, they'd managed to save up for a small two-up-two-down near town. They'd been trying for a baby but told themselves they'd been lucky not to have been successful up to this point – not before they'd moved into the new family home anyway.

8

Roy surveyed his garden through the glass patio doors. Really, he ought to move his chair to this spot, he found himself standing there so often. He liked to watch the birds – their quick, sudden movements, their inquisitive head tilts. He liked seeing them knock food from the feeder, and then gather it up again from the lawn. Food knocked from the feeder offered Roy the prospect of something to do. It would need restocking, for the next batch of birds, or for the same birds, next time.

There was life in the garden. When Roy turned, he would be back in the house, alone and in the silence. When Enid had lived with him, they had enjoyed the garden, but in a different way. They had grown grapes and made English wine. Roy had tended to the bushes and flowers while Enid hung the washing out. They had lived in it, been a part of it, making movement along with and among the birds, the ants and the spiders. Now,

Roy just watched. A separate entity. Nature the play, and he the audience.

It would be May soon. Spring had come early, and the grass was long. Before Enid had moved out, Roy had mowed regularly, keeping both the grass and the shoots of wild garlic that sprang high between the blades, short and under control. Now the lawn was high, and the garlic even higher.

'A new lawn season,' Roy said, out loud and to himself. The last time he had cut it would have been September, he thought. He would likely have been alone then too, but Enid would have been inside, and she would have come out when he'd finished and commented on his work. The knowledge of her presence in the house would have made the work less lonely. Today he would be cutting the lawn only for himself, and the birds.

'Well, someone has to do it,' he said to himself by way of motivation, and walked slowly through the kitchen and out of the side door towards the garage. He heard the familiar chime of bells coming from the string of birds which Enid had hung on the door. A familiar sound, which, for the past forty-five years, he had never paid much attention to, but seemed to hold so many memories now.

Sunlight shone through the garage window, illuminating the workbench and the old wine fermenter sitting on top of it. Below the bench, Roy could see a few bottles of homemade white in a crate, keeping cool and saving refrigerator space. The gardening tools were in the shadow at the back.

Roy stretched his legs in preparation and found that they ached a little in the thighs. He leaned to the left, and then to the right. His back was tight. Not painful, but stiff. Maybe he shouldn't mow the lawn – not today. He should wait until his body has loosened a little. He picked up one of the bottles and looked at the label. It read *'Wine'*. Enid's handwriting.

'Alright,' he spoke aloud, turning to leave the garage. He'd mow tomorrow.

The first sip tasted sour. Roy was in the lounge, facing his blank TV. He had no interest in watching anything. He grimaced at the wine and placed the glass back down on the coffee table. After a minute, he picked it up again and had another sip. Not good, but not as bad as the first. Again, he placed it down on the coffee table. When he picked up his glass for the third time, it was for want of something to do, rather than for the wine itself, but he found that he was acclimatising to the taste. By the time he'd finished the glass, he wanted more.

In the kitchen, Roy poured himself another glass before returning to the lounge. Enid would love this, he thought. They always enjoyed drinking homemade wine together, usually in the garden, but sometimes in the house. He wondered what she would be doing now. He pictured the room in which she now slept, the dining room where she ate her meals with the other residents, and the conservatory which was considered the 'social room'. She would be in the conservatory, he thought, if she was happy. If she was scared or worried, she'd be on her bed. She should be here, with a glass of the wine they'd made together last summer.

Roy had protested and fought to have his wife home again, but there had been nothing he could do. A group of professionals, along with Barb, had excluded him from pretty much all their discussions, and yet, still, Roy felt guilty for letting this happen.

The glass was empty again. He wobbled slightly on his way

to the kitchen and had to steady himself using the dining-room table. He reached up to the cabinet and brought down another wine glass. He filled it, along with his own, and carried them both back into the lounge. He placed them both on the coffee table next to each other, one in front of his spot on the sofa, and the other in front of Enid's.

They weren't heavy drinkers; just casual. They'd only normally drink if they had company or were enjoying a peaceful night together. Rarely would they pour themselves anything just to watch *Strictly* on a Saturday night. Roy remembered one Christmas at Barb's when Enid had accidentally had one too many and lost her earring in the toilet. Barb and Alex still laughed about that Christmas now. That was before Barb and Calvin had split up. Calvin had offered to drive Enid and Roy home, though he'd had a drink himself. In the end, both Enid and Roy had stayed in the spare room.

He wondered if things would have been different now, had Calvin not left Barb. Probably not, he concluded. Enid would still have suffered the strokes and moved into a dementia home, and if anything, Roy would have had even less of a say in things.

He yawned and looked at his watch. It was only 6.30 but he could barely keep his eyes open. Picking up Enid's untouched glass and his own empty one, he stumbled to the kitchen, swaying slightly. He'd only had three glasses, he thought, indignantly.

Roy threw the full glass of wine down the sink and washed them both. He dried Enid's glass and put it away, leaving his own to dry on the draining board. He felt stupid for pouring his wife a glass of wine in her absence, and he didn't want to be reminded of it in the morning.

9

The toilet seat lid was down. Enid held on to one of the bars on the wall and lifted the lid. She jolted her head back in disgust. The water had been covered up with toilet paper and whatever was underneath emitted a foul smell. Some people can be really disgusting, Enid thought, frowning.

Once she had finished her business, she stood, pulled her trousers up, only managing it on the third attempt, and went to flush. Other than a silver square on top of the cistern, there was nothing. No handle to push down, no chain to pull.

'Well,' Enid said to herself, before groping, with trembling hands, down both sides of the toilet. She stood for quite some time, staring at the toilet, before decisively ripping piece after piece of toilet paper from the roll and dropping them into the bowl. When every inch of the contents was covered, Enid put down the toilet lid, and washed her hands.

Olivia always felt bad leaving Martin at the end of visits, but Martin himself didn't seem to mind. He'd smile and tell them to pass his love onto the children. They really should bring Dillon and Oona soon. It was always just so much easier when they were at school and nursery, but Olivia knew that Martin would like to see them.

'See you next week, Martin,' she repeated, as she and David left his room and headed for the exit. At reception, one of the carers, Duncan, leapt forwards to open the door to them both.

'See you both soon,' he said. Olivia walked out first, thanking him. As she did, she felt Duncan gently usher her through with his free hand.

'Yep, OK, bye,' she heard David say behind her. They walked down the steep drive to the car, David slowly overtaking Olivia with each stride. 'Know him, do you?' he asked.

'Who?' Olivia asked. 'Your dad?'

David turned abruptly. 'The good-looking fella at the door,' he said.

Olivia was taken aback. 'The carer?' she asked, genuinely confused. 'Sort of, I suppose. He works at the home.'

David snorted, turned and started walking again. 'He was a bit touchy-feely, don't you think?'

Olivia didn't know what to say, so she didn't say anything – just followed, several feet behind David, to the car. She hated it when he acted like this, especially in public. It gave such a bad impression of him when he could be so charming. She found herself wishing that Dillon and Oona were with them. David never snapped at her with them around. He was such a good dad, though she often wondered whether she would still feel the same way when Oona grew up, into a young woman.

Anyway, Martin would love to see the kids. Next time, she decided, she would bring them.

A knock.

'Enid,' a voice called from outside the bedroom door. Enid stood in the bathroom and tried to reply, unsuccessfully. Another knock. 'Enid, my lovely, can I come in?' It was a woman's voice. The door handle was being pushed down when Enid re-entered the bedroom.

'Hello, Enid, how are you?' Kara, one of the carers, beamed at Enid and walked over to where she stood. 'I'm just here to change your bedding.' She smiled again and started changing Enid's pillowcases in a silence that was surely intended to be comfortable, but that Enid found oppressive.

'Oh, Enid,' Kara said, holding up some cutlery from inside Enid's pillowcase. 'I'll need to take these back to the kitchen when I'm done.'

Enid stammered nervously.

'N…uh… I have…n…no I…d…think.' She stopped to steady her voice, looked at Kara, and spoke firmly. 'Mine.' Kara smiled a scrunched-up smile.

'I think they're from the kitchen,' she replied. 'They're yours when you're eating.' She pushed her hand back into the pillowcase intrusively and bought out a plastic fish. 'This is from the dayroom,' she said, 'but you can keep it in your room for the time being. Shall we take it out of your pillowcase though, eh?'

Enid didn't respond. It felt like shakedown. She didn't want to admit to anything, and she didn't want to be in any more trouble.

'Mine,' she repeated. This time, Enid fully believed herself.

'Alright, my lovely,' Kara agreed, pocketing the cutlery. 'Have you just used the loo? I thought I saw you coming out after I knocked.' If only Enid could find the words, she would give this young woman a lesson in manners. 'Did you have trouble with the flush this time?' Kara walked past Enid and into the bathroom, throwing the last pillowcase on the bed as she passed. 'Nothing to be ashamed of, Enid; they're tricky things, these flushes.' Kara walked back into the bedroom. 'Do you want me to show you?' Enid stood silently, defiantly, so Kara went back into the bathroom to flush without her. 'I'll just have a little tidy-up in here too, while I'm doing it,' she called out.

Enid walked to the open window. The sky was a clear blue, tinted at the horizon to suggest that the sun would soon set. Enid recognised the shape of the rocks jutting out into the sea, and she recognised the pier that could only just be seen poking out behind them. She was close to home, and she was close to Roy. Enid knew that, but she didn't know how she would get there.

There was a clock on her chest of drawers now. Barb had brought it for her at some point, but the numbers were meaningless to Enid, no matter how much she concentrated on them. There were other ways of telling the time though, she found: the colour of the sky; the number of visitors in the conservatory at any one time; the heat and flavour of the meal she was eating. Now the sky was telling her that soon, someone would come and help her change her clothes and get her into bed, much like she had once done for Barb.

She could hear the gentle waves lapping in the bay below,

and the occasional seagull laughing at the thought of whatever it would steal next. Chips, maybe a fish.

Footsteps interrupted the gentle sounds of nature. Enid peered out. She could see David further down the drive. He was partly concealed by the bushes outside Enid's window. He looked angry – or busy. It could be busy.

Kara came out of the bathroom.

'All sorted,' she said, busying herself behind Enid. 'Now, would you like another pillow? You've only got one at the moment.' Enid didn't reply. 'What are you looking at out there?' Kara walked over to Enid, stood just behind her, and looked out of the window.

'It's a lovely room you've got here, Enid,' Kara stated, seemingly without any need for Enid's opinion on the matter. 'It must be lovely to have this view whenever you want.'

Enid ignored her and frowned, focusing hard on David's back, the only part of him she could see through the bushes. It looked like he was opening the car door for someone.

Kara touched Enid's shoulder and turned to leave. 'Right, Enid,' she said. 'I'll be back in an hour or so, to get you ready for bed.'

Enid didn't lose her focus though, or acknowledge Kara's departure. David stepped back slightly, still holding onto the car door, and Enid saw Olivia standing on her toes, kissing him quickly. Just a peck. She watched David tapping his wedding ring on the car door impatiently. She heard the clicks. Click. Click. Click. She saw Olivia bend down to get into the passenger seat, and then she saw David look around, before slamming the door, hard, onto his wife's shoulder.

Enid jumped back and made to duck low, though her body wouldn't allow her to. She peered out again and saw a bright macaw flying from the bushes by the road. Olivia was outside the car again, standing there, while David examined her shoulder. He looked apologetic. Maybe it was an accident, Enid thought, doubting herself, always doubting herself.

She watched Olivia bend down again to get back into the passenger seat. David looked around once more. It was softer this time, and more subtle, but there was no mistaking it. Enid saw David close the door, as before, onto his wife's shoulder before she was in the car. He apologised, before closing the door completely.

David clambered into the driver's seat with yet another slam of a door. She could see him inside the car, holding onto the steering wheel, gently tapping his forehead against the top of it. Then he leant back against his seat, arms stretched out forward, hands against the wheel, pushing his body as far back as possible. He shook his head, seemingly annoyed. Eventually, the engine rolled over and finally, after an amount of time that Enid couldn't quantify, the car pulled away.

She watched a glorious cacophony of red, blue, and yellow macaws fly high from the trees, spread into formation, and head out to the horizon.

10

In her youth, Enid had kept the books for five different men at a printer's. She'd enjoyed the work, but always found it hard to get excited about it around Donald. He tended to fixate on one of the men she worked with, although not always the same one, and ask silly questions about their families and grow irritated if they sat anywhere near Enid. In truth, she found his jealousy flattering, but she did wish she could share her excitement when a new contract came through.

'You won't need to work when the little one comes,' Donald told her, and he was right, of course, but Enid wished he wouldn't talk like that before she'd even fallen pregnant. They'd carried on trying after the move into the new house. Together, they'd made a concerted effort, each month after her period, to be intimate, but lately Enid had been losing hope, and she knew that Donald was too. The effort had become more strained, and afterwards, neither talked. They weren't talking much at all in fact, and when they did, Enid felt Donald's general disappointment in her.

He and his friends had been carrying out various projects in the garage where he worked, and he'd begun to return home later and later. Enid found herself sitting alone in the living room, or visiting her parents, pretending that she wasn't feeling just that tad bit lonely.

Despite the pressure she felt placed on her body to fall pregnant, Enid found herself looking forward to the nights that she and Donald would be intimate. It served as a reminder that she was a wife, and he still her husband. They were a married couple. Sometimes, she worried that if she were to fall pregnant, they would lose that last shred of intimacy, even though the act itself was just a means to that very end. The thought made her recoil with guilt.

It wasn't long before Donald was working weekends too. His expertise seemed to be required almost around the clock. If his friends at the garage had been coupled up, Enid thought, then maybe she could have spent time with their partners, but they weren't, and Enid's life became lonelier still. She couldn't keep visiting her parents – it was embarrassing.

Donald was always in such a bad mood in the mornings before work. He excused himself to Enid by telling her that he wasn't a morning person. But he had been, once.

'But that's the only time I get to see you,' she'd protested, but he would grumble something about working hard for her, and ungratefulness. On weekdays, Enid left for work thirty minutes after him.

They still shared their monthly week of intimacy, though even on these nights Donald often came home smelling of bitter. It was as if the constant underlying disappointment had become too much for him. The chore of sex had forced him to drink just so he could see the act through. He would talk down to Enid and blame her for their apparent infertility. He said that she was trying to remain barren so she could stay at work, and that she was an embarrassment to women. When Enid fought back, asking how she would even be able to do that, he became remorseful.

'I don't even understand,' he would say. 'You were so keen when we met. You basically begged me to court you back then. *You* asked *me* out.' He'd hold his head in his hands, the emotion from drink catching up with him. 'You must have wanted children back then – you must have – so what's changed? It can't be your parents; they adore me.' Then he'd look Enid in the eye. 'Your mum would love to knit little jumpers and socks and bonnets,' he'd say, full of spite.

Enid and Donald shared a different history these days. She could remember Donald approaching her on her way home from work four years ago, but she couldn't remember if it had happened or whether she had dreamed it up. It was true that she had fancied him at school, so it did make sense that she would have approached him, didn't it? Likewise, she remembered being disappointed by her mum's reaction to Donald in the early days. Wasn't that why they had lived at Donald's own mother's house? But then, she couldn't clearly remember how her mum had acted with her before meeting Donald, and they rarely met up, the four of them together, so perhaps Donald and her parents did get on. Perhaps her mum did adore him. To a certain degree, Enid hoped that Donald was right. But was she intentionally barren? Could she possibly be doing this all to herself?

She honestly didn't know.

Then, one night, Donald came home at gone eleven, bitter on his breath, an unsteady swagger in his step. Enid had been reading.

'Come on then,' he'd said. 'Let's do what we've got to do.' He barely stifled the wind behind his words. Enid sighed deeply. She didn't want to initiate a fight, but she couldn't help herself.

'I wish you'd come home just a little earlier,' she told him. 'So we can talk...about...' Enid went to say something else, but the words failed her. Donald had squinted his eyes at her, presumably to focus.

'I'm working, Enid,' he said, 'and I'm normally home earlier than this. Can't I get a night off every once in a while?' He was swaying, and Enid just watched. 'I was home early Monday...' he looked at his fingers, raising them with each day, '...Tuesday, Thursday.'

Was he right? Enid couldn't remember a night in the house with him that week, but he looked so fed up with her. Perhaps she was mistaken, and if she was, he must be so fed up with her lies.

'What am I coming home for anyway?' he asked, practically spitting the words out. Then he backed out of the room and started stamping his boots up the stairs.

'Donald,' Enid called.

'Hang on,' he shouted down the stairs, 'I'll be with you in a minute, love. I'm just tucking the kids into bed.' Enid heard his boots coming back down. 'Oh, fucking wait,' he said, back at the doorway. Enid couldn't look at him. She felt the tears prick her eyes. He'd been unpleasant to her before, but she'd never seen him aggressive like this. She could hear him fumbling with something over by the record player as she closed her eyes, feeling stupid for allowing herself to cry.

There was a smash against the stacked table nest, and she jolted her head up to see what had happened. Pieces of black vinyl were scattered across the floor, the other side of the room to where she was sitting. The cover of her new Tom Jones record lay, dented, below the tables.

That night, Enid slept downstairs. After four and a half years of marriage, she visited her parents and confided in them that she was unhappy, and that she wanted to leave Donald. She didn't give them the details – she didn't know what the details were any more – but she told herself that even if she had remembered their history incorrectly, she knew that she wasn't happy in the present.

11

SOME NIGHTS, IN THE care-home bed, Enid would try to list her memories. She couldn't write them down and she couldn't count them, but if she relived them, as often as possible, hopefully they would remain with her. Her memories were her identity, and it felt as if her identity was slowly slipping away from her.

She remembered her wedding day. So long ago now. Back then, she and Roy had been different people. Enid had been young and fashionable, with her hair done up like the girls in the magazines. Her mother had done it; she'd made the cake too. Enid had tailored her own dress, but it was no less beautiful than any other. She'd taken extra care to make space at the waist for the bump she was growing. Years later, she'd tailored Barb's dress too.

Roy had worn his work uniform, a basic suit, grey and

pinstriped, with his hair brushed into a neat side parting. They had been quite the handsome couple.

Enid couldn't remember everyone who had been at the registry office that morning, but she recalled a small gathering – just a few friends and family. It wasn't her first wedding, or marriage, so they hadn't invited many people; too many judging faces for the happy day. Enid was expecting, and she knew that the timing between her divorce and the wedding had left the town talking.

She couldn't remember the service, or any of the speeches – or anything that anyone had said that day in fact – but the feeling she'd had as her father's car pulled up to the registry office, and the butterflies she'd felt when she first saw Roy standing waiting for her were still fresh, as if her whole life was about to begin.

Enid opened her eyes. She was back in her room, in the new reality, uncomfortable and alone. She would soon be asleep though; sleep wasn't hard for Enid any more. She had even caught herself nodding off in the day recently, through boredom presumably.

She turned onto her side. That was no more comfortable, so she rolled onto her back again and closed her eyes.

Enid imagined walking through her own home. The hall first, with the phone on the left, before the stairs. A picture given to them on their wedding day hung opposite. The coat rack only ever had two coats hanging on it, and Roy's old shoehorn leaning against the bottom. Enid had often thought the coat rack unnecessary. She walked through the hall, past the stairs and into the kitchen. It was small, but then the boiler dominated a good portion of the work surface. A kettle, a toaster, the hob and a chopping board took up the rest. How many cups of tea had that kettle made for her and Roy? Such a simple pleasure from her previous life. Roy must still use it presumably. Enid hoped he would use less water now, what with bills as they were.

She walked through the kitchen and into the largest room of the house, which acted as both the dining room and the lounge. That isn't to say they ate with the television on – they never did, except for maybe fruit or a biscuit during *Countdown*.

They'd had their wedding picture taken against the glass dining-room patio doors so that the photographer could see the garden behind them. Roy was ever so proud of their garden. Chardonnay wine grapes grew against the greenhouse, and Roy grew courgettes and tomatoes, rather successfully, at the end, beyond the lawn. Enid wondered if he still did.

The resulting wedding picture stood in a frame on the mantelpiece below the glasses in the dining room. Enid couldn't remember all the ornaments they had up in the house, even though they hadn't changed for over a decade, but she remembered the picture, or a version of it, or maybe the feeling from when it was taken.

The lounge she remembered from her usual position on the sofa. Roy would be sitting next to her; the television would be on, and a small wooden table would sit in front of them with two teas and a small plate of biscuits. There was a record player to the left of where Roy would sit, with old Tom Jones and Elvis records resting against it. Once, Enid had thrown her knickers at Tom Jones.

She didn't venture upstairs in her thoughts. There were memories upstairs that would be too intimate for her to bear now. It would just serve as a reminder of all the nights spent alone since her forced departure. Worse, a reminder of the nights that Roy now spent upstairs in the house, alone. Instead, Enid completed the circuit of downstairs, through the lounge, back into the hall, and out of the front door. She walked past the caravan, down the drive and out to the road. She could remember the shape of the neighbour's neatly trimmed hedge but, she realised now, not his name.

At the end of the road was a bus stop. Only one bus ever stopped there, a single decker which circled Clevedon, every day, over and over. Enid could picture the bus, along with the route number on the front; two digits. She could remember the shapes of the numbers, but not their value.

Back in the care home – the real world – Enid held onto this memory for as long as she could. The value of a number listed on the front of a bus wasn't important; it was the shape of the number that mattered. She opened the drawer next to her bed, her body stiff from lying down, and searched for a packet of tissues. The drawer was empty. She glanced over at the chest of drawers on the other side of the room. Her tissues were probably in one of those. Enid stood up, slowly and painfully, still picturing the shape of the numbers she had seen on the front of the bus. Halfway to the chest of drawers, she turned. The packet of tissues was on the bed next to where she had been lying.

The arthritis in Enid's fingers wouldn't allow her to pull out just a single tissue, so she pulled them all out. Then she rifled through her bag.

At some point, it had become important to Enid to gather items that didn't belong to her. Out of her bag, she pulled a pop-up book about birds, several forks, a spoon, someone else's hairbrush, and a raw potato from the kitchen. She shuffled her haul of smaller contraband around in the bottom of the bag, until she found what she was looking for. A felt-tip pen.

She arranged one of the tissues on top of the drawer next to her bed, held the pen with her entire fist, and drew two numbers across it shakily.

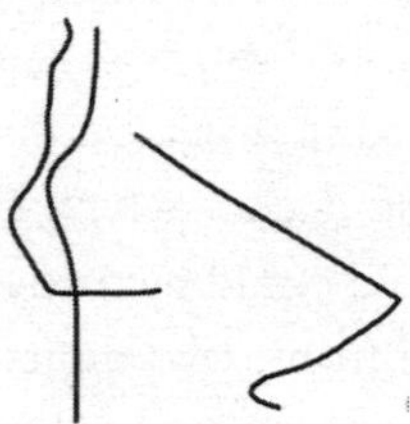

12

On what had been her last holiday with Roy, Enid had found herself sitting inside the caravan, watching rain trickle down the window. They'd gone down to Devon, as they often did. It was less than two hours from home. It had been sunny when they'd left Clevedon early that morning, but at this point they'd decided, if the weather didn't pick up, they would head back the next day.

The caravan didn't have a television. There was a radio, but Enid had turned it off shortly after they'd arrived. It would have to do for entertainment if the weather carried on like this, so they'd best save it for the evening.

Being stuck inside a caravan didn't matter too much to Enid. She talked with Roy about the same things that they always talked about: Barb and Alex, and how well Barb was doing since her divorce; *Strictly Come Dancing*; their old dog.

They talked about whether they should get another dog. Their last one, Ken, had died about five years before and Enid still missed him dearly.

'His dopey face,' Roy chuckled, 'when I used to get back from the shop and he'd be at the door, still jumping up and down, even in his old age.'

'He was lovely,' Enid agreed, 'but you know if we got another, it wouldn't be the same. Ken was special.'

'I know, and we'd have to train it, and there wouldn't be any promises that he'd be as well-behaved as our Ken.'

The conversation was well trodden, but comfortable. They fantasised about getting a new dog, and then gave each other lots of reasons not to: the night wakes; the vet fees. Enid couldn't bring herself to say what they were both surely thinking: if they got a new dog, there was a strong chance that it would outlive them.

The rain continued through the early afternoon. The small box of teabags they'd brought with them rapidly depleted, and the caravan grew darker. Enid thought of the seagulls who had greeted them so loudly when they'd arrived. She wondered where they went when it rained. In hiding, she presumed, under bushes, in dense shrubs, clinging close to the trunks of the thickest trees. For now, she thought, much like Roy and herself, they were trapped.

'I'll pop down the shop,' Roy announced, taking his time to stand up from the low caravan bench. 'We're short on teabags, milk…well, everything, and I want another paper.' Enid watched her husband put on his wellies and coat. He pulled his hood up, kissed her on the cheek and stepped out, into the driving rain, leaving her in the dim light of the afternoon.

Enid turned the radio back on and decided to cook a

few slices of bacon so that she and Roy could have an early dinner when he returned. She pulled out four slices of bread from the packet and spread margarine across them, took the ketchup out of the cupboard, pulled a few mixed leaves from a supermarket pre-washed bag, and then she turned on the gas.

She peered out of the window at the weather. Underneath the bush next to the water tap outside, Enid noticed a few of the leaves moving. A flurry of movement and then stillness. And then again. Movement and stillness. A bird, she thought, or an animal. Maybe seagulls. She watched for a while longer, and then grew bored as the regularity of the movements died down.

She looked at the buttered bread and realised that the bacon would be done far too early if she started cooking it now. Roy wouldn't be long, the shop was only down the road, but bacon took just a few minutes to cook. She relaxed a little and sat back down on the sofa, and at some point, she must have fallen asleep.

Enid woke to a noise outside. Her neck ached from the awkward sleeping position, and she wasn't sure where she was. Slowly and painfully, she turned her shoulders to look around the narrow room, all four walls feeling too close. She was in the caravan, which meant that she must have been sleepwalking.

There was a rustling outside, and heavy footsteps, the sound of someone trudging through thick mud left by rain. The sky looked blue through the window, with a few grey clouds scattering the canvas. Enid stood up, scared for her safety, and picked up a plate from the worktop. She hid behind the door, plate raised.

Enid heard her own name as she brought the plate down on the intruder, hitting him hard on one of his forearms. The brute.

'What are you doing?' Roy said, and Enid felt her face turn from anger, to fear, to realisation. 'It's OK, love. It's me; it's Roy.'

'Oh,' Enid said, and then her body began to shake. She lowered the plate to her side and then dropped it. 'Roy. Oh. I'm so sorry. I thought…'

Roy held onto one of her arms, put his other around her shoulders, and led her gently to the sofa. Enid saw him turn the gas off on the way.

'It's OK, love,' he told her again, as she began to cry. 'It's OK. I shouldn't have gone to the shop. It was my fault, love. It's OK. I promise.'

Enid looked up at her husband. His eyes were wet, focusing on the hob. Outside, she heard a seagull caw, then echoed by the rest of the flock. She felt Roy's arm around her shoulder, her body being pulled closer into his.

'It's my fault, love,' he muttered again, but it wasn't. She knew he was wrong.

Roy turned on the radio that night, but he didn't really listen to it. Although the rain had stopped, the wind blew hard, and as a result, the show was barely audible. He pretended to be engrossed though, and he knew that Enid was doing the same.

They didn't often hold each other in the evenings like this – not any more. He would have enjoyed it, had he not been so desperately unhappy. The evening ticked on without much conversation, but with compassion, and reassurance. The wind died down after dark, and around nine, he forced a chuckle.

'Early night, love?' he asked.

'I liked our cuddle,' Enid said, by way of reply.

'Me too.'

Roy changed for bed in the small caravan bathroom. With his top off, he looked at himself in the mirror. His skin drooping downwards. Some grey hairs remained on his chest. Enid hadn't hit him hard, but a large bruise was forming on his arm. Just a few years ago, he'd have barely marked. He pulled a vest over his head, buttoned his shirt and walked back into the lounge-cum-bedroom.

'You normally sleep in your pyjama bottoms,' Enid accused him from the bed. 'Why are you wearing a shirt?'

Roy smiled at her apologetically and lifted his arm to show the bruise. He saw the guilt flash across Enid's face.

'Oh,' she said quietly, sadly. She looked away from him as she walked past to take her turn in the bathroom.

'It doesn't hurt,' he told her through the bathroom door. 'Ow.' He forced a laugh. 'Unless I poke it, that is.'

He slowly lowered himself onto the bed and began tapping his chest, thinking.

'Enid, love,' he said. She never normally took this long in the bathroom. How long had it been? Twenty minutes? 'Enid?' Roy lifted himself back onto his feet, at the only pace he could manage these days, and walked the few steps to the bathroom door.

'Enid?' he asked again, but the only reply was the familiar sound of muffled, secret, tears.

Roy had woken to a bright sun the following morning, and he and Enid had gone for a short morning walk. They talked about breakfast and about Barb and Alex, *Strictly Come Dancing* and their old dog, but neither had mentioned the incident with the plate. Back in the caravan, they'd carried on as though nothing had happened. Roy made several cups of tea for them both and read his paper. Enid prepared sandwiches for lunch. They ate them on the chairs outside. By the second glass of lemonade, the sky was turning grey again, and it wasn't long before Roy noticed spots of rain on his newspaper.

By the early afternoon, the rain was heavy once again, but by that time, they'd already decided to stay at least one more night. Roy wasn't ready for the holiday to end – not yet.

For the second afternoon in a row, he found himself sitting in the caravan, waiting for the storm to pass. At ten past two, he found his mind drifting to *Countdown*. It would be starting now, a daily ritual which he wouldn't mind missing if they were able to go outside. He told Enid as much.

'I've got an idea,' she said, and she took a small pad of paper and a pen out of her bag. 'Here,' she passed the pad to Roy. 'I'll have a consonant please.' It took Roy a second to understand, and then he laughed. Enid continued. 'A vowel, another vowel, and then a consonant please, Roy.' Enid looked like she was thinking for a second. 'Maybe…yes, one more vowel and then four consonants. That's nine?' Roy nodded with a knowing smile and showed her the pad.

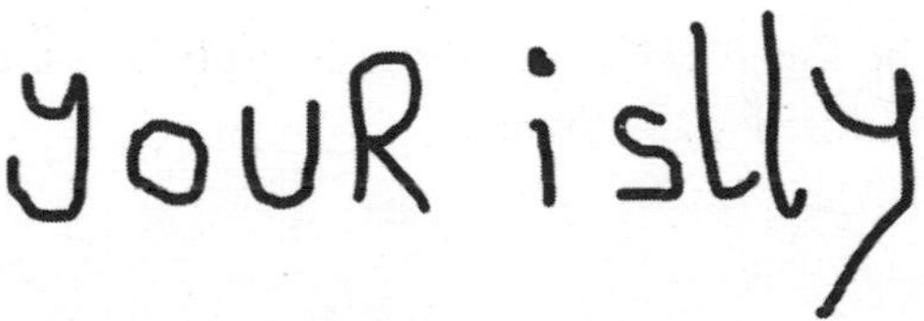

The game lasted much longer than the usual fifty minutes, with both Enid and Roy trying for points while at the same time leaving little messages to each other in the clues.

Maybe they wouldn't leave for home tomorrow either. Maybe Roy could persuade Enid to stay a few more nights – a week, even. Roy felt desperate for the holiday to continue. He hadn't told anyone about their last-minute trip to Devon. It had been on something of a whim after Neil had found Enid crying, and despite the fun they were having, the air felt oppressive, suffocating. Like at the end of the old movie, *Butch Cassidy and the Sundance Kid*, life was caving in. There was a finality to the event, and Roy wasn't ready to let it end.

13

'Had to bring him this time, didn't I, Mum? You two will be the death of me.' Barb was in forced good spirits. As far as she could tell, so far, her mum hadn't noticed that Roy never visited by himself any more, and she didn't want to raise suspicion in Enid. She pulled a chair up to where her mum was sitting, leaving the spot next to Enid free for Roy.

'I'm fine,' Roy said, with slightly too much phlegm in the back of his mouth, blocking his words. He was still on his way to the chair, and Barb could see that Enid was watching him closely. Roy cleared his throat. 'I'm fine,' he repeated. 'I wish you wouldn't worry.'

'I know, Dad. I know. Here, sit down.' Slowly, Roy did as he was told. 'How are you, Mum?' Barb asked, but Enid didn't respond. She was staring at Roy with her mouth ever so slightly open. Barb was used to this sort of behaviour by now.

'Alex wants a tongue piercing,' she said, and then paused to no response. 'She's not getting one though; she's only fourteen.' Enid was now looking at Barb, but it was obvious she hadn't taken in what had been said. Barb noticed that her mum had placed her hand on top of Roy's hand. Sweet, she thought. 'I would never have been allowed something like that when I was fourteen. You would never have let me. Mum. Mum?' Enid was looking back at Roy again, and clearly struggling to say something. Barb was quiet. It was important to give her mum time to form sentences.

'Love,' she said eventually, and after some effort. Barb smiled.

'Love you too, love,' Roy said, and then he shuffled in his chair. 'Lovely tomatoes this year – growing right up to the top of the greenhouse, they are.' Enid gave him only half a smile. Barb wondered if she should leave and give them some privacy. They were married after all. Her mum's lips started shaking.

'Limping,' she said, and Roy nodded at her.

'Him and his garden,' Barb interjected nervously. 'I'll have to find a care home for you too soon, Dad.' She instantly regretted saying it. She'd hoped they'd laugh. As long as there was someone to bring Roy to see Enid, and to help with the shopping, he'd be fine at home. Barb could do those things. She had been doing them in fact. She looked at her parents, who were both staring at her with deadly serious, expectant faces.

'I was joking,' she said, but they didn't change their expressions. 'Look, Mum, it's just a limp. Dad's fine, but when the time comes, I'll make sure he moves in here, so you can be together.' Both her parents softened. Enid lifted her hand to touch her chest, every feature of her face smiling, and Roy exhaled with relief.

'Good, good,' he mumbled.

'It'll be fewer trips for me anyway,' Barb continued, reassuring herself that by the time this eventuality came, they'd both have forgotten the conversation.

'You and your bloody garden, Dad,' she said under her breath.

Enid walked into the kitchen; her face purposely nonchalant.

'Enid, lovely, you can't be in here.' The chef sounded worried. Enid pretended she hadn't heard, looked up at one of the shelves, pointed her finger at nothing in particular, and then nodded. Pretending to be satisfied, she turned around and walked back out of the kitchen and sat on one of the armchairs in the corridor.

Time passed, probably. A buzzer sounded. A carer let in some young people before shutting the door again. Even if Enid knew the code and could decipher the numbers, the arthritis in her fingers would never allow her to press the buttons, so she never tried.

The young people had a dog with them. As they passed, Enid went to stroke the dog, and the dog leaned in to be stroked, but the young people pulled it away by its lead. They hadn't come to see Enid.

More time passed. Not much; lots. Enid couldn't tell.

She walked into the kitchen, this time looking around her as if she'd lost something.

'Enid,' the same chef said in the same tone. Enid looked away.

'Enid,' the chef said again, this time standing directly in front of her. There was no escape. Enid huffed, frowned, and growled angrily at her oppressor. Then she left.

Back in the armchair, Enid wondered when Roy would be moving in with her. She imagined him now, sitting in the chair next to her, holding onto her hand. She thought of him sleeping, with one hand on his chest and his other touching her leg, like he used to. He would do that again, she thought, when he moved in.

She wondered what Roy would think of the outings they had at the home. The residents were allowed out, but never without supervision, and never of their own choosing. Still, Enid enjoyed going out and she hoped that Roy would too.

They went to a supermarket café sometimes. It was the same supermarket that Enid used to shop at most weeks in her previous life. She liked peeking into how she used to live, and watching other people living something similar, a million worlds away from her life now.

There was also a tearoom near the beach which she and a few of the other residents were taken to occasionally. Barb had taken her there once without the other residents. Enid remembered this outing better than the others. She'd enjoyed it so much that when the time had come to leave, she'd held on tight to the table and refused to move. Poor Barbara had to call one of the carers to come and help her prise her away. Enid wondered why she had to remember this outing over the others. It was one memory she wouldn't mind losing. She was so ashamed of herself; it would never have happened if Roy had been with her though. She'd have happily come home again then.

If Roy didn't like these outings, Enid told herself, it would be due to the lack of independence, but he would surely like the bench. One or two of the carers would sometimes take a select few of the residents down to a bench at the bottom of the drive. There was a bus stop next to the bench, but it was rare that a bus would stop there.

From the bench, they could look down some steep steps which none of them would ever manage again, over a little cove and out across the sea. They wouldn't do much there – just sit, and occasionally eat sandwiches that had been pre-prepared by the kitchen. Enid pictured herself there now, next to Roy, eating a picnic and enjoying the fresh air. The wrinkles on his face had disappeared, for the most part at least, and his skin was smoother than she remembered. There were shopping bags on the floor, and for a split-second, Enid watched as her fantasy turned into a long-forgotten memory. Fizzy water, crisps and ham. Then it was gone again.

Enid stood up and walked into the kitchen, her eyes on the floor this time. She walked over to the stainless-steel worktop on the opposite side of the room to the chef, although still only a few steps away, and swept one of many carrots into her bag.

'Enid, dear, I'm sorry, you really can't be in here.' Enid felt two hands being placed gently onto her shoulders. They ushered her backwards, turned her body to face the door, and with the lightest of pushes, directed her back out of the kitchen.

Enid sat back on the same armchair that she had left less than a minute ago, as the chef closed the kitchen door behind her. She looked in her bag at the carrot.

Victory.

The next time Enid saw Olivia, she was with the whole family visiting Martin in the home. Olivia was sitting next to David, with a little girl laughing on her lap. A rusty-haired young boy was pulling at his shoelaces as hard as he could on the floor. Enid smiled, happy to see Olivia's two children. How lovely, she thought – a girl and a boy. The little girl was smacking herself in the cheeks repeatedly and joyously, turning them a faint shade of red. Enid decided to move seats to be closer to them.

She stood up, looked out of the window so as not to be so obvious, and then sat down in the chair next to Olivia, behind the boy on the floor. She was close enough that an onlooker might think she was part of the family. The children didn't notice. Olivia gave the smallest of smiles, and David frowned at the intrusion, but didn't verbally object. He was dressed in a suit today, and his bald head shone. If it weren't for everything that Enid thought she knew about him already, she would say he looked handsome.

'Blimey, Dad, it's hot,' David said, before blowing exaggeratedly through pursed lips. He took off his suit jacket, revealing a neatly ironed shirt and tie, and placed it, along with his briefcase, onto the floor next to Olivia, and, Enid noticed, next to her.

Enid didn't know what she was hoping for by listening in on their conversation – proof of what she had seen out of her window perhaps, or a stand-off between David and Martin. Whatever it was, it didn't come. David talked at length and Martin listened. Martin said little and David didn't listen to the little that Martin said. David talked about a quiz. He talked about his work. He talked about one of his friends – a top bloke, actually. Enid drifted in and out.

She started thinking about Roy, and when he would come again. Barb still visited as often as she ever had, but Roy wasn't always with her any more. His presence was becoming ever rarer, and Enid couldn't remember the last time he had come by himself. On the few occasions that he would be with Barb, he would grunt a few times in response to something Barb would say, but he wouldn't have much to contribute himself. When Barb asked him a question now, she tended to shout it, and then still have to repeat herself. She never used to have to do that. Enid knew that Roy would be living with her again soon, though she didn't know when. She told herself that when he was, she would help him with his hearing.

The little girl had stopped hitting her cheeks and both were red. Olivia was holding onto the girl's arms and playing a quiet version of patter cake with her on her legs. Enid noticed the blue in the toddler's fingers, and the yellow feathers that were sticking out from her back. Had there been feathers when they'd first come in?

Click.

Enid squinted at the toddler, her claws now weaving in between Olivia's own, her cheeks bright red and textured.

Click.

'Uh,' Enid said, and then, 'Uh...oh.' David looked at her as if she were old furniture, coughing dust into the room. Enid looked away, waiting for the ringing in her ears to stop. When it finally did, she raised her head to see that Olivia had stopped playing with her daughter. She was looking down and concentrating on nothing. David laughed at Enid's interruption and rolled his eyes. The little girl smiled at her dad, pale skin and featherless. The rusty-haired boy was no longer pulling at his shoelaces. He absentmindedly played with the coded lock on David's briefcase instead. Opening it, closing it, opening it, closing it, opening it. Click, click, click.

'We went to the tearoom down by the seafront the other day,' Martin said, clearly trying to change the subject. David laughed and looked at the other residents around him, Enid included.

'I bet that was fun,' he said, sarcastically. 'I bet you had a proper party, did you?' He was clearly joking, and in truth Enid could see his point, but she still found it offensive.

'Will you leave my briefcase alone,' David snapped, and the little boy jumped, and then sat on his hands. David turned back to his dad and started talking about some sort of deal his company was working on.

Enid looked down at the briefcase. It was open. A pad of paper, a laptop, and a pen, each held neatly in place by elastic. She leant down, pretended to tie the laces on her lace-less slippers, and slyly pulled the pen out of the briefcase. She looked at David as she placed his pen in her own bag. He was absorbed in his own conversation, even if his dad didn't appear to be. She rummaged around in her bag and pulled out the carrot.

When no one was looking, she placed the carrot in David's briefcase.

A few minutes later, David rose to his feet. 'We'd best be off,' he said.

Olivia stood, holding her toddler in one arm, pulling her son up from the floor with the other.

'Bye, Grandad,' the boy said, before being cut off by his dad.

'Close my case,' David ordered. Olivia picked up the case for her son, peered inside and closed it on his behalf.

'Bye, Martin,' she said, and then she nodded at Enid, smiling.

14

'You've only been married two minutes,' Enid's mum had said when Enid had told her she wanted to leave Donald. 'You work at a marriage. That's what it is all about; loving your husband despite all odds.'

Enid didn't see how she could work on her marriage. Donald was rarely there, and when he was, she no longer felt like working on anything with him. The thought was too unpleasant. What's more, she honestly couldn't decipher whether her mum wanted her to stay with Donald just to keep up appearances, or if she genuinely liked the brute. It was true that Enid had never known anyone to get divorced. It just wasn't done.

One Saturday, following her mum's advice in the only way she could see was possible, Enid decided to visit the garage that Donald worked at. She would dress well and wear make-up, and then ask him to go on a date with her after work, instead of socialising with his friends. She would suggest No. 5 The Beach again, as it seemed to be the only part of their history they agreed on.

When she arrived at the garage, she saw a man standing in the small room which served as reception. He had a grubby but friendly face.

'Is Donald here?' she asked. The man looked uncomfortable.

'Donald?' he asked, coyly. 'Well, no.'

Enid knew she was looking good, and tried to play the part, the trophy wife, making her husband proud. 'I'm terribly sorry,' she said 'I'm Enid. When will he be back?'

'Enid,' the man said, though it wasn't clear that the name meant anything to him. 'Well, I'm sorry, Enid. Donald won't be back 'til Monday.'

It was gone midnight when Donald returned home that night, long after the local pubs had closed. Enid had wondered whether he'd return at all. She'd spent two nights on the sofa now, and she suspected that the man from the garage would have called him about her visit.

When Donald did walk in, drunk, but not as drunk as expected, Enid had quietly informed him that she wanted a divorce.

'You can't,' he'd told her, picking up her glass of water from the nest of tables. 'I won't allow it.'

Enid had laughed despite herself. 'Donald,' she said, 'you're not happy either.' Donald stood up and started pacing circles around the living room.

'I'll make the decisions,' he said, the control in his voice slowly disappearing, talking as if to himself. 'I'm the man. I'm the husband, your husband. I'll make the decisions. We're not getting a divorce.'

'Donald,' Enid said sadly, sympathetically.

'What?' he shouted, stopping dead in front of her, towering over her place on the sofa. 'You turn up at my work dressed like a slut, and you expect me to trust you?'

'Trust *me*?' Enid screamed back abruptly, shocked, but on the back foot. 'Trust *me*?' Louder. 'Where have *you* been all night, Donald? All day even? And you have the nerve to say I'm untrustworthy?' She saw Donald's face turning red, his body itching with built-up tension, a bullet waiting to be fired.

Enid heard the curse at the same time as she felt the glass hit her face, sharp and instant above her right eyebrow. She raised her hand to her forehead and bent forward until she was touching her knees. The pain grew more intense with each second, she could feel the blood in her hands, the skin throbbing in her palm. She didn't look up for a long time, unsure of whether another attack was coming. When she did, she saw Donald was still standing in front of her, a few steps back, still red, breathing heavily, less tense. There was broken glass on the floor and on the sofa cushions. He was watching her.

'I…' he said, looking for his excuse.

'At least this is something we can *both* lie about,' Enid said, standing and pushing past him upstairs, her hand still holding the cut on her head.

The bathroom door didn't lock, but even now, Enid didn't see Donald as a threat. He'd exploded, but he wouldn't again – not tonight. She looked at herself in the cabinet mirror and lowered her hand. The cut was deep. In normal circumstances,

Enid would call an ambulance, but it wasn't an option.

She opened the cabinet and pulled out surgical plaster, bandage and tape. She inhaled through her teeth as she compacted the wound as best she could through the pain. Then she wrapped the bandage around her head to hold it in. The job looked messy, and she could see blood drying on her hair, but it would hold the wound until it scabbed, and besides, the worse it looked, the better. Enid wanted Donald to feel it. She wanted his guilt to be unbearable.

When she returned downstairs, she found Donald in his chair with his head in his hands.

'I never meant it to hit you,' he said, looking up at her.

'But you meant to intimidate me,' Enid told him, without any doubt that he had meant to hit her. 'That's just as bad.' She sat on the other side of the sofa, opposite her husband, brushing the glass onto the floor.

'So,' she said. 'Where have you been going?'

'Just a friends house,' he said. 'We've been working on the bike.'

'Which friend?' Enid asked, and Donald slouched back in his chair, sighing – possibly playing for time, Enid thought.

'Edward,' he said. 'Just Ed.' Enid didn't reply. She knew he was lying, but it didn't make much difference any more. 'It doesn't matter what her name is anyway.'

So, there it was, Enid thought. *Her* name. She didn't point out his mistake.

'I'll be moving back to my parent's house in the morning,' Enid said flatly. Donald's begging felt only a gesture; she didn't really believe that he wanted her to stay. It stung when he talked of the family they hadn't yet had, but Enid knew that she'd made the right decision.

The next morning, she listened as Donald left the house before the sun rose. It was no different to any other day, except today, there wasn't the pretence of going to work. She packed what she needed and left shortly after.

She didn't tell her mum the details of the previous night, though clearly she would be able to see the cut above Enid's eyebrow. Her mum had been more than a little disappointed with the news.

'No one will want you now,' she'd stated matter-of-factly, and then exhaled as if a divorce would take its toll on her, rather than Enid. 'Damaged goods.'

After that, Enid found herself spending her evenings and weekends alone, much as she had in married life. She chose to spend her time in her room, upstairs, rather than with her parents, because she found happiness in solitude. She would have to wait a whole five years before the divorce would be accepted by the courts, but even in the act of waiting, Enid found solace. There was less pressure on her, and less to worry about. Small pleasures such as reading and embroidery became enjoyable again, and there was always her job at the printers for company. She looked forward to weekdays when she'd find herself occupied at the office, and when the new man, Roy, started, she began to look forward to those days even more.

15

These days, Enid could no longer decipher the large, green, neon letters that were stuck above the entrance, but she knew that if she could, she'd read the word ASDA. It was a word that she had seen so many times throughout her life, and yet now had become nothing more than bright, meaningless shapes. She had been lucky enough to be picked for an outing that day, as had Evelyn, Frank and Betty, three of the other residents.

Once they were all inside and seated at one of the small rectangular tables, Kara asked what they each wanted, in a roundabout way.

'Evelyn, coffee?' Evelyn nodded, more than she normally did.

'Frank, the same?' Frank looked up, over the frames of his glasses and made a noise to imply that he hadn't heard.

'Coffee, Frank?'

'Uh, oh yes. Yes, thank you very much.'

'Enid, a cup of tea?'

Enid smiled at her.

'Betty, tea as well?' Betty never replied to anything, but Enid knew Kara would buy her a cup of tea anyway.

Kara brought the drinks on a large brown tray and sat with Duncan on the next table over from the residents. Apart from the two carers, no one said much. Enid found conversation hard, and she suspected that Evelyn did too. Betty never seemed to say anything more than an inaudible mumble, and Frank couldn't hear anything that was said, unless it was shouted. Still, Enid enjoyed people-watching; imagining their lives, and wondering what they might do after they left the supermarket.

The others too, except for Betty, would look around at their surroundings rather than at each other. Betty just looked down.

Enid watched a mother peel a banana and hand the flesh to the reaching arms of a toddler who sat facing her in the trolley. Enid fantasised that the woman would return to her childhood sweetheart in a one-bed semi. They'd have had some troubles in their relationship to begin with, Enid decided, but then they'd have grown stronger, just before the baby came along. Now they would be going through what every couple with a new child goes through. The stress, the arguments, the lack of sleep. The companionship, the strength, the love. Enid thought about Barb when she was a baby – how she and Roy had managed.

Over by the canned goods, Enid could see a man hunching over his trolley, leaning on it while pushing. He was facing away from the café, but Enid could still see the back of his head. It was a mix of thinning grey hair and sun-blotched baldness. He was wearing a suit and there was a briefcase placed in his trolley. He must work. Enid wondered who he would be going home to that night, and how much time he would have left with that person before his body completely gave way and they, too, were separated.

A short, dark-haired woman was rubbing the back of her shoulder on the other side of the aisle. The pain must have been under the blade because she really had to reach to get it. She was wearing a colour that Enid couldn't remember the name of, and her trolley was full – a mix of vegetables and packaged snacks.

The woman let go of her shoulder and turned around. Enid inhaled quietly but sharply. Olivia. The small, rusty-haired boy whom Enid had sat in front of back in the home ran up to Olivia holding something undoubtedly sugary. Olivia smiled, shook her head, and patted the boy's back, ushering him away. As he ran off to put whatever it was back on the shelf, Olivia's smile gave way to a pained expression, and her uninjured arm quickly jolted up to continue rubbing the back of her shoulder.

Then, almost as if she'd noticed Enid's gaze, Olivia looked up at the residents. She gave a small wave and the tiniest of smiles before looking away again, as if guilty of something. Enid saw David walking up the aisle behind Olivia, head tilted, and looking quizzically in the direction his wife had waved. He was holding his daughter in one arm, blonde, pale and obedient. Enid moved back in her chair and looked away. On the table next to the residents, she could see Duncan waving.

Enid looked around the table, as if she were re-joining a conversation. Evelyn was drinking her coffee, shaking the cup slightly, but drinking without help. Betty looked at her own legs, murmuring something inaudible and potentially nonsensical, and Frank just stared out of the café, and into the shop. Enid looked closely at him. That must be how she looked to other people.

When Enid dared to look back into the shop, Olivia had been re-joined by the boy. David's free hand was holding onto Olivia's shoulder, gripping close to her neck. In her minds eye, Enid saw the car park outside her window at the home, a flash of red and yellow, the car door landing on Olivia's shoulder, and again.

She felt the anger burning, first in the back of her head, and then in her eyes, shooting daggers at David. She started spitting, growling, scrunching her nose up angrily with hate. Somewhere in the periphery, she could hear Duncan's voice.

'Right then,' he said cheerily. 'Shall we make a move back home?' Enid could sense Kara pushing her chair back and rising to her feet, but she kept up the noise; a low, threatening growl. 'Enid, lassie, are you ready?' Duncan asked, now standing directly in front of her. Enid looked at him, all the hate she'd previously felt, now gone. She lowered her voice.

'Oh, uh,' she fumbled, reaching up to wipe the spit from her chin. Then she looked at her only half-empty cup of tea. 'Um.'

'It's time we went back now,' Duncan said, softly.

'Eh?' Frank asked, loudly.

'I said it's time we went back, Frank.'

The six of them shuffled to the exit, past security, past the tobacco desk, past the magazines and the ready-made sandwiches. Enid looked back into the shop, causing Duncan to stop as he waited for her. Kara went on with the other three. The toddler had finished her banana now, and she was complaining about having her mouth wiped. Her mother persisted, but ignored the mess left on her daughter's clothes. The hunched man was still holding onto his trolley, he was speaking with a shop assistant. Enid wondered what he was looking for. Nothing important, she thought; he'd be going home to whatever his important was.

Further down the aisle, Enid saw Olivia. She was looking down now and facing away. Next to her, Enid noticed a toy dispenser. Twenty pence for a rubber ball or a rubber puppy, left to chance. The plastic base was a bright orange, a clear top to show the prizes and a silver mechanism below. Two men, each holding a crate of beer, walked past the dispenser, laughing.

When it came back into Enid's view, the clear window had been replaced by bars, and the toys had disappeared. In their place, Enid saw dark black eyes, glaring at her through the crowd. One blue wing shook, hitting the cage, testing them, attempting to break free. The hollow beak opened and remained silent for a fraction of a second. Enid felt deafened by the scream that followed. She closed her eyes, and when she opened them again, Duncan was holding onto her shoulder and her elbow. He was looking into the shop. David, it seemed, was looking back at them, and he was smirking.

Olivia had managed to hoover upstairs, tidy the playroom, and even clean the kitchen. She had an hour before she needed to pick Dillon up from school and was deciding whether to make meatballs or bolognaise. These moments were rare. It wasn't often that she found a little time of her own to enjoy, and she loved cooking. Normally she'd find herself chucking something in the pressure cooker, or worse, a ready-made packet in the oven. Olivia remembered a time before the children, before the rush of everyday life, when she and David would throw dinner parties and entertain old friends. The effort she used to make back then had been legendary.

She started up a Mowtown playlist and found herself singing along to Sam Cooke. While the mince defrosted in the microwave, she ground some thyme in a pestle and mortar, along with salt and pepper. The thyme had been bought dried and pre-ground, but it was the action that Olivia savoured, the care that time had allowed her. Still undecided on what was being prepared, she pulled some pre-washed spinach from the fridge and washed it in the colander. The water from the tap gave the leaves an extra freshness as she chopped them slowly on the wooden board.

She was mixing the contents of the pestle and mortar with the chopped spinach when the door slammed shut in the next room.

'David?' she called. He wasn't supposed to be home for another two hours. Olivia would make bolognaise; much quicker than meatballs, and it could always be rushed if he was in a bad mood. He saw anything other than basic cooking as a luxury these days, where once it had been Olivia's hobby. He stormed into the kitchen, his face red, forehead beating.

'A fucking carrot,' he shouted, accentuating the fuck. 'That meeting was important. The sale of the whole fucking firm could have been on that, and someone's replaced my pen with a fucking carrot.' Olivia didn't say anything. She ducked her head low on her shoulders and tried to make herself as small as she felt. David looked at her, and then the pestle and mortar. 'Is this what you do all day?' he asked, clearly not expecting an answer, his eyes raging. 'Fucking cooking and listening to

Baby Love?'

'No, I...' Olivia started to protest, but David interrupted.

'A fucking carrot,' he repeated, heading back out of the kitchen, much to Olivia's relief. 'I'm going upstairs. I'll find out who did it – some kind of a fucking joke. They'll pay with their job.' He looked back into the room, at Olivia, and pointed at the ingredients on the kitchen worktop. 'I fancy a takeaway tonight anyway.'

'I've got to pick up Dillon soon,' Olivia said quietly as her husband left the room. She knew that by the time he came down again, Dillon would be home. David was always pleasant around the children.

She could hear her husband upstairs, speaking irately to some poor soul on the phone. A carrot, she thought. She remembered the woman sitting next to her at the dementia home, and the open briefcase between them. She began to laugh, first under her breath, and then, gaining a little confidence, louder.

She pulled down the breadbin from the shelf and started tearing small chunks from the loaf into the bowl of spinach and thyme.

'Meatballs,' she said, shaking her head, still laughing. 'Fucking meatballs.'

16

Little Barb often sat on the carpet, close to the TV, cross-legged with her hands on her knees. Roy should probably tell her to move back, but he was a soft touch, and he knew it. He could see the fresh smudged finger marks on the white plastic around the dials where she'd turned them after the morning's buttery toast.

It was Saturday and Emu was on. Barb giggled as the tinselled bird pulled flowers out of a vase and threw them at the presenter. The bird's keeper, Rod, pretended to look shocked, but really, he was laughing.

Roy was sitting at the table, wearing his usual white shirt with braces and pinstriped suit trousers. Even at weekends he liked to look smart. He leant back on his chair and looked over at his daughter. Her childish laugh made him smile.

'Barb,' he said, but she was lost to the chaos on the screen, to a world of bright colours and slapstick humour. 'Barb.'

Barb made the slightest of movements with her head, which Roy took to mean she could hear him.

'What do you want to do today?' he asked, and Barb made a noise that couldn't be described as a word. 'Park?' he suggested. Nothing. 'The usual park over the road?' he prompted again, but again he received nothing.

'I love you,' he said, raising the intonation at the end and not expecting a response.

An audience clapped, a camera pulled away, and red, yellow and blue graphics shot across the screen. Barb stood up.

'Daddy?' she asked.

'Barb?'

'I love Emu.'

Roy laughed. 'I know,' he said. 'What shall we do today?' Barb looked up at the wall behind him, and thought.

'Umm...'

Enid walked into the dining room, holding her hair, and pushing in a clip.

'Don't forget I have to start cooking at three today,' she said.

Roy turned. They discussed how long the chicken would take, when they should sit down to eat it, and what they could do with the leftovers. That would affect the seasoning Enid should use today, see. Then they digressed. Enid bought up the neighbour's new dog – a Labrador, who had started howling in the early hours of the morning. Barb was so taken with the birds outside, Roy pointed out, wouldn't a dog be lovely? Barb interrupted with an excited squeal, and Enid told her that she couldn't have a dog. That discussion was for another day, she said. Back to the chicken. They agreed that it would probably take around two hours, and they would probably be hungry by five, so yes, Enid should probably start cooking around three.

Roy often found himself lost in small talk with Enid.

'So,' he turned back to Barb, 'we've got five hours.' He stopped short. Barb was back facing the TV. The image on the screen cut from eagle to owl, from hawk to buzzard. A middle-aged straight-faced man in a thick rainbow-striped jumper spoke directly to the camera. A parrot stood on his shoulder, eyeing him.

'Join us at Birdland, for hundreds of spectacular displays,' the man said, before the parrot pecked his ear, 'and the finest exotic birds in the world.' The parrot extended its neck, put its head to one side and picked at the presenter's hair with its beak. 'Like this fine beauty here,' the man said, as he leaned away from the bird. The screen filled with a logo, followed by the directions needed to visit Birdland.

In one movement, Barb stood up and turned towards her parents.

'Can we go there?' she asked, her face beaming with excitement. Roy began nodding. He loved it when Barb's eyes went wide like this. He'd created such a level of excitement in one single nod. It was exhilarating.

'Of course, we ca…' he started, but Enid interrupted.

'Not today we can't, no,' she said, sounding shocked at Roy's naivety. 'Maybe another day.' Roy turned to see his wife scowling at him. 'Why must I be the bad one?' she asked. 'You know we can't go today. We'd have to leave as soon as we arrived.' Enid walked purposefully, but apologetically towards her daughter. Barb was already showing signs of a meltdown. Her face was red, her eyes were wet, and her bottom lip was wobbling.

'But Dad…Dad…Dad said I could,' Barb stuttered, and then

she screamed as she stomped out of the room. Roy watched as Enid tried to hold onto their daughter, but missed. Barb slammed the lounge door shut behind her, catching Enid's wrist on the handle as she did.

Enid sucked in air through her teeth, held onto her arm, and then turned to glare at Roy. He felt guilty, the bliss of the morning shattered in one misguided utterance.

'So,' he said coyly, and a little cheekily, 'what *should* we do toda…' His sentence trailed off, but Enid rolled her eyes, and he could see them already softening.

The bird was next to her partner when the first of her three eggs shook. The movement was subtle, but it was enough. They looked at each other, and then they both looked somewhere else, then at each other again, and then at the nest. Then she hopped onto the edge of the nest and flew down to the bottom of the garden.

She gave little thought to the little girl watching them from across the patio. The girl was often there, eating, singing, fidgeting. The bird rummaged in the soil in one of the beds. It didn't take long to uncover a fat worm. She yanked it up into her beak and flew back to the nest, placing it on the floor next to the moving egg. Then pecked at the worm until it lay still.

She nudged the egg with her beak. The movement was sharp, and the egg looked fragile, but it didn't break. She wanted her chick to feel its first movement from the world beyond the confines of the egg. She wanted it to know that there was something more outside.

The egg moved again of its own accord, and the blackbird welled up with pride. There was a tiny crack forming. She looked at her partner and saw that he had puffed out his chest.

She looked around, down the garden and then back at the egg. Along to the side gate and then back at the egg. Into the sky and then back at the egg. Up the patio and then back at the egg. And then back up the patio again.

The girl was standing now, up on her tiptoes, eyes wide, biting the side of her bottom lip. The bird looked at her partner, his blazing orange beak aimed at the little girl. He tweeted a warning and raised his tail to show that he meant business. The girl lifted herself higher and leered closer to the nest. He warbled; long, low, and melodious, defending what was his. The female blackbird knew she was lucky to have him, but she felt compromised.

There was a sound from inside the building, and the girl hopped inside, frantic and fast. The blackbird knew that the girl had heeded her partner's warning, and she felt her heartbeat steady. She looked at the egg silently, and then back to the male bird. He was turning his head quickly this way and that, scanning for other predators or unwelcome guests. Then he looked at her. Then they both looked at the egg.

The crack had widened now, and she could see the pink skin of her eighth chick. A featherless wing, thin, fragile and swaying side to side, like a worm reaching for its next patch of soil. She pecked the egg one more time. Slowly, delicately yet forcefully, the chick pushed the crack on the shell to create a hole, just large enough for her wing, neck and back to be exposed. The bird watched as her chick felt the warmth of the morning sun for the first time.

This was good progress, she thought. She had lost four this year, raised three, and was hopeful for what would be her final attempt. She raised her head to the sky, then looked across the patio, back to the gate, and then to the lawn. Then, again, she looked at her partner, her head ever so slightly to one side. He had protected her eggs, and she was grateful.

She held onto the loose piece of shell with her beak, and pulled it away softly. The chick's head fell backwards out onto the nest floor, the weight too heavy for the unpractised muscles in the neck.

The bird saw her chick's beak open, hungry for the worm she had just gathered from the lawn. She recognised the yellow crusting around the chick's tiny beak, and the pus seeping from its swollen eyes.

She heard the little girl jumping back out onto the patio behind her, and she felt the rush of wind as the girl ran to the nest. She sensed more people there, and she heard them talking.

Neither blackbird fought the intrusion this time. Neither turned, and they didn't tweet or warble. They did nothing to defend their nest. The female bird picked up the worm from the nest floor and pushed it, hard into the chick's open beak, but she'd seen crusting like this before, and she'd felt a similar swell. She knew there was nothing she could do.

That night, three pink, almost translucent chicks fell about the nest floor, fighting for the food that had been gathered for them. One neck would extend, beak wide and eyes shut, and then it would fall back to the nest, neck stuffed with worm. Then the next would emerge from the pile of wriggling limbs. Two of the chicks raised their heads more regularly than the third, and their mum noticed. When the third did lift its head, it looked desperate – more a struggle for survival than a request for food. The crust had already grown wider, and the eyes were now bulbous and wet.

She fed whichever beak was presented to her, but on the occasion that the infected beak reared itself to the feast, she couldn't help but feel disappointed; for herself, for her poorly chick, for its siblings and for the waste of a worm.

In the morning, Barb woke to the loudest of birdsong. She rushed outside excitedly to see how the new arrivals were. Both parents were in the nest when she jumped out onto the patio, the brown one patting something down with her foot. Barb stayed back. The yellow ring around the darker bird's eye seemed to dart from one spot to the next, never leaving the inside of the nest. Finally, she watched him raise his tail and hop across the nest wall, taking to the sky, over the fence and out of the garden.

Barb crept forward; her bare feet cold against the tiles, still wearing her summer pyjamas as late as August. Not so close as to alert the remaining parent, she stood on tiptoes and looked over the bird and into the nest.

Her bottom lip pouted out from under her top involuntarily, and she fell back onto her heels, her body swaying. The brown blackbird patted the nest again with her scaled foot. While two of the chicks moved and stretched, and writhed and twitched, the third lay underneath them, limp.

Barb thought of the new Labrador puppy next door, howling during the early hours of the morning. The dog must have been outside for her to have woken from the noise. She thought of the nest's low position in the weeds. She clenched both her fists, her arms rigid by her sides. Her bottom lip remained, but the rest of her face contorted from despair to anger.

The bird sang loud as Barb bent down, a sound which she took to be gratitude. When she placed her hands around both sides of the nest, the small bird jumped and jumped, she beat her wings, she screamed the most beautifully haunting song. It wasn't until Barb was about to lift the chicks, the nest and the tumble of weeds surrounding it that she stopped.

'Barb,' her mum called from the patio doors. 'What do you think you're doing?'

Barb stumbled from the shock of hearing her mum's voice. Still angry at the dog, overcome by emotion for the chick, and now confused by the pain shooting up her leg, Barb started bawling. When she opened her eyes, she found herself on the ground. Her mum was running towards her, panicked. The world was blurry though tears, but Barb could see the nest propped at an angle, and the limp chick lying on the patio.

Only Enid joined Barb in the ambulance, and she was a little embarrassed at having called one. By the time the paramedics had arrived Barb had stopped crying. Red tracks of tears could still be seen marking her cheeks, and the occasional sniff escaped, vigorous enough to shake Barb's whole body, but she would be alright.

When Barb had first tried to walk after the fall, she hadn't been able to put weight on her foot, so Enid and Roy had waited with her in the lounge, Barb sobbing on Enid's lap and Roy attempting to make jokes to cheer Barb up.

Roy had offered to come with them, but Barb had said no. Instead, she'd asked him to look after the birds, with a sincerity in her eyes that only a child can manage. Roy had smiled and agreed. No one had touched the nest since the fall, and since the birds meant so much to Barb, it had seemed a reasonable request.

Before Enid and Barb had left, Roy had told his daughter that he loved her. Barb had replied that she loved him too, and that she loved birds. Roy had just nodded. Enid had attempted to stifle a laugh.

'What a weekend,' Enid said to her daughter in the back of the ambulance. The sirens weren't on. 'With your Birdland tantrum, the chicks, and now this.' She wasn't cross.

A few seconds of silence passed, while Enid contemplated the ups and downs of family life.

'The bird is dead, Mum,' Barb whispered. 'It's dead.' Her head dropped, and again, she started to cry. Softer now; deeper. Enid put her hand on Barb's leg and shook it gently. 'I…I was trying to help,' Barb stuttered.

Enid didn't lift Barb's face, and she didn't talk. Instead, she allowed her daughter to experience the sorrow of death. Sorrow leads to healing. After a while, her daughter looked up at her.

'I'm sorry I hurt you with the door,' she said, and Enid nodded.

'You didn't mean to.' She gave her daughter a half-smile. 'Even if you did, I'd still love you.'

17

ENID FELT AS IF SHE WAS forever being told she wasn't a prisoner, but she certainly felt like one. No one else ever brought it up, but when asked how she was, she would often reply that she was stuck, or trapped. She brought it up, a lot.

'Oh, Mum,' Barb had laughed, kindly. 'You're not trapped. They're nice here – you said so yourself – they're nice people, and they're helping you.' Enid knew that Barb felt uncomfortable on the subject, but she also knew that this discomfort was because, fundamentally, Barb knew that Enid was a prisoner.

There were codes on the doors that Enid would never be able to remember – that was if she'd ever been told them in the first place, which she was sure she hadn't – and there was always a carer by the main door. Beyond that door was a reception area, with offices, before another coded door. Enid *was* a prisoner, and she, Barb, and the carers all knew it.

On the odd occasion that Roy had visited with Barb, he agreed. He was the only one.

So, when Enid, along with a selection of the other residents, was allowed to sit on the bench at the bottom of the drive, she would pretend she could still enjoy freedom. She'd imagine that she was waiting for a bus, and when a bus did come, which was rare, she would imagine boarding it, as if she had just finished her shopping and was going home to Roy. Soon, she realised, she would not have to imagine going home to Roy. Soon, he would be home with her.

The memory of her old home was fading. Enid could still remember specific scenes from her life in each room, but she couldn't imagine walking through it as she once had. She could remember the elaborate cake she'd once baked for Roy sixtieth birthday. She'd carried it from the kitchen out to the dining-room table, where Barb, Calvin and Alex had all been seated with Roy. Everyone was dressed up. They'd just come back from a meal at the posh pub at the beach, with the nice views. Enid could remember this, and the memory included her dining room and kitchen, but at the time they had just been background details. Now, they seemed more important to her.

Today, much like other days, no one on the bench talked much. Enid could hear Duncan and Kara chatting a few paces away, over by the gate. It was the height of summer; the sky was a sheet of blue and the bushes before the bay a random pattern of pinks and greens. A seagull landed on the pavement a few metres away from the residents. The bird tilted his head and then looked down at Enid's bag. Defensively, she picked the bag up and rooted through it, looking for the photograph of Roy that she sometimes carried with her.

A breadstick, some spoons, lots of quilting squares (that's useful, Enid thought), a scarf that she didn't recognise but which was made from a lovely fabric, a tissue with something scribbled on it and a plastic fish. The picture wasn't in there.

The calm sounds of the sea below, and of the birds above, were interrupted by a vehicle coming round the corner. The seagull, which Enid had noticed edging closer, probably after food, took to the sky as a bus pulled up at the stop next to the residents. Enid picked up the tissue from the bag and rubbed it against her dry nose, more out of habit than necessity. She looked at the scribble on the tissue.

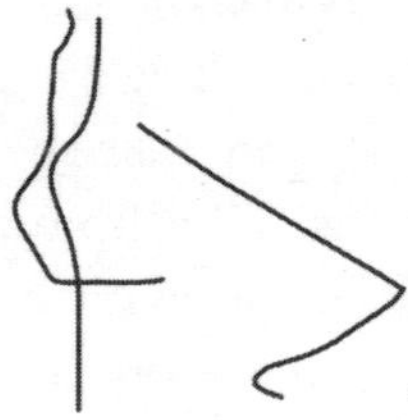

Then she looked up at the bus. There was a shape on the front of it.

47

Once again, Enid glanced at the tissue. The shape appeared… could it be the same as the bus? It wasn't a click as such, but a slow realisation that swept across Enid. She scrunched up her face and clenched her fists with joy. She knew how to get home. Without a moment to lose, she rose to her feet. Unfortunately, she lost a million moments in the time it took to prepare her joints and straighten her legs. As always, she worked through the pain, but by the time she was up, the doors had closed, and the bus was inching forward to leave.

'Time to go back in for dinner,' Duncan called over from the gate. Enid felt like she'd been punched in the stomach.

The seagull landed again; this time so close that Enid could have touched it with her foot. It studied the area around the bench while the other residents started to rise. Enid began to bend down to pick up her bag, whose zipper top sagged open, but before she could, the seagull swooped its head down, plunging its beak deep inside the bag. Enid froze as the bird ran away, wings lifted over its back, plastic fish in its beak.

18

Roy had been alone for four months now; the house silent for four months. It felt like years. Enid had been taken to the hospital a few weeks before that of course, but those first weeks had been bearable, her space on the sofa temporarily vacant. Roy had known it was likely that she wouldn't be able to come home, but there had been hope, and it had been enough to cling onto, just enough to believe. When the decision was finally made, when Roy's worst fears had finally been confirmed, the house fell into a permanent, overwhelming silence.

It wasn't a literal silence – he had visitors. Neil popped in now and again offering to pick up milk and groceries, which Roy regularly took him up on. Barb often came over too, making the same offer and staying for a cuppa. Roy knew how busy she was, and he was grateful for the visits, but even with people there, even when Barb had Alex with her, the house felt silent. It pushed an absence on him, every movement they made a reminder of other movements that were missing.

On the telly, *Countdown* had just begun. Roy chuckled as Rachel Riley placed suggestible letters on the board. Rachel herself looked a bit uncomfortable. Roy still played *Countdown* every day, with the same notepad he'd used when he'd played with Enid before. Enid's own paper was still on top of the record player, her pen beside it. Roy sat in the same spot on the sofa, despite the fact that Enid's had a better vantage point, and he still prepared a cup of tea and five biscuits for the programme. Five were always too many, even when Enid had lived there, but five was what they had, and so it remained.

Roy found his *Countdown* skills had depleted since he'd lost his opponent. He didn't feel the same pressure from the clock that he once had. Some days he hadn't even bothered trying. Today though, he found himself wanting to find a sensible word from the overly suggestible letters, and well before the minute was up, he'd managed it.

TRISQUARE. All nine letters. A victory to share with no one.

He picked up his cup and swilled the dregs in the bottom, before finishing the last mouthful, the sweet, sunken sugar now cool.

Roy spent the entirety of the end credits shuffling his weight on the sofa, both palms down, preparing himself for the push to his feet. They were introducing the next programme, *Moneybags*, by the time he was up. It hurt to bend as he picked up the three remaining biscuits, along with his mug, and it hurt to straighten again to stand. Roy could feel himself growing old, fast. He made his way to the kitchen, sliding each foot forward rather than stepping, his left worse than his right.

In the kitchen, he placed the three biscuits back in the barrel, washed his mug and plate, and then made his way back through to the lounge, stopping for a while to steady himself at the dining-room table. By the time he'd managed to lower himself back down onto the sofa, slowly at first, with a heavy drop at the end, *Moneybags* was halfway through the first adverts. The whole ordeal, Roy estimated glumly, must have taken him twenty minutes.

He turned the TV off. He wouldn't normally watch *Moneybags* anyway, so it didn't matter that he'd missed the beginning. Barb would be coming again tomorrow, and Roy worried that she'd noticed his increasing lack of mobility. He wasn't stupid: Barb had the best of intentions, but Roy knew that if he was ever going to live with Enid again, he would need to develop some form of dementia. How one developed such a thing intentionally, he didn't know.

Suddenly, he found that he needed the toilet. It was always sudden these days, just as his legs were slowing, the speed with which he needed to be upstairs and in the bathroom was increasing. Again, he placed his palms either side of him on the sofa and shuffled into what felt like the most stable position available. He held his breath and pushed himself up.

On the way to the hall, Roy considered the need for a toilet downstairs – not that he had the room. Even suggesting it to Barb would be a trigger. Would it be cheaper to instal a toilet, or to move him to a care home? Would Barb see it as an unnecessary short-term solution? No, he wouldn't bring it up. Best to stay at home until dementia set in. Maybe, when it started, he could ham it up.

He held onto the banister with his right hand and paused before taking the first step. It was the first step that did it. He lifted his leg and placed his toes on the edge of the stair. He rested his weight on the sole of his slipper and felt his toes bend up as his heel fell backwards to the ground. In an attempt to keep himself upright, Roy pulled himself forward on the banister, but his arm couldn't hold his weight, and his wide frame fell forwards. He watched the step hurtle at his face, and he felt the corner dent his chin before he fell, slowly, to the ground.

Small, quaint, and old-fashioned, No. 5 The Beach had been designed to suit the Victorian pier it overlooked. Olivia had rung Martin's home that morning and been told that he, along with a few of the other residents, would be having afternoon tea at the café that afternoon. She had a two-hour window in which to see her father-in-law before she needed to collect the children, and so, here she was. She didn't love that she would have to speak with him in front of the other residents but hoped that she could communicate what needed to be said without being too explicit.

Martin was sitting with two other residents, only one of whom Olivia recognised. They each had a drink and a slice of marble cake. There was an empty chair by the wall. She hesitated.

'Can I get you anything?'

Olivia jumped and turned. Duncan, the care assistant, was sitting on a separate table with Kara.

He laughed. 'Apologies, I didn't mean to scare you. Cup of tea? Cake?'

Olivia touched her chest. 'Sorry, thank you,' she said. 'Yes, a cup of tea please.'

'Please, sit, sit. I can get that for you.' Duncan pulled the free chair out for Olivia and introduced everyone at the table. 'This is Frank; he won't hear you unless you shout.' He gestured to the small bespectacled man sitting opposite Martin. Olivia smiled and lifted her hand in a small wave, but Frank didn't respond. 'And this is Enid,' Duncan continued. 'She finds it quite hard to remember words.' Olivia watched Enid open her mouth and then close it again.

'Hi, Enid,' Olivia smiled and redirected her wave.

'Everyone, this is Olivia,' Duncan announced.

'Yes,' Enid nodded, as if confirming. Duncan walked to the counter.

'Hi, Liv, love.'

'Hiya, Martin,' Olivia replied, sitting down next to him.

'You're looking lovely. Are you going somewhere later?' Olivia looked down. She was wearing make-up, and she knew it must look overdone for mid-afternoon. She'd worn an awful lot of make-up these last few days: thick foundation; blusher; heavy eye shadow.

'Nowhere special,' she replied, wondering whether Martin's question had been loaded.

'Here you go,' Duncan said softly, placing a cup of tea in front of Olivia. She looked up at him, making a point of eye contact, and thanked him before he returned to Kara on the table behind.

Olivia started telling Martin about Dillon's progress at school. Martin nodded, making intermittent noises to imply understanding, but he didn't ask any questions. When her monologue had come to an end, he smiled at her. Olivia had always loved Martin's smile, which extended to his eyes, today laced with water along the bottom lid.

'And you, love,' he said eventually. 'How are you doing?'

'Good,' Olivia lied. She didn't know why she'd said it.

'You never visit without David. You don't have Dillon today?' Martin paused, thinking. He looked confused. 'Or Oona,' he said eventually, and Olivia tilted her head and smiled at him. He'd forgotten his own granddaughter. 'I love that you're here, love. Of course, I do.' Olivia didn't reply. 'But,' he continued, 'am I wrong?' Olivia clasped her hands tightly on her lap.

'You know me,' she said, choosing her words so as not to cause offence. David was Martin's son after all. 'I'm OK.' That wasn't what Martin had asked, she thought.

'I do know,' Martin said, and Olivia looked up at him. She lowered her voice, though she suspected she hadn't needed to, based on the company.

'It's not as bad as before,' Olivia confided quietly, in an attempt to soften what she needed to say. 'I'm OK.' She paused again before the words piled out at speed. 'Could you have a word with him though, Martin? He's drinking quite a lot, and…well, it did a world of good last time, when I was preg…' She trailed off, and lost eye contact again, '…before Dillon came along.'

Poor Martin. At his age, and in his condition, to have to hear this about his son, again. Things had improved after Dillon had been born; they really had. David had improved for a while. Never perfect, but she had never asked for perfect. He was a doting father, but something had changed recently. He'd switched back to the jealous, angry man he'd once been, and Olivia didn't know why, so she couldn't do anything about it. Martin had been a pillar of support before. She needed him again.

'I don't think I can, Liv,' Martin said. He looked so sad, Olivia couldn't bear it. 'David doesn't visit me without you. When would I?' Olivia gave him an apologetic and understanding smile. It was a smile which she hoped would suggest an end to that particular conversation, but Martin continued. 'He's a good boy, David. You just have to hold your ground with him.' Martin looked so sad, and Olivia felt guilty for even thinking of burdening him with her own problems.

'Oona's potty training,' she said, attempting to change the subject, before she was interrupted.

'Um, uh,' said the woman across the table. Olivia and Martin looked at her. 'What, oh.' Enid shook her head. 'What drink?' she asked.

Olivia touched her chest. 'Me?' she asked, then looked down at her cup. 'Tea.'

'No, um. No.' Enid rolled her hand in front of her, gesticulating. 'You know.'

'David?' Olivia asked, frowning. Enid was looking at her expectantly. 'Beer, mainly, I suppose.' Olivia hadn't noticed Enid listening to their conversation until now. 'But who doesn't like a drink?' She forced a laugh, shifting uncomfortably in her seat.

Enid didn't laugh. She raised her hand to touch her forehead, running her fingers along a pale white line, diagonally from her hairline down to her eyebrow, and then back again. A scar; old but still prominent. Olivia remembered noticing it before.

Enid looked down at Olivia's teacup. Olivia followed her gaze, but then quickly looked back at Enid, who had started making a funny noise.

'Caw, caw.'

Almost like a bird. Olivia leaned back to the table behind where Duncan and Kara were sitting.

'Enid,' she said.

Enid stopped making the noise and shook her head. 'Oh... um, uh,' she stammered.

'It's OK,' Olivia said, glad that Enid had stopped. Again, Enid gesticulated in front of her, this time towards Olivia's drink.

'It's red,' she said. 'Red, and, oh, red.'

'It's just tea,' Olivia told her.

'Red and, um, red and blue.'

Roy's back hurt, his legs hurt, his chest hurt. He felt a consistent dull pain in his chin, which he expected to worsen when the shock faded, but when would that be? He'd been in roughly the same position all night. He'd moved his arms after he'd fallen, and tried to push himself up, but to no avail. He'd held onto the spindle closest to him, in order to lift himself, but he didn't have the strength. He wouldn't have had the strength before the fall either and he knew it. Eventually, he focused on finding the comfiest position, but as the late afternoon drew into evening, it had become apparent that there wasn't one. Lying on his front, on the hall floor at the bottom of the stairs, unable to roll onto his back, he would spend the night repeatedly moving his limbs in an attempt to relieve the cramp setting in. He drifted in and out of consciousness for hours. By morning, he could barely tell which pain had been caused by the fall, and which had grown in the night.

His thoughts tormented him more than the physical pain. What if Barb didn't come that day? How long would he be lying there? But then, what if Barb did come? Would she move him out of the house like she had Enid? And to where? Not in with Enid, surely. You hear these stories of elderly people found dead on their own floors, don't you? You read about the smell through the letterbox. He scolded his over-active mind for being so melodramatic.

To add insult to injury, the hallway table, the one with the phone on it, was digging into his hip. He couldn't reach the phone. He'd tried. Of course he'd tried.

The doorbell rang.

At first, he didn't reply. His eyes re-adjusted. His sight wasn't what it used to be, and although he was lying directly in front of the door, he couldn't make out the handle, let alone the shape through the window. When he did try to call out, he found he couldn't talk.

The bell rang again, and Roy lifted his arm and dropped it again to draw attention to himself. 'Hello,' he managed, in only a whisper. He heard the letterbox open, and then Neil, the neighbour's voice.

'Roy?'

'Hello,' still a whisper.

'Roy,' Neil called, alarm in his voice. Quite rightly, Roy thought. He heard the letterbox spring snap shut. Then, nothing.

Had Neil not seen him? The silence was too much. How many more hours would he have to lie here? Neil had always been useless, Roy thought. Pleasant enough, but useless; just about managing to bumble through life. He was always wearing Lycra, and swimming in the estuary in winter. No survival skills. It was no wonder he hadn't noticed Roy.

Then he heard the key in the lock, the sound of the door handle being pushed, and he felt a rush of air enter the hall as Neil barged in.

'Neil,' he whispered. 'Neil, thank you.'

Neil knelt on the carpet next to Roy, his mobile phone in his hand.

'Roy, are you OK?' he asked, and then, without waiting for an answer, 'I'm ringing an ambulance.'

'No,' Roy replied. 'No, don't be silly,' but Neil was already speaking into his phone. When he'd finished, Roy grabbed his arm. 'Help me up,' he said.

'The paramedics will know what to do, Roy. We need the paramedics.'

'Please Neil,' Roy said, looking him in the eye and speaking slowly, 'don't tell Barb about this.'

'Oh Roy,' Neil replied. 'You know…' and Roy did know.

19

After she'd moved back in with her parents, Enid found that not having to worry about Donald's whereabouts came as a relief. She thrived in separation. Knowing that she was alone was less painful than missing someone who should have been by her side.

Some places felt lonelier than others. The walk from the pier along the seafront made her think of happier times – her first date with Donald and getting to know him. The café at the other end of the seafront reminded her of his proposal; her joy as he'd dropped down onto one knee, and how the kiss that had followed had seemed to last forever. Truly, she had been smitten.

But Enid also found herself thinking of their final night together, and as she did, she'd touch the slowly healing wound above her right eyebrow. The fight wasn't about the fight. It wasn't about Donald not going to work. It wasn't even about his affair – an affair still unspoken between them. The fight had stemmed from disappointment, a growing seed that had sprouted between them, forcing them apart with each unsuccessful month. Donald had been an unhappy man.

The first letter Enid received came only a week after she'd moved back in with her parents. By then, she'd divulged to her mother more information about the cut above her eyebrow, and had taken comfort in her mum's outrage. The envelope had *'Enid'* written in Donald's handwriting. She'd opened it in her bedroom, alone.

Donald wrote that he was sorry, and that he missed Enid, though Enid wondered how much of that had come from his own mum not wanting a divorce in the family. She noted that while he was sorry, he never stated specifically what he was sorry for, almost as if it would be too painful for him to write, or to admit, either to her or to himself.

The second letter came exactly one week after the first. The contents were similar, but with the addition that Donald's mum had requested to meet Enid. It was a request that wouldn't be granted. Both letters asked her to go back to him. She knew she should be angry, but Enid found herself pitying Donald.

There were six men working with her at the printers now. Roy, the new boy, had settled in well, and everyone, Enid included, found him hilarious. Occasionally, Enid had the feeling that Roy was flirting with her, but she knew that he couldn't be, and regularly scolded herself for thinking so. She had been married once already. The men at the printers were polite about it, but Enid knew, as far as they were concerned, she was damaged goods.

This feeling was regularly reinforced by her mum, though

she no longer tried to persuade Enid to make things work with Donald.

'Marrying him was the stupidest thing you ever did,' she'd say. 'It was never going to end happily. He was only ever interested in himself.' She had been right. She always was, and that's why, when she told Enid that 'no decent chap would ever want her now,' Enid had believed her.

'Go on,' Roy had said, playfully, one day, just before lunch. 'Come for a drink with me.' Enid blushed and shook her head.

'You don't mean it,' she said, believing her own words. Her least favourite thing about Roy – perhaps his only flaw – was his persistence in asking her out. Enid suspected that the others had put him up to it.

'Fine,' Roy replied with a grin. 'I'll go alone.' Enid knew that he wouldn't. He'd have lunch with his partner, if he had one, or his friends. Enid always ate lunch at her desk.

'How was your lunch alone?' she asked Roy when he walked back into the office, putting a mocking emphasis in her words, attempting to own the joke.

'I *was* alone,' he replied, eyes wide, faking injury.

'Mm,' Enid looked back at the papers on her desk.

By the fourth letter, Donald's tone had changed completely. The begging, which was frankly pathetic, had been replaced by a stronger voice, one that Enid found threatening. He reminded her that he knew where she was staying, and regularly commented on the five years in which he would still have her as his wife. Legally, you're mine, he'd written.

In the fifth letter, Donald acknowledged the affair, claiming that he would end it if Enid came back to him, though Enid had the distinct impression that his new woman was living in their house. It was at this point that Enid decided to show her parents the correspondence. She couldn't keep it to herself any longer.

The sixth letter demanded that she came home. He was telling her, as her husband – not requesting. The ink had been pressed hard into the paper. It had been written in anger. The overall effect was a man who wasn't in his right mind. One minute remorseful, the next angry. Sometimes he loved Enid, sometimes he hated her.

'Why doesn't he just talk to me?' Enid had asked her mum that night.

'Because he knows what I'll do to him if *I* answer the door,' had been the answer. It was nice to have her fighting Enid's corner.

'I've been speaking with some of the boys at work,' her dad interjected, 'and I don't think you need to wait five years to get a divorce.'

Enid doubted this was true but she couldn't help feeling hopeful. 'Why?' she pressed.

'Well, one of them reckons that you can get an early divorce if you can prove cruelty or adultery – and what with these letters, you can prove both, can't you?'

Later that week, a solicitor confirmed this to be the case, and Enid, with support from both her mum and dad, started proceedings. She received only one more letter from Donald, clearly posted before he'd been notified. It was vile. A fantasy in which he and his new woman had three children together, and Enid grew old, barren and alone.

'He's hammered the final nail into his own coffin there,' Enid's dad had reassured her, after finding her crying in her room and reading the letter. Enid saw his face when he was reading. He seemed as repulsed as she was.

The following week, Enid stood up to Roy. His persistent jokes were bordering on bullying now, and she didn't need more of that in her life.

'Fine,' she said, calling his bluff. 'I'll meet you for a drink. Where?' She'd expected Roy to backtrack, to apologise and acknowledge the cruel joke. He'd be polite about it, but ultimately, he'd reject her. She hadn't expected him to provide a place and a time, like he'd been waiting for this moment, like he'd been planning for it.

20

By the time she reached the drinks aisle, Olivia's trolley was close to full. She found she had mixed feelings about choosing wine that day. Normally, she enjoyed picking the wine – three bottles of red and three of white. On such a day, with the kids at school and nursery, she'd take in the labels and savour the choice, Sauvignon Blanc being their joint favourite grape, and New Zealand being a preferred region. Today she found herself reluctant even to pick up a bottle. God knew that she needed a glass every now and again, but what with David being as he had been recently, buying alcohol just felt like locking herself in. Into where, she didn't know. If she didn't buy wine at all though...well, that would just be throwing fuel on the fire. She picked up six bottles and threw them quickly into the trolley, before heading over to the checkout almost on autopilot.

In the queue, she took her phone out, as usual, more for the false feeling of solitude than anything else. There were no notifications. She opened the news, ignored the headlines and then closed the app again. Then the same with Facebook, the weather app, and then Facebook again. After that, she just started scrolling between home pages.

The phone vibrated and Olivia watched David's name flash onto the screen. She didn't open the message, and instead lowered her hand to her side. For all David knew, the phone could have been in her pocket.

She looked up, behind her and then around the shop. She told herself that she'd had enough of staring at the screen, and wanted to take in her surroundings, but who was she kidding? Somewhere deep inside herself, where her unconscious collided fleetingly with her conscious, Olivia knew that she was checking to make sure David wasn't near her, that he hadn't seen her ignore his text. Luckily, his lack of presence allowed Olivia to tell herself that wasn't the case.

Just then, she noticed Duncan and Kara at a table in the café. She looked around for Martin, but the care home residents, seated two tables away from the carers, consisted of the same motley crew as before: an old gentleman and two elderly women, one of whom, Olivia remembered, was called Enid.

Even without Martin there, Olivia considered walking over to say hello after paying. It would be nice to speak to someone – about anything really – but the thought was only fleeting. What would she say, and to whom? Kara and Duncan were the two nearest to her in age, but she suspected David wouldn't like her talking with another man. He'd been so jealous in the past. Sure, he'd improved, but she didn't want to encourage the relapse he seemed to be going through recently. Something inside her acknowledged the absurdity of her decision, but she pushed it down, ignoring the claustrophobic sensation tightening around her stomach.

She lifted her phone again and tapped into her messages.

Off out tonight. I won't be too late xx

Olivia felt her chest deflate. He would be late, drinking no doubt, and he would expect her to be awake when he returned. He'd be drinking from stress, and he'd be violent. This last point wasn't a given, but she felt likely to say something he wouldn't like, and then the crescendo of booze and stress would be hers to weather. She tapped the keyboard.

Have fun. Love you xx

Even if he came home in a good mood, which did still happen sometimes, she would find herself a nervous wreck all night, waiting.

When it was her turn at the till, Olivia bagged up her shopping and paid, her body weightless, as if she was watching her movements rather than controlling them. When the bags were in the trolley, she walked past the café towards the exit, giving a small wave over to the carers' table so as not to seem rude. Both Duncan and Kara appeared to be deep into some paperwork, and neither noticed, so Olivia diverted the wave to the residents' table.

She noticed that Enid, the elderly woman with the scar above her eyebrow, wasn't sitting at the table as she had been. Rather, she was shuffling towards the checkout, away from the other residents and the carers. 'Enid?' Olivia called, and Enid paused and turned to look at Olivia, who left her trolley and walked over. 'Enid,' she said again, softer. 'Where are you off to?'

'Oh…um…' Enid frowned, and Olivia could see her

determination to speak. 'Roy,' she said, and then, 'how, oh. It's you. How are you?'

'You don't need to ask about me,' Olivia told her, though she was surprised to find herself flattered that Enid had.

'Worried,' Enid said. Olivia's mouth opened slightly, and for the first time she and Enid had direct eye contact.

'Worried?' Olivia repeated. Enid began to stutter.

'You know,' she replied, clearly trying to find the words, 'oh…uh.'

'Your friends are there.' Olivia gestured to where Enid had been sitting, just a few metres away from where they were standing now.

'No,' Enid said, and nodded pointedly at Olivia. 'Worried, you.'

'Worried about me?' Olivia asked in a whisper. 'I'm fine. I am fine. Do you mean Martin is worried? You can tell Martin that I'm fine.' She felt heat rise inside her, but then continued, 'and give him my love.'

Enid looked flustered, and Olivia felt guilty for causing it. 'Come on, Enid,' she said in a recomposed voice, 'let's get you back with your friends.' She lifted her hand to Enid's upper arm, flinching from the pain in her shoulder. It was still recovering, taking an age after David had accidentally caught it in the car door. Enid lowered her head.

'What, um…your, should…um. Shoulder?'

'Just lifting,' Olivia replied, as she always did. She turned Enid around to face the table and helped her down into her chair.

'Now, where were you going, Enid?' It was Duncan. He didn't wait for Enid to reply, and instead looked up at Olivia. 'Thank you,' he said. 'She never would have gotten very far.'

He smiled, and Olivia smiled back. He was probably worried she'd think they might lose Martin, but Martin always seemed happy with them, so they could do no wrong in Olivia's eyes.

'Roy,' Enid muttered.

'Cuppa?' Duncan asked, and Olivia shook her head. She regretted coming over at all.

'No, thank you,' she answered, already turning to leave. I've got to...' She paused, thinking of an excuse, '...pick up the kids.' It wasn't even an excuse. She heard Duncan cheerily wishing her a good day as she returned to her trolley, the supermarket a wall of noise surrounding her, the air outside deafening her on the way to the car.

Once in the driving seat, Olivia found herself unable to cry. She held onto her shoulder with her hand. It was one thing lying to people about how she'd hurt her shoulder, but she'd started lying to herself. Of course it hadn't been an accident. He'd hit her with the door twice. Accidents don't happen twice, within the same few seconds.

He'd hit her with his hands at home too. He'd held her against the wall and spat at her. Most of the ways in which David had hurt her could be hidden – from the children, from society and from himself – when he was playing a better version of a husband.

Olivia had wanted to sit down with Enid, or Duncan, or Kara, but she'd run, scared of what David might do if he found her with them. What had Duncan said? Enid never would have gotten very far. He was right. Enid found it hard to move quickly, and she found it hard to talk. More than that, had Enid confessed to being worried about Olivia herself?

Olivia found herself desperately lonely. She should go back. She should walk back into the supermarket and sit with the residents. She should talk to Enid, not about the pain in her shoulder, or in her stomach, or on her side, but just for the company. Just to remember what it was like. If David saw her, then so what?

But she didn't. Instead, she turned the key in the ignition, and drove out of the car park.

21

Roy watched the school doors dutifully. He knew a little about some of the women that surrounded him, waiting for their own children to finish school. Enid talked to them regularly when she waited for Barb, and she'd often relay the gossip to him in the evenings when Barb was asleep. It was all so inconsequential.

Roy never found himself chatting though. Maybe it was because he was a man, or maybe it was simply the fact that he only picked up Barb once a week, due to his working hours not allowing him more. Either way, he didn't mind, but he did always feel slightly self-conscious before the door opened. He tried to keep his head down, while at the same time scanning the faces, searching for the parents of Barb's friends, just in case they approached him.

He recognised one of the mothers, a brunette woman,

standing a few feet away from him. Little Peter's mother. Roy couldn't remember her name. R something. He knew that she'd needed a plumber last week, and that she'd had to wait three days for one to come. That wasn't useful to him. She was engaged in conversation with the woman next to her anyhow. It was unlikely he'd need to remember her name.

A little further back, he could see Julia. According to Enid, Julia had had to mend her Andrew's school uniform twice in the past month; boys hey, and… Wait. Roy raised his head, peering above the crowd. It was an action he wouldn't normally dream of, but he recognised the slicked-back hair, the flat shapeless forehead; another man in the crowd of women. He squinted to make sure he wasn't mistaken, but he wasn't. It was Donald, Enid's ex-husband.

Roy ducked down again, but saw Donald's head turn just before he did, and for the smallest of moments, they had direct eye-contact. What was Donald doing here? Roy knew he didn't have children of his own, and he couldn't imagine anyone trusting Donald enough to pick up theirs. That must be it though, surely, he thought.

Still, Roy moved closer to the front, apologising to the women he overtook as he did so. He felt his heart-rate increase and took a second to regulate his breathing. He wanted to appear calm and unassuming. He would make it so that when Barb came out, he would be right there, next to the door. He would pick her up and they'd go home. They were having beef for dinner. They liked beef.

The door opened, and Roy allowed himself to glance behind him, back towards Donald, but when he did, he saw that Donald had gone.

Barb liked it when her dad came to pick her up from school. He made her feel like she was the only kid in the playground. He'd pick her up, swing her around, and then joke with her on the walk to the car. Today had been different. He'd held onto her hand so tightly, thanked her teacher under his breath and then ushered her to the car before she'd even had time to say goodbye to her friends.

Barb sat still in the car. Normally she'd kick her feet rhythmically against the car seat and chat aimlessly with her dad about her day at school, or she'd hum some melody and he'd ask her what the tune was. Usually, it was a hymn she'd learned at school, and then she'd hear him humming along, giving away that he already knew it. Today, she didn't kick, and she wasn't humming. Her dad wasn't chatting with her. Barb was acutely aware of her own stillness. She didn't know what was wrong with him, but she sensed her dad's stress, and feared that if she moved, she would make it worse.

'Sorry, Daddy,' she said, quietly.

'Hmm,' her dad replied, not paying attention. She tried to think why he could be cross with her. She'd apologised for trying to hold the birds and been told that it hadn't been her fault; she wasn't to know. And he'd left for work that morning happy, Barb remembered, he'd been singing his own made-up song about keys. She'd giggled.

'Do you want to play jokes?' she asked, tentatively.

'Yes,' he replied. 'You tell one first.'

Barb sucked her bottom lip and thought. She wanted to tell one of his favourites, though it was hard to know which ones were, because he laughed at them all.

'Knock, knock,' she said.

'Who's there?'

'Twit,' she smiled. She knew he'd know the punchline now.

'Twit who?' he asked.

'Did you hear an owl, Daddy?' Barb broke into a giggle, expecting her dad to join in, but instead he tapped his steering wheel, in thought.

'Hm,' he said. Barb felt lost in the break from their usual rhythm, but she tried to bring it back again.

'Your turn, Daddy,' she said, but he didn't reply. She could see his eyes in the rear-view mirror, darting this way and that. He was in his own world, his lips moving every now and then. Occasionally, she'd hear a word or two of his mutterings, but they meant nothing to her.

'Doing there… What… Why would… Hasn't seen her for… Why at school…' Barb started to fiddle with the material on the chair beneath her legs.

'Are you cross, Daddy?' she asked. Her words seemed to jolt her dad back into reality.

'What?' he asked, and then, 'Cross? No, of course not.' They rode in silence for a while, and then he said, 'I love you and your mum very much – more than anything in fact.' Barb watched his eyes look at her through the mirror and she smiled back at him.

The words were reassuring, but Barb could only focus on the distance in his tone. She couldn't wait to get home and see her mum.

22

Bloody Neil. It wasn't as if Roy had fallen down the stairs; he'd just fallen on his way up the stairs, on the first step, no less. He couldn't help but feel like it had looked worse than it was, but Neil had insisted on telling Barb, and Barb had insisted on telling a social worker.

They'd prodded and poked him. He'd spent two nights in hospital, listening to Barb talking with doctors and social workers and all those professional types and what-have-you. They'd discussed him and his future right there, in front of his face, always asking what he thought about it, but never listening. He knew that no one had told Enid about his fall. Apparently, it would be 'for her own good', but Roy suspected she would want to know about the wellbeing of her husband.

Eventually, when he was up and walking again, it was agreed that he would be allowed to come home. He had been assessed as mentally capable, which was the exact opposite of what Roy wanted. He wanted to be mentally incapable and living with Enid.

Barb had been visiting daily, and Roy was grateful. He enjoyed her company and cherished the visits, but they also served as a hammer, waiting to fall. He knew that Barb was checking up on him, making sure that he wasn't on the floor, that he wouldn't be left alone again, helpless on the floor. He ought to be happy to have this kind of love in his life, and he was, but he was also distinctly aware that if Barb did come in one day to find him on the floor, that would be it. He would be shipped into the wrong care home. A home for the mentally capable, and he would never live with his Enid ever again.

But Roy had a plan. He'd started kicking up a campaign of fuss. On the fourth of Barb's visits, when he began to realise the main purpose of them, he began to forget people's names.

'How is Sam?' he'd asked.

'Sam?' Barb had shouted.

'Oh, you know, Sam,' Roy had said, imitating the way he'd seen Enid waving one of her arms around when trying to communicate something. 'Sam, your son.'

'You mean Alex? My daughter?'

'That's the ticket.'

When Roy couldn't hear something that Barb was saying, which for Roy was often, he'd talk about printers, at length, forgetting the names of all the various pieces of machinery and of his former colleagues.

'Well,' he'd say, 'back then everything was manual, you know, and the…um. Well, I'd have to operate that while… oh, the boy in the cap – what's his name? He'd have to hold onto the…well…you know. It was different then, wasn't it?'

'I asked if Neil had brought you round a paper this morning, Dad,' Barb would reply, looking annoyed.

One Saturday, Barb had offered to pick Roy up the following day and take him to hers for a roast. Roy had said yes, and Barb had confirmed that she'd pick him up around midday. After Barb left, Roy walked to the shop and bought a raw chicken and placed it in the fridge before bedtime. He set his alarm for half-past eight, and when it woke him, he shuffled downstairs and turned the oven on. He put the chicken in at nine. At twelve, when Barb turned up, there was a distinct smell of burning throughout the house. Barb had sat on the sofa.

'Why does it smell of chicken, Dad?' she shouted so that Roy could hear.

'Hmm,' Roy responded. 'I used to put the paper in, you know, and then I'd…well it depended on what I'd been asked to print, you see.'

'Dad,' Barb interrupted, this time louder, more annoyed. 'Chicken.'

'Oh, yes, I'm cooking a chicken for dinner. To help out, you know. Now, when did I put the oven on?' Roy made a show of talking slower than normal. Barb stormed angrily into the kitchen to turn the oven off, but she didn't bother taking the ruined chicken out.

'What the hell, Dad?' she said on her way back into the lounge, just loud enough for Roy to hear. He bit his bottom lip and looked straight in front of him, out of the window. Barb pulled the footstool up to his chair and sat facing him.

'I know what you're doing, Dad,' she said loudly, and Roy gave her a sad smile. He knew, deep down, that she would. 'You can't fake dementia.' She gave him the same sad smile in return. 'You're not doing a bad job of it – I'll give you that –

but you wouldn't be able to keep it up.'

Roy exhaled. 'I would, love,' he replied.

'You know where Mum is,' Barb continued. 'It's expensive, Dad. Really expensive. They specialise in dementia. If we want Mum to be able to stay there, we've got to make sure we can afford it.' Roy had never thought about it like that, and he understood what Barb was saying. If he was to move, it needed to be somewhere cheap. It wasn't Barb's money of course, it was his and Enid's, but Roy did want Enid to have the best care possible, and Enid did seem increasingly comfortable where she was.

'I miss her,' he said. 'I miss her so much, love.'

23

Enid was no stranger to buses. She and Roy had received their free passes when they'd retired, and they'd made the most of them, exploring villages and towns they'd never been to before. You could only travel on the small local buses, but if you planned it well enough, you could visit towns quite far afield by taking two or three. Enid and Roy did plan well enough.

One Friday, they'd managed to take three buses all the way down to Wells, where they'd booked a room above a pub, then they'd caught another two buses the morning after to spend the day in Glastonbury. After a night in a hotel room, from which they'd had a view of the Tor, they'd taken four buses to Weston-Super-Mare (via a few hours in Bridgewater), slept in a classic British seaside bed and breakfast, and then, finally, they'd caught the single bus back home to Clevedon on Monday. Bus travel had become something of a game for Enid and Roy.

Of course, the free bus passes also had more practical uses. Enid started taking the bus to ASDA rather than driving. Once they'd both retired, Roy tended to come shopping with her. They didn't always talk on the bus; they'd been married a long time and they didn't always want to, but sometimes they did. Sometimes they talked a lot. Once they talked so much on the way back from ASDA that they missed the stop outside their own house.

'What on earth are we doing here?' Roy said, looking out of the window. Enid followed his gaze and saw the beach, with the silhouette of the pier jutting out from behind the cove.

'Oh, dear me,' she laughed. 'I don't want to walk back with all this shopping. It's heavy. We'll have to get off at the next stop and get another bus back.' It didn't feel like an inconvenience.

'Well, if we're getting another bus,' Roy said, his eyes smiling, 'let's go a few more stops and find somewhere nice to sit. We have the makings of a picnic.' He nodded down to the shopping bags at their feet.

'We have a week's-worth of shopping,' Enid corrected him. She loved being carried away with Roy's whims, but she'd never found it easy to get on board with them straight away.

'We've got bread, ham, mayonnaise, crisps,' Roy said. 'The only thing we don't have is a drink.'

'I bought fizzy water,' Enid interjected, by way of agreement. The bus continued on for another ten minutes, past the bandstand, past the leaning tree and the tearooms. It turned away from the seafront, drove up a hill, around a grassy patch, and down a small wooded road to a spot which overlooked a bay and out to sea again. Enid watched Roy put his finger in the air dramatically, putting on a show. He opened his mouth and inhaled, as if creating suspense for an announcement.

'Here,' he said in one big exhale.

It was mid-afternoon, the sun was still high but not intrusive, and the sea was calm. Across the road stood another bus stop beside a small, empty bench. Looking around, Enid realised that the area was completely deserted.

She made sandwiches as Roy stored the shopping under the bench in the shade and then they sat, side by side, eating their picnic.

After they'd finished, Enid and Roy chatted and watched the waves bob gently up and down. Occasionally a car would pull into the old Victorian building perched on the hill behind them, and then leave about twenty to thirty minutes later.

'Nice place to live,' Enid had commented.

Before they knew it, the sun was setting. How long had they been sitting on the bench? Roy had put his arm around Enid.

'We should get the next bus,' he'd said, and two buses later, they went home.

Barb placed a packet of biscuits on Enid's dresser, gave her some updates on the family, then pulled a bin bag full of her mum's underwear from under the cupboard.

'Why do you keep hiding your clothes, Mum?' she asked.

Enid looked surprised. 'I do no such thing,' she said, and rubbed her wedding ring, anxiously. She seemed agitated.

'It's a beautiful ring,' Barb said, trying to distract her. 'Is it real silver? Could you and dad afford silver back then?' Barb knew that it wasn't, she'd had this conversation with her mum many times before. They'd bought what they could afford. Enid had been pregnant with her when she'd married Roy, but she used to like telling the story, and Barb enjoyed hearing it, so she asked anyway.

'Yes.' Enid said. 'Silver, yes. I think. Beautiful, isn't it?'

Barb smiled at her. 'It is,' she said.

'How long…?' Enid asked, not finishing the question. 'How long…you know?'

Barb watched her wave her hand up and down, as if trying to wave the words out of her mouth.

'Long, Mum. You and Dad have been married all my life, and I'm fifty.' Barb knew that the number would mean nothing to Enid, but suspected that the word 'long' would, and she noticed her mother welling up. 'You're getting so much better at talking,' she said.

They sat in silence for a while. Barb touched Enid's wedding ring and they both looked at it.

'When…oh…um,' Enid started, 'when's Martin coming? Oh…no. Not Martin.' She looked at Barb and Barb looked patiently back. 'Roy.'

Now it was Barb's turn to hold back the tears. She hoped upon hope that Enid wouldn't remember their previous conversation, when she'd joked about Roy moving into the home.

'Mum,' she said, and then paused, searching for the right words. There weren't any. Barb hadn't lied to her mum since she was a teenager, and she wasn't going to start again now. 'Dad's finding it hard at home by himself. He can't really walk anywhere any more, and you have to shout if you want him to hear anything.' Barb watched her mum's face fall; her mouth, her cheeks; worst of all, her eyes.

'He's alright, Mum, I've found a place for him to live.' It was true. She had. It was a shabby, run-down building, grand on the outside and sickly on the in. Crucially, it was close to here, and that mattered. Barb looked around Enid's room. 'It's like this,' she said, and was happy to see her mum's face brighten.

'Oh,' Enid smiled, 'this.'

'Just like this,' Barb confirmed.

Enid nodded. 'This,' she repeated, and Barb felt the guilt deep inside her stomach.

'How are you feeling this morning, Enid, my lovely?' Kara walked into Enid's room confidently and opened the little window, as if the room were hers. Enid didn't mind. Kara's face was familiar, kind and soft. She was there to help Enid get washed and dressed. Enid didn't like being washed or dressed by someone else, but she found it difficult to do it herself these days. The number of times people had told her she'd forgotten to put a bra on, or that her trousers were inside out, had become embarrassing, so she'd succumbed to the carer's help a long time ago.

At the side of her bed, Enid fumbled with her nightie and tried to wish Kara a good morning. She never managed to say any words at all straight after waking up, but she still tried, nonetheless.

'It's alright, lovely,' Kara interrupted Enid's stuttering, 'let me get that for you.' She helped Enid out of her nightie, chatting merrily as she did.

'Oh…um…how…you?' Enid managed eventually, interrupting. Kara stopped in her tracks as she was leading Enid to the bathroom.

'I'm very well thank you, Enid,' she said, with a grateful nod of the head.

'I...' Enid began, and then thought about how to finish the sentence. 'I...I'll be having a visitor soon,' she smiled. Kara would surely know she meant permanently. Barb would have had to go through all the procedures to move Roy in. Kara would probably spend the rest of the day preparing for his arrival. Kara helped Enid into the chair in the shower.

'Probably,' she said, as she turned on the shower in Enid's en suite and checked the temperature with her hand. 'You have a lot of visitors, Enid, and it's no wonder. You're fun to chat with, and you have such a lovely personality.'

Kara showered Enid, starting with her shoulders and working down her whole body to her feet. Enid had grown used to the right movements to make: mouth closed; arm in the air; other arm; foot up; other foot. Kara swapped flannels and wetted the new one with soap while Enid closed her eyes tightly.

'Almost done,' she said, but Enid knew that. 'Alright then, Enid, my lovely, up you come. Careful you don't slip.' Kara helped Enid to her feet, wrapped her in a clean towel and dried her gently. 'It's chilly today,' she stated, 'you can wear that new cardigan that Barb brought you last week.' Enid didn't remember the cardigan but agreed and thanked her for the help.

Once Enid was in the cardigan, she noticed that the carer was looking closely at her face.

'Where did you get the scar on your eyebrow?' Kara asked. 'I've noticed you touching it sometimes. It doesn't ever hurt, does it?' Enid didn't respond. 'You don't have to answer,' Kara confirmed. 'It's just me being nosy. Click.' She smiled and looked away.

Click.

One of the curtains blew into the room and Kara walked over to the window to close it.

'Chilly,' she said. 'Click.'

Enid scrunched her eyes up tight.

'Stop,' she muttered to herself.

'Enid?' Kara was close to her again, and Enid felt a palm on the top of her back. She raised her own arms to place her hands over her ears. Despite the closed window, she found that she could hear the sea once again, and she focused hard on it, blanking out Kara, blanking out her incessant clicking.

Among the waves in Enid's hands, she could hear a scratching, light and distant. The scream, when it came, was up close to Enid's ears.

Catching her breath in a deep and sudden intake, she opened her eyes, and then froze. The noise had gone. Kara was up close to Enid's face, her eyebrows worried and her mouth moving as though saying something, but she was silent. Silent and out of focus.

Over Kara's left shoulder, on the drawers next to Enid's bag, stood a magnificent, brightly coloured and glossy macaw. The yellow feathers shone like neon, the red and blue feathers circling them rending the rest of the room dull and emphasising its mundanity. Enid could only see one eye on the parrot's tilted head, but the deep emptiness behind it was directed straight at her, and she felt naked. The glassy black otherness seemed to be examining her. The silence was broken by the bird's toe.

Tap.

And then, a soft caw.

Caw.

'Enid?' Kara's voice slowly echoed back into the room. Enid blinked and let out a disjointed string of syllables.

'I...ja...bi...couj...ya.'

Kara was holding onto both of Enid's shoulders now, her young but wrinkled face obscuring the parrot behind her. Enid looked at the faded red of Kara's lipstick, her dark eyes full of concern, and the pretty, but dull sapphire earrings that she wore every single day. Kara was familiarity. Kara was safety.

Enid's shoulders relaxed and Kara stepped back. The macaw wasn't behind her any more. Enid looked around the room, but there was nothing out of the ordinary. The sounds had gone.

'Donald,' Enid said.

'Donald?' Enid touched the skin above her right eyebrow. Kara nodded and stepped back. She couldn't have known what Enid had meant. Enid had called Roy 'Donald' before. Enid felt terrible about that, but Roy would understand. Kara must have assumed Enid had meant to say Roy this time too.

'Let's hope Roy will be able to visit again soon,' she said.

In a flash, Enid remembered what Barb had told her the night before. Roy would be moving in with her soon.

'Oh good,' she said, wondering if it would be later that day.

24

FOR THEIR FIRST DATE, Enid had met Roy at the pier where, five years earlier she'd had her first date with Donald. Thankfully, she hadn't had a chance to think about that because Roy had been so full of questions. Where had she grown up? What were her family like? How many siblings? Her favourite places to eat, music, films. He listened too, seeming genuinely interested in Enid and what she had to say. They walked along the seafront.

'You know I was married before,' Enid said, still not convinced that this wasn't a prolonged joke, 'very recently in fact.' Roy nodded. Enid had only just separated from her Donald when Roy had started at the printers, so she knew he must have at least some idea. 'I'm a divorcee,' she continued, hammering the point, and Roy nodded again. Enid looked away from him, embarrassed. She was going to have to say it.

'If you've asked me out for a joke, Roy,' she started, but didn't finish the sentence. Roy swooped his head down in front of her so that Enid couldn't help but face him. She was forced to stop walking.

'Look at you,' he said. 'Why would I care if you're divorced? You're beautiful. Any fool can see that.' Enid blushed. 'But it's not that, Enid; you're funny – really funny in fact.'

'Quiet,' Enid replied, again embarrassed.

'Do you still love your ex-husband?'

Enid shook her head.

'He's a fool to let you go.' They carried on walking in silence. 'This is the place,' Roy said eventually, gesturing towards a café; No. 5 The Beach. Enid laughed. 'What?' he asked.

'I'll tell you inside,' she replied, deciding whether she would or not. She was relieved when they sat at a different table.

'Tell me about your scar,' Roy probed. 'I bet there's a good story there.'

'Oh, not really,' Enid replied, her answer prepared, rehearsed and repeated. 'I just fell over with a wine glass in my hand. I guess that's why you shouldn't drink wine.' She laughed as she always did and wondered whether Roy believed her. He nodded and didn't press further.

'What are you drinking?' he asked, and Enid gave him a knowing smile. He'd set the punchline up too well to ignore.

'Oh, I don't know,' she said, looking at the board. 'Well, they don't serve wine, so that's me at a complete loss.' Their laughter was interrupted by a familiar voice.

'Enid?' It was her mum. She was calling across the tables from the door. Enid put her head in her hands, hiding her face from both her mum and Roy. She didn't want her mum to think she was loose, and yet, here she was on a date so soon after Donald.

'That's my mum,' she whispered, embarrassed for herself, and by her behaviour. To Enid's further dismay, Roy stood and walked over to the door.

'Roy,' she heard him say, and then looked up through her fingers to see him extending a hand. 'Enid's mother?' Her mum nodded and took his hand. Enid lowered her hand and watched. Frozen to her chair.

'Roy,' her mum said. Roy's smile was always cheeky, like he might be about to do something he shouldn't.

'You've raised a wonderful daughter,' he said. Enid's mum didn't respond. 'I work at the printers, with Enid.' Still there was no answer. 'Would you like to join us?' Roy's voice sounded shaky now, and uncertain. He fetched both Enid and her mum a cup of tea and a slice of fruit cake, while she quizzed Enid about the secret relationship which she seemed to have walked in on.

'This is the first time I've met with him,' Enid scowled at her, guilty for being with a man, and mortified that her mum had found her. 'He's a friend from work,' she'd explained, but when they all stood to leave, Enid noticed her mum gushing a little.

'Won't you join us for dinner this weekend?' she asked, and Enid's eyes widened.

'I'd love to,' Roy replied. 'That is, if Enid would like me to.'

Not only were Roy and Enid seeing each other every day at work, but now they would often meet in the evenings too. Enid insisted that they didn't show affection in public; she didn't want people to talk, or for rumours about her to spread.

For the most part Roy agreed with her, but he refused to hide away completely, so Enid found herself eating out with him and sharing long, slow walks along the seafront. Every Sunday they ate lunch at Enid's parents' house, and Enid was amazed to see how well Roy and her parents got on. Her mum asked Roy questions. He was nothing short of charming in his answers, but he also showed an interest in learning about her parents too. Enid began to recognise why her mum had been so wary of Donald from the start.

After much deliberation with her parents, Enid had shown Roy the letters from Donald, and explained the truth behind her scar. She didn't want to hide anything from him. She could tell, just from those last few weeks, that he wouldn't lose his head over it, and she had been right. He hadn't. Rather, he'd contemplated the facts overnight and suggested the following day that they tell Donald about the two of them – only if Enid was in agreement, which she wasn't.

'It might be better if he finds out from us,' Roy had reasoned, clearly having given it much thought. 'Or you, rather.'

'I think he probably knows,' Enid said. 'It's a small town, and I'd be surprised if he didn't check up on me from time to time. Mum wrote to him saying I'd moved out , but he'll have checked. He'll know I haven't. He's probably seen you.'

'If you're sure, then I'll do whatever's right for you.'

Enid fell for Roy further with every sentence. The relationship became harder to hide when her belly began to swell. A mere four months after they had started courting, Roy invited Enid to move into his home . It was a muted affair as Enid didn't want the neighbours to talk. They would anyway; she knew that.

'Let them talk,' Roy had said. 'Let them scream it, and let

us scream it with them.' Enid had never known anyone so genuinely happy as Roy appeared to be, and his happiness was infectious.

Just three days after the move, Roy surprised Enid by cooking her dinner: coq-au-vin. Melon for starters and a treacle tart for dessert. Enid felt her spoon tap against something hard in the tart. It didn't surprise her – the food had been terrible – but she didn't say anything. Roy had made such an effort. She shuffled the object out of the topping secretly, hoping Roy wouldn't notice. It wasn't easy, he was taking an unnatural amount of interest in her eating.

'Oh,' Enid said when she saw the ring. She said it again when she saw that Roy was already down on one knee.

'Enid, I would have taken you out,' he said, 'but I thought you'd prefer it if I did this here, in our home, in our family's home.'

Enid smiled, and cried, both uncontrollably. 'Oh,' she said again. 'Hormones.' They both laughed. 'Yes. Of course, yes.'

Roy stood up and they hugged.

'I haven't asked you anything yet,' he whispered in her ear.

'But,' Enid said through her tears, 'you were going to, weren't you?' Roy laughed.

'You're silly.'

That Sunday, at Enid's parents' house, Roy and Enid shared the news.

'A shotgun wedding,' her mum had said, clearly distressed. 'Oh Enid, what happened?' Enid had been expecting this response, though Roy had told her not to worry.

'No, Mum,' she said. 'It's not a shotgun wedding. We're getting married because we're in love, and we're having a baby for the same...'

'Stop.' Enid's mum scrunched her face up tightly. She exploded in an open-mouthed smile. 'I'm sorry Enid.' She looked at Roy: 'Roy.' Her shoulders dropped and she exhaled. 'I'm so proud,' she said. 'Really, I am.'

25

Olivia went through her plan one final time before pressing the buzzer on the large wooden door of the dementia home. She looked down and focused on her breathing. It shouldn't be this scary. On the surface of it, all she was doing was visiting an elderly person in their home. In different circumstances, this would be considered charity work. She heard footsteps the other side, exhaled, looked up and smiled, prepared as though she were going to preach religion.

'Olivia,' Duncan said with a cheery Scottish lilt. 'How lovely. Come in. Martin will be happy to see you.' He turned and started walking back into the building, the implication being that Olivia should follow. 'No David today?'

'Actually,' Olivia said, one foot in the door, 'I'm here to visit Enid.' Duncan turned, surprised.

'Enid?'

'Do you have more than one Enid here?' she asked, trying to remain nonchalant, 'I mean the lady I spoke to in ASDA the other day.'

'No, no, we only have the one,' Duncan confirmed. 'She's in her room right now.' Olivia tried to hide her relief. Enid's room was sure to offer privacy.

'I said I'd visit when I spoke with her in the supermarket,' Olivia lied and then she laughed and shook her head. 'I don't know why, but, I'm a lady of my word.' There was a pause and Duncan looked unsure what to say. He studied her face, and she hoped that he wasn't dissecting her heavy make-up, contemplating what could be underneath. She wore make-up so often these days, and she hoped it likely that he'd just think that was her style. It wasn't. 'I'd love to see Martin too, of course,' she said to interrupt the silence, 'if he's around?' What a stupid thing to say – of course he'd be around. It was early evening; they never had outings at that time.

'He's in his room as well,' Duncan replied. 'Who would you like to see first?'

'Enid,' Olivia said, confidently and with a nod. She followed Duncan through the next coded door and along the main corridor. The visiting rooms were empty either side, and most of the resident's bedroom doors were closed. A few staff were walking about purposefully, caught up in a daily routine that Olivia – and family members – would never usually have seen. All the carers still made the effort to greet her as she walked through with Duncan, and Olivia did her best to return the gesture.

Beyond visiting Enid, Olivia didn't have much of a plan. She didn't have a grand scheme to confide the depravity of her marriage with David. She didn't want to replay David coming home the other night – the same day Olivia had spoken to Enid in ASDA. She didn't want to wipe the blusher from her cheek and show the yellowing underneath, or for Enid to see the faint black eye shadow she'd been wearing below her right eye involuntarily since. She just wanted some company, away from David. She knew he would never allow her to get back in touch with her friends. On the surface he would – sure – but there would be repercussions; ones that would seem unrelated, but that Olivia would know weren't.

An elderly woman in a care home wasn't obvious company, but Enid would have time on her hands. Olivia didn't intend to pour her heart out, but if she did, Enid would be there to listen, and better still, she would be unlikely to remember. Even if she did remember, Olivia knew that Enid would find it hard to tell anyone.

Duncan knocked on a door and waited. Olivia looked at the picture of Enid hanging on the handle. Her hair was dyed ash blonde and she looked a little younger, though it was hard to tell as the picture had clearly come from a printer with a low ink supply.

'I'm coming in, Enid,' Duncan called, his face close to the door. 'You have a visitor.' Then he stepped back, before slowly entering. 'Are we alright to come in?'

Olivia heard Enid stammering some vowels before saying yes.

'Hi, Enid,' Olivia said on entering, and then, 'Do you remember, I said I'd visit?' Enid didn't reply, but that was as good as she could hope for. She felt bad for lying to Enid and worried that she would further confuse the woman's already muddled memory, but she promised herself that this would be the only time.

Enid looked disappointed, and Olivia couldn't blame her. She must have been expecting family.

'I'll leave you two to it,' Duncan said, leaving the door open behind him.

Olivia sat down on the chair opposite the bed where Enid was sitting, more to put Enid at ease than anything else.

'Do you remember me?' she asked.

'Yes,' Enid said. 'Uh, I, um.' Olivia waited, giving her the time to form her words. 'I, uh…Roy.' Enid smiled apologetically.

'It's alright, Enid, take your time.'

'Roy is coming,' she said, 'moving in – you know – here.' Her face lit up, eyes smiling and cheeks raised, her body started bopping up and down, like a child.

'Tonight?' Olivia asked, and Enid nodded. "Roy, your husband?' She tried to take this in. If it was true, she shouldn't be here ruining such an event for Enid, and it could be true, she supposed. 'I'm so happy for you,' she said. 'That's why I came, to say how happy I am for you.' Olivia found that she was happy for Enid. She felt deflated for herself, but genuinely happy that Enid and her husband would be reunited. 'I best be going then,' she said. 'I don't want to get in the way.' As she stood to leave, she noticed Enid's expression changing. She stopped bopping up and down, and her smile became pained. All the tension in her muscles seemed to have moved from her cheeks to her brow as she studied Olivia. For the second time, Olivia felt conscious of what lay underneath her make-up.

Enid opened her mouth and then closed it again.

'Worried,' she said, the same as she had said in the supermarket.

'Honestly, Enid, you don't need to worry ab…'

'Wed…married…ing,' Enid interrupted. It didn't make any

sense, and it was Olivia's turn to frown. 'Used to be,' Enid continued. 'Not, oh…not now. Before.' A long pause. 'Before Roy – I was married before Roy.'

Olivia sat down again. She had a vague memory of Enid's daughter telling Enid that she'd been married before.

'I…uh, love. You know. Not love.' Enid touched her chest with her hand. 'I thought, you know…I loved him.' There was a long pause while Olivia allowed Enid to gather her thoughts. Then Enid stuttered for a while, frustrated, but determined. 'Not love. He loved himself, I think, you know….more than… you know.' Enid used her hand to gesture at herself. 'You can't…you have to look after, you know,' and she nodded towards Olivia.

'I know,' Olivia whispered, willing Enid to go on. Instead, Enid reached up and touched the scar on the right side of her forehead, above her eyebrow.

'Can I ask?' Olivia probed.

'Fall,' Enid replied poignantly. 'Fall.'

'Enid, why are you telling me this?' Olivia asked, dreading the answer. If Enid had noticed the flaws in her and David's relationship, she couldn't be the only one. 'You've got Roy coming soon, I should get out of your hair.' Enid's face visibly lit up at Roy's name, but then she shook her head.

'You mistake,' she said, 'not the, um, not make the same.'

Olivia didn't reply, because she didn't know what to say, but she wanted to leave, and she wanted to cry. Enid continued.

'Oh…uh… He was…bad,' she fumbled.

'Bad?' Olivia asked shakily, and Enid shook her head.

'Oh…um…no. Not bad,' she corrected herself. 'Stupid, you know. I never saw him. He never, you know, never…came home.' Olivia felt she understood Enid, even without the details. Enid's first husband didn't sound as bad as David had become, and she was glad of that.

'Men,' she said, and Enid laughed.

'We,' Enid paused again and then put her hands together before pulling them apart.

'You broke up,' Olivia guessed. 'Divorced?' Enid smiled confirmation that she'd guessed right.

'And…you know…long time.'

'Of course,' Olivia caught on. 'Divorce wouldn't have been so common then.' They sat quietly for a bit, Enid rubbing the scar on her forehead again.

'Not fall,' she said eventually, and Olivia felt Enid's eyes lock with hers. 'Him, you know. Throwing…things…him…lots, you know.' Olivia did know.

'Oh, Enid.'

'Now…Roy,' Enid interrupted, the joy springing back to her face.

26

Barb watched the two remaining chicks in the nest with their mum. They were waiting for the male to return. His scurries for food were taking longer than they used to, and Barb had made the fair assumption that he was going further afield. The chicks were growing and presumably they needed more to sustain them. When the male did return from his various excursions, he always brought worms with him, and Barb had noticed that they'd become fatter and livelier.

He now took the same route out of the garden each time, along the patio, up onto the garage roof and over the fence. Where he went after that Barb did not know.

The nest was still surrounded by the same weeds as before, but now the weeds were disturbed, and some were bent. Since her dad had moved the nest back, it hadn't been level. Barb hadn't noticed it at first, but after another half a day of watching, she saw that if the chicks didn't continuously shuffle up the twigs, they would end up squashed together at the bottom. She'd mentioned it to her parents but been told that they'd meddled in the birds lives enough. Perhaps, they'd told her, the chick's wings would gain strength faster than nature had intended due to the constant shuffling. Perhaps they would fledge the nest sooner. Wouldn't Barb like to see that? She surely would, she'd agreed.

The biggest chick padded its feet down on the floor of the nest, regaining balance as its smaller sibling struggled up the miniature straw hill. Barb watched as its neck lifted to the sky and it stretched muscular and, thus far, unused wings, knocking the other chick as it did. It shuffled its newly formed tail feathers left, and then right, and then both ways again. Slowly and clumsily, its small round body raised itself up onto the edge of the nest. The smaller chick fell back down into the lower corner of the nest behind.

Barb clung to the edges of her patio chair, eyes wide in awe, as the biggest chick reached out to almost the entire width of the nest with its wings. It flapped once, as if experiencing an unexpected twitch, and then again, loosening its bones ready. It was happening. Barb wiggled her bum further forward in her seat, almost tipping the chair forward. The chick flapped repeatedly, as it prepared to take off. Its body was propelled forward in a gallant attempt at flight, and then it hit the patio – neck first, body and head after.

For a second the chick didn't move. The female bird hopped onto the nest wall and peered down at her baby. Barb stood up, but then remembered what her dad had told her about interfering with nature, so sat back down again.

She noticed a twitch in the chick's wing, and then another,

but it looked like it was struggling. The littlest chick chirped loudly from the safety of the nest, but was drowned out by a ringing sound from inside the house.

Barb stood up, excited, and jumped inside through the glass patio doors. She had been told that she could answer the phone now. She was six, and six was old enough.

'Hello, um…Oaktree Avenue. Barbara, um…Barbara. Speaking,' Barb said into the handset in the hall. She could see her mum smiling at her from the kitchen door but made a point of looking at the phone ring-dial as she had seen her parents do on the phone.

'Barbara?' a voice said through the receiver, and then nothing.

'Mummy and Daddy call me Barb,' Barb replied, aware of her telephone voice, putting on a posh accent. She placed her finger in one of the coils on the cord and twiddled it. She was a grown-up.

'Oh,' the voice came back, eventually. 'Oh wow. Barb.' No one said anything for a while, and then Barb heard the person on the other end of the phone exhale. 'Barb,' the voice said, 'I'm your dad.'

Barb giggled.

'Who is it?' her mum asked from the doorway.

'Daddy,' Barb replied, laughing, almost in fits now. Her dad was so funny.

'Good,' her mum said, walking towards her daughter, 'I need to speak to him about tea tonight.' Barb held out the receiver to her mum, who was now also laughing, seemingly at Barb, though Barb didn't know why.

'Hiya, love,' she heard her mum saying into the receiver as she ran back outside to the nest, still giggling to herself. She fell into the chair, now at an angle where she'd left it, and looked across to the nest. The fallen chick wasn't on the floor any more. It was back in the low end of the nest with its sibling, and both parents now. The littlest chick shuffled up the nest. The female bird helped it using the bulk of her body. The male picked up a red berry from a small pile of three in the nest and placed it forcefully into the largest chick's beak.

'He didn't say anything,' her mum said, holding onto the door frame and leaning out. 'He must have hung up.' She shook her head. 'Your father, Barb, I swear. Sometimes I just don't understand him,' and then she left, heading in the direction of the kitchen.

Barb's bedroom glowed pink from a horse-shaped nightlight plugged into the corner of the room. Her shelves were lined with the soft toys she'd collected over her six years. The pink bear she was given at birth sat next to the blue bear she was given at birth. Lots of cats, all in a row, together; they were friends. There were three horses: two little and one big, all pink, and there was one small multi-coloured toucan that her dad had bought her recently. She wanted an emu and a blackbird to join her cuddly bird family.

The oldest soft toy lay next to Barb in her bed. A classic teddy, with one lopsided eye and several bare patches up its arms. It used to be her mum's when she had been a little girl. Barb had first seen it sitting in the wicker chair on the landing, and then taken a fancy to it when she was three. She remembered sitting on her knees in front of the chair, leaning forward and talking to the old bear about an imaginary walk that they were going to take to the beach. Since then, the bear had been Barb's.

The room was quiet, but Barb could hear her mum in the next one across, putting away some newly ironed clothes, shaking the bedding, fluffing the pillows. Barb had bathed and enjoyed a story about a baby swan who thought he was a duck. Her mum had kissed her goodnight, and now she was waiting for her dad to come up and tuck her in.

'Night love,' Roy said, pushing the door from ajar to open, flooding the room with the light from the landing. 'Did you enjoy your story?' he asked, sitting on the side of Barb's bed, and resting his hand on the other side, close to the wall. A comfortable and safe tunnel of hairy arms and fatherly breath. Barb smiled at her dad and nodded.

'Yes,' she said with a tired voice, and then, mustering energy and fighting sleep, she grinned, lifted her head up and opened her eyes wide. 'Do the funny voice again,' she said.

Her dad frowned and smiled at the same time, a question in his expression. He held his thumb against his forefinger to form an imaginary mouth and stuck his other fingers up for the ears. He scrunched his nose.

'I'm Mr Rabbit,' he said, tightening his voice to make it smaller and higher-pitched than usual, 'and I think it might be time to go to sleep.'

Barb laughed. 'Not that voice,' she said, 'the one you did on the phone,' but her dad just shook his head, and kissed her on the forehead.

'I don't know what you're talking about,' he said, 'but it's time to sleep now.' He stood to leave. 'Love you.'

'Love you, Daddy.'

27

Olivia had left Enid in her room, excited about the prospect of seeing Roy. After the tale of Enid's first marriage, Olivia had asked about Roy.

'And he's good?'

'Oh.' Enid had scrunched up her face, held both hands up, balled into fists, in front of her. 'Yes.'

They'd talked a little about Roy moving in. Enid had told Olivia that Barb – presumably Enid's daughter – had told her he would come, and Olivia had told Enid, once again, just how happy for her she was. And she was.

Now she was alone though, back in the corridor, Olivia was filled with thoughts of Enid's first husband, and of her own current husband. Enid had already known that something was wrong; she hadn't needed to spill her heart out.

Head down, Olivia headed through the now mostly empty

corridor, and through the first coded door. She was about to open the second when she heard the familiar cheery voice.

'Did you see Martin?' Olivia turned and watched Duncan's face change to concern. 'Here, here,' he said. 'Take a seat.' He ushered her to the sofa in the reception between the two doors. She felt compelled to follow his lead, feeling a dampness on her cheeks and wanting to leave. If she ignored him, it could raise even more suspicion.

'Try not to be so hard on yourself,' he said, before asking again in a hushed tone, 'Did you see Martin?' She shook her head.

'I'm just being silly.'

'No, you're not.' Duncan said matter-of-factly. 'You already have Martin to deal with. It's a lot. Try not to take too much on.'

Olivia looked at his thin tinted glasses perched on top of a square nose. He was quite young, with a thick neck that suggested he didn't mind the gym.

'So, you only saw Enid,' he continued. 'I understand. She's a lovely lady, but she does have family who visit.'

'She was telling me about Roy,' Olivia said quietly, hoping for the conversation to end.

'Her husband,' Duncan smiled. 'A lovely chap.' There was something soothing about his Scottish accent, warm and low. They sat for a few seconds and Olivia considered the etiquette of standing to leave. She decided to ask a question in an attempt to make her exit feel more natural.

'Did I notice you have some time off?' She picked up her bag and wiped her eyes dry.

'Aye,' Duncan said in a large, tired exhale. 'My dad – well he's not got dementia, but he became very old, very fast.'

He paused, looked down at the floor, and then back up again at Olivia, who hadn't yet stood up, surprised by his answer. She'd thought maybe he'd been travelling or something. 'He's moved into what they call a retirement community and, hey, I got signed off with stress, so, look, don't take too much on, hey?'

'I'm sorry,' Olivia said, and she really meant it.

'Being signed off didn't help anyway,' Duncan continued, with a shrug and a smile. 'I just spent more time in an empty house with nothing to do. Dad didn't need looking after any more. Better off being at work I reckon.'

'You lived with your dad?'

Duncan tightened his lips in a forced smile.

'Look,' he said, his composure coming back to him. 'There are things to laugh at with dementia, and I don't think Enid or Martin, or my dad, would mind us saying that. I think they'd all laugh along in fact.' He paused and folded his muscular arms. 'But a person with dementia will be complex, and that can be hard, for anyone. Do you know how many people we see here, like yourself, who have to watch someone they love going through what Martin is going through?

'You're not being silly; just don't take on too much. If you want to visit Enid, I won't stop you, but don't feel like you have to, and don't be too hard on yourself. Take it from me, you're doing a grand job.'

Olivia was taken aback. Of course, Duncan had the wrong end of the stick. Olivia was visiting Enid for purely selfish reasons, but she still wasn't used to being spoken to so kindly. She didn't know what to say, so she didn't say anything.

'Back to it.' Duncan clapped his hands together and stood up. Olivia remained on the sofa.

'Thank you,' she said, hearing the main door open behind her.

'Ah, look who it is.' Duncan looked up and almost shouted. 'How are you, good sir? Are you here to see Martin?'

'Maybe,' a voice came from behind Olivia. 'I'll just have a word with my wife first.'

David.

'Well,' Duncan replied, either oblivious or choosing to ignore David's emphasis on the word 'wife', 'I'll leave you both to it. Let me know if you're coming in.' Olivia watched him leave through the coded door and head back into the home. She felt the fear seep through her body as if it were physical, as if she had drunk it. She hadn't told David that she was coming here; he must have followed her. Feeling his hand on her shoulder she spun around to face him.

'What are you doing here?' she asked, hearing her own voice; hollow, flat.

'I thought it was about time I visited Dad by myself,' David replied casually, and then he nodded to the coded door. 'He seems nice.'

'He's a carer.'

'Yes.'

'I was visiting Martin.'

'Yes, and how was he?'

Olivia felt her breath catch. She didn't know how Martin was. She hadn't seen him.

'Good,' she said, horrified at her inability to lie under pressure. David smirked.

'I'll go in then, shall I? I'll make sure he remembers you.' David's eye twitched, sneering. 'Of course, he will; you were just there.' Olivia stared at her husband, frozen, unable to speak. 'You can go home. You've already seen him. I'll let him know I saw you on your way out.'

David offered a forced, tight-lipped smile before entering the code and leaving Olivia standing in reception, eyes unable to focus, skin icy pale.

28

There was nothing outside Roy's new room – not as far as he was concerned. People had come and gone through the door over the past few hours, but there was nothing on the other side. When he'd been brought there the previous day, by Barb and some people he hadn't recognised, he'd seen the outside of the house, the corridors, the lift, the small alcove which housed the door to his room, but he only vaguely remembered any of it. He'd found it all rather distressing, and he'd been pushed in a wheelchair. It was hard to take in. The overall impression had been of a formerly grand house, with run-down interiors. A property fallen from grace.

Roy's room was already old and well-used before he moved in, but it seemed comfortable enough. Most importantly, it was warm. He always felt so cold in his and Enid's house. Mind you, he could never put the heating on – not at the prices he read in the newspaper.

He knew he was on the top floor because the ceiling at the end of his bed was slanted, and he could see the sky when the blind was pulled up. With better eyesight, he might have been able to see the seagulls that flew above him, searching the earth for adventure, or a child with a pasty to pinch, but they were just blurry moving black dots to him. No bother, there were pictures of birds, cut out and stuck on the wall next to his bed; they would have to do.

It wasn't just the fall that had prompted Roy's move (though, bloody Neil, anyway), his sight was worsening, and his hearing had become almost non-existent over the past year. That last fall had affected his ability to walk though, not straightaway, but he'd felt his legs deteriorating quickly. By his final few days at home, Roy had found himself sitting on his chair, struggling to get up and waiting for Barb to bring food.

Now, he was sitting in a different chair. Large, with huge armrests, placed next to a bed. The television was too small and far away for Roy to make out the people on it properly, and although he'd been told that the volume was high, it was not high enough. The previous night, very early in the evening, Roy had been moved from the large chair into the bed. A team of people had assisted him, changed his clothes and brushed his teeth, and the same team had washed him this morning. He'd only been here one night, but already they'd changed his underwear four times.

Barb had told him that she would visit again that day, but he doubted she would bring Enid. Roy had seen Enid become violent at times over the past year or so, and he understood that Barb was finding it hard. He doubted she would ever bring Enid.

He liked the people who had moved him to the bed and back to the chair, and he'd heard there was a PAT dog that visited every now and again. He looked forward to that, but Roy knew he would never leave his new room. He couldn't move, and he wasn't going to try. That was why he was there; that was why he would never see Enid again; and that was why, to Roy, there was nothing outside his room.

29

ENID TRIED HARD TO LOOK into Kara's eyes, but Kara didn't seem to notice. She was hurriedly tugging a blouse around Enid's back and fishing for Enid's arms through the sleeves. Finally, she buttoned her up. Enid had already been hastily washed next to the sink in her bathroom, before being rushed back into her bedroom. Kara was talking with urgency, but as far as Enid could tell, she was talking about nothing.

'I hope you slept well Enid, my lovely,' she said for the third time, almost out of breath and not expecting a response. 'Lovely blouse this one. Lovely. You want to be looking nice today.' It was true. Enid always wanted to look nice.

Kara pulled her up onto her feet.

'What trousers would you like to wear today?' she asked, while pulling out a loose-fitting pair of harem trousers from the bottom drawer of Enid's wardrobe. 'Very trendy.' Holding onto the frame she used every morning to get dressed, Enid lifted one of her legs. No one talked while Kara yanked the trousers up, but the quickness with which she tightened the waist made Enid grunt with discomfort. She wondered if Kara had dressed herself with such haste that morning. Her uniform was wrinkled, it was true, but maybe Kara had been there all night. Maybe she hadn't dressed herself that morning at all.

'Sorry Enid,' Kara apologised, and then she turned back to the wardrobe. 'Socks.' She paused for a second, thinking, then moved slightly to her right and opened the top drawer of the chest, just below a new picture of Roy, and pulled out a pair of long, thick, once-white socks.

Again, holding on to the frame, Enid lifted her feet, one after the other.

'Right,' Kara said, touching Enid's shoulders gently, and finally allowing Enid to gain eye contact. 'Are you ready for the day?' Enid looked back at Kara's eager but tired face and didn't respond. She felt too flustered now. How long had she been awake?

'Good,' Kara continued. She was studying Enid's face now. Enid felt lost. 'You're seeing Roy today, remember?' Enid lit up. She did remember. Roy was moving in with her. She vaguely remembered previous disappointments when he hadn't turned up, but today must be the day.

'Oh, um,' Enid nodded vigorously. 'Yes.'

'Barb is already sat in the conservatory waiting for you. You'll like it, Enid. I've heard they have three hot meals there every day – even breakfast – and don't worry, you'll be back in time for the lily-pad painting before lunch.'

Enid attempted to take everything in. None of this made

any sense. Barb was here, but only Barb? Hot meals and lily pads? When would Roy be there?

She allowed herself to be walked out of her door and along an empty corridor with several more doors coming off it. Through each door, Enid could hear talking, but she could not make out any precise words. She focused on having Roy home with her. She pictured their afternoon, sitting side by side in her – no – in their room. They walked into the conservatory and Enid saw Barb.

'Morning, Mum.' She stood up, cheerfully.

'Uh,' Enid nodded, by way of reply. She looked around the glass walls and thought about Roy's tomatoes. Maybe he would grow some here, once he was settled in. Gently, Kara let go of Enid's arm.

'We're going to see Dad,' Barb said.

'Uh.'

'Mum?'

'Yes, my Roy. Today?'

'That's right, today.'

Enid beamed. She felt the relief fill her stomach, her legs became weightless, a happiness she hadn't felt for years. 'We're going to see Dad, in his new home, do you remember? It's only three streets away, it won't take long.'

Enid froze. Her stomach dropped, her legs became lead and she felt tears prick her eyes. Roy's new home? She did *not* remember. She tried to protest but started stuttering. Both of her arms began to shake.

'It's alright, Mum,' Barb said. 'We've talked about this. Dad's moved and he likes it there.' Barb placed a hand on her arm. Enid could feel herself shaking with anger. Anger at her daughter. After all, wasn't it Barb who had moved her here, against her will? And now she was moving Roy to a new home, a different home. He wouldn't be moving in with Enid, not now and not ever. She felt so stupid. Stupid and betrayed. Stupid and betrayed and angry. So angry.

She let out a low growling sound and felt her face distort into pure hatred. She couldn't form any words and her attempts turned into small specks of spit on the floor. Enid pulled her arm away from Barb's hand abruptly and hit her daughter hard in the face.

Enid watched Barb go to defend herself, using her arms as a shield, but it was too late. Enid had already struck. She felt Kara holding onto her body from behind, restraining her. Enid thrashed but couldn't break free. Eventually, she stopped fighting. She could see the tears on her daughter's face.

'It's alright,' Barb said, gently. 'I'll come back later.' She sniffed and Enid scowled. 'I know you didn't mean to hurt me then, Mum,' she said, 'but even if you did, I still love you.'

That night, Enid sat up in bed, unable to sleep. Mind you, it hadn't been easy getting into a sitting position. She'd attempted to shuffle up from lying down, but her back hurt too much. She'd ended up rolling onto her side, and then back again, onto her side, and then back again. Eventually, she'd managed to pull herself out of bed, walked to the window, opened the blackout curtains, considered leaving through the window, and then returned to bed in the required position. Her body was at its weakest in the mornings and evenings, but in the evenings her mind was active, maybe due to the amount she was nodding off in the day.

It was light outside – not sunlight; it wasn't day – but from the stillness of the night. Maybe a distant streetlamp, maybe a bright moon. From where Enid was sitting, she couldn't tell. She could hear the sea, but she couldn't see it. It comforted her to know that it was there, just outside her window and down the hill. She had lived near the sea all her life.

She was certain that she forgot most of what happened almost every day these days, maybe because her mind was failing her, and maybe because nothing worth remembering ever happened any more. It was hard to tell, but she remembered that morning in all its miserable, vivid detail. She remembered Barb telling her that Roy had moved into another home nearby, and she understood that she and Roy would never live together again. He had been so good to her, Roy. He would want to be here with her. No, this was Barb's doing. But then, she remembered the hurt on her daughter's face, and that too pained her. She'd spent the best part of her life protecting Barb. She didn't want to hurt her.

She couldn't remember the last time she'd seen Roy. Barb would never take her to see him now – not after that. She so desperately wanted to leave, to find him. She wanted to climb out of the window, take Roy's hand and stroll back to their house with him, back to their old life, back maybe a dozen years, just so they could have a dozen more years together.

She listened to the waves gently lapping outside. Somewhere nearby, she thought, Roy would be listening to the same waves. There was comfort in that, but summer was fading, and the rain would soon blanket the shared sounds of nature. Then they would be completely alone. Two people who once knew each other, living separate lives.

30

Olivia and David hadn't spoken about their meeting in the dementia home since it had happened a week ago. David hadn't brought it up and Olivia didn't know how to. In fact, on the surface, home life had become more civil. David had been friendly – loving even – but for Olivia, that was worse. The calm before the storm. It was the waiting, because the storm would come, it was just a question of when. She knew that David would never approach the matter in front of the children; they were everything to him. When they were there, she felt safe, but as soon as they were in bed, she found herself on tenterhooks. It didn't feel good using the children as protection, but it worked, and they were certainly coming to no harm. They placated him. Olivia knew that if it ever came to a court battle, David would have a strong chance of gaining custody. He would be charming and easily able to demonstrate the genuine relationship he had with them, whereas she would be a nervous wreck. She knew how useless she was, and he'd be adept at demonstrating that too. If, by some pure fluke of chance he didn't gain custody, it would crush their worlds. Olivia knew she could never let it come to that.

David was in good spirits – a curious thing the morning after a quiz, particularly a quiz in which his team had lost. He was singing Otis Redding into the cupboard while searching for the jam. Olivia had spent the night before sitting up, waiting for him to come home from the pub quiz, worrying about the mood he would be in when he did, but he had practically skipped through the door. He'd fumbled with his keys as usual, and he'd been drunk, but instead of the spite and anger that Olivia had been expecting, instead of the accusations and unfounded theories on why she'd been at the home that day, without seeing Martin, David had come in laughing. He'd gone to the fridge, pulled out a beer and sat on the sofa next to Olivia.

'We're on our way up, Liv,' he'd said.

'Yeah? Did you win?' She'd forced a smile, knowing that the fear would still be showing in her eyes. Fear doesn't disappear that quickly; it's a physical emotion. David paused before answering, a pause long enough for Olivia to assume that she'd misread his good mood.

'No,' he said finally, 'but we had a good day. Some productive meetings.' He took a swig from his bottle, slowly swallowed, and exhaled happily before continuing his sentence. 'Do you know, I think we might get this acquisition through quicker than I thought?' He put his feet up on the coffee table.

'That's good,' Olivia said, hoping that she didn't sound too distant, or too objectionable in any way. It *was* good though, she thought. When David wasn't stressed, he became more predictable and less angry.

Later, they'd gone to bed at different times, Olivia had made sure of that. She'd retired halfway through *QI* and then listened to David laughing downstairs on the sofa. From their shared bed, she tried, failed, and then pretended to be asleep.

Now, David was making Olivia and the children breakfast. Not a first, but a rarity. Toast and jam (with the option of lemon curd). It was nothing spectacular, but he'd been openly affectionate with her in front of the kids and was clearly enjoying playing the role of the doting husband, a role that better men played every day. Olivia sensed that Dillon, her eldest, had noticed a shift in normality too. David was being even more attentive than normal, almost like the cartoon of a perfect dad.

He kissed her forehead as he placed her toast on the table. Olivia smiled and sipped her coffee, feeling on edge, hiding from eye contact. He kissed both children on their respective foreheads and gave them their breakfast. Olivia watched as Dillon winced. Oona only paid attention to the toast. Two-year-olds are so blissfully oblivious. Olivia envied her daughter, and then she pitied her, before finally loathing herself for allowing this dysfunction into her little girl's life.

'I enjoyed last night,' David said to Olivia. The children weren't paying any attention. Olivia smiled at him – not an explicit reply, but not a disagreement either. She knew that he was referring to them sitting on the sofa together after he'd come back from the pub, but there hadn't been anything to enjoy. They'd shared what Olivia considered to be some fairly forced small talk, and then watched half a quiz show together.

'It was like the old us again,' he continued, 'when we were

younger.' Olivia made a noise which, again, only implied agreement. 'Before all this,' David said with a flourish of his hand.

Before all this. What was he referring to? He couldn't mean the children. Did he mean the bruises he'd inflicted, that they'd worked together to hide? Olivia wondered if his jovial mood was born of pride. Was he proud that he had nothing to apologise for this morning? He hadn't taken out his frustration on his wife, he hadn't pushed her or held her arm or her hair. To him, perhaps this deserved celebrating.

Olivia had once enjoyed David's cheery morning moods, but that was before, when they had been brought about by dinner parties and nights out with their friends. This time she felt nothing, it was too fake. David would go out to work, and maybe he would have a good day, and maybe he would have a bad day. It was always a gamble. Olivia could still feel a dull pain when she closed her right eye. She touched the lid with her thumb. The bruise was no longer visible, but it was still there.

'Finish up kids,' she said abruptly, even though Dillon had already finished, and Oona was yet to eat more than one mouthful. She wouldn't indulge David in this fantasy of a perfect family. She looked at Dillon, 'I need you ready for school in five.' Dillon stood up, grateful, and ran upstairs. 'Oona,' she said, softer now, looking at the jam on her daughter's fingers, forehead, and clothes. 'Oh Oona, I need to clean you up. It's a nursery day.' She started to wipe the jam away, noticing with some annoyance the lack of jam around her daughter's mouth.

The fear that seeped through Olivia as she spoke her next words was completely disproportionate to their content and meaning. She felt light-headed and stupid for feeling so.

'I'll take them a little early today, Dave. I think there's something going on at nursery.' It was casual. Perhaps too casual. She never called him Dave. David looked at her, surprised, but not cross.

'Of course,' he said, faux genuine. 'Liv, love, I can see you later.'

Olivia had grown up popular. She'd been confident, which had helped her get on with the cliquey girls at school, but she was kind too, and that made her more accessible to the less popular girls in her year. Boys tended to fancy her, then get to know her and want to stay friends with her after she'd turned away their advances.

She left school after her GCSEs, preferring to look for work, and maybe, if she found the right man, start a family. She remained friends with the same cliquey girls who, by this point, had become much less cliquey. She still spent a lot of time with a few of her male friends too, and it was through one of these friends that she first met David.

David was funny, intelligent and already successful within a large financial firm. He had dreams of starting his own business in the future and got on well with Olivia's once-cliquey friends. He liked her male friends too, showing just enough jealousy for Olivia to feel special, but not so much that she felt trapped. It wasn't long before they were married.

Olivia and David were as sociable in marriage as they had been before; they held dinner parties at their house and met up with their friends in restaurants, drank together in pubs and found new friends in strangers. When the working day was over, Olivia's friend Susan knew she could pop in uninvited and would always be welcome. Most days, she did.

With Olivia's encouragement, David's dream of starting his own firm became a slow reality, and life only seemed to get better. The dinner parties became more lavish, and they found that they could treat themselves to small European holidays. They became accustomed to a life that neither of them had previously known. Although far from rich, they had money and found they no longer had to worry about spending.

It was around this time that Olivia fell pregnant.

She insisted on saving the spare money they had for the baby, and she told David that they would probably have to stop holding quite so many parties. She found herself tired all the time and she couldn't drink anyway. She never suggested that he should be teetotal, but she did point out that while she was drinking herbal tea in the evenings, he could join her.

Around fifteen weeks into the pregnancy, David started showing a mood that Olivia hadn't seen before. Markets had been low, he'd told her, and business was bad. He blamed her for pushing him into starting the new business. He began to spend most of his time at the office, and when he was at home he didn't want to talk about the baby, despite regularly complaining about being bored.

The night Olivia had asked David when he was going to paint the nursery had been the first night she'd seen just how far his temper could push him. He'd been in a bad mood that night already, but it was a job that needed to be done, and Olivia was wary of the paint fumes harming the baby. He'd put his foot right through one of the cot bars, breaking his own previous handiwork.

'The baby isn't going to care about the colour of the room,' he'd said, clearly having frustrated himself further, knowing that at some point, it would be his job to fix the now-broken cot.

'But David,' Olivia felt on the verge of tears. She was emotional these days anyway. 'The cot.' David had stormed past her out of the nursery, kicking her in the shin on his way out. It had been the start of an unpleasant pattern, which Olivia grew concerningly accustomed to.

After that night, the dinner parties became less frequent. Olivia started turning down the invites she received from her friends to go to restaurants. If Susan knocked on the door after work, Olivia would either hide in one of the upstairs rooms, or answer with a smile, and then turn her away. She could cover the bruise that had formed on her shin, and those on her other limbs, but not the shame. She wasn't in the mood for socialising anyway; she was too tired from the pregnancy.

By the time the baby came, Olivia and David had stopped receiving invites at all, and Susan had stopped knocking after work. Presumably, their friends thought they were setting up family life, and that they needed their privacy.

After everyone had met the new baby, Olivia's social life died completely.

Olivia closed the door and breathed a sigh of relief. She had just over six hours to herself. She would hoover and clean, empty the dishwasher, cook tea, water the plants, stick some washing on, fill the dishwasher – all the things she needed to do to keep the house running – but she would do it all alone. There were precious few hours in a week where she didn't feel on edge. Without them, she didn't know how she'd survive.

She walked through to the kitchen, on her way to the kettle, to coffee, but froze in the doorway.

'Alright, gorgeous,' David said, tapping away at his phone. Olivia realised she was holding her breath, and let it go in another useless attempt to relax her body and appear casual.

'Hi,' she managed.

David looked up. 'I'm not needed in the office today.' He pushed his glasses up his nose elaborately, jokingly, and then started tugging at his tie. 'I am ready to party.'

'I've got things…' she said meekly, not even finishing her sentence.

David pulled a bottle of wine from the fridge. 'Come on, what have you got to do, Liv?' he asked, without any inclination of wanting an answer. He laughed. 'I think life will go on with a dusty light switch.'

'I wasn't going to…' Again, she couldn't finish her sentence.

'Let's spend the morning together,' he carried on, picking up two wine glasses from the cabinet. 'Let's skive off work, like old times.'

Olivia couldn't feel her body. She was completely weightless; numb and empty. She took a seat. The thought of having to endure a day, even a morning with David and no children was too much to bear. She couldn't force a smile for that long, her body wouldn't be able to take the worry, the wait, the anticipation of the storm. His tie was hanging low, and he'd undone his top button. The less than subtle sexual undertones made her skin itch. She felt powerless.

'David,' Olivia said, doing everything she could to hold the tremble in her voice, 'I don't want you to drink,' and then, catching herself she said, 'Not this early, please.'

David laughed again, and then scoffed. He walked across to the table where she was sitting, the confidence in his movements filling the room.

'I wasn't going to,' he said. 'I was going to offer you a glass.' He exhaled spitefully. 'Someone's got to pick the kids up later, Liv, fuck.' He turned away. 'Sorry, that was a little defensive. You know how work's been lately.'

'It isn't an excuse.' The silence that followed filled the room. Olivia had surprised herself. The words had been born from deep seeded anger, though they'd come out quiet and unexpected. David turned and sat opposite.

'No,' he replied, full of remorse, but a familiar remorse. Olivia used his apparent weakness to build up her own confidence.

'You're not at work now,' she said, 'so it's not an excuse.'

'Liv, I've apologised, I always do. I can't keep apologising. I don't know what else you want.' They were talking about more than the outburst now.

'I want you to be nice to me,' Olivia replied. She'd often wondered how this conversation might go, never expecting it to ever happen. In her imagination, she'd been much stronger. As it was, she felt like she was hurting herself, signing her own health away. She sounded so young, so naive.

'What are you talking about?' David hadn't raised his voice yet, but Olivia knew she needed to divert the conversation and she hated herself for starting it. 'What about last night? We had a good night.' Olivia held her hand up, to ask him to stop. She was scared. At least the wine hadn't been poured.

'I want you to be nice to me, all of the time,' she said. She sounded just as pathetic as before. Why couldn't she shut up?

'It's not like I hit you every fucking night.' There it was. He'd said it. He knew. A clock ticked. Someone down the street started up a lawn mower.

David touched Olivia's hand and of course she let him, for the children. They needed their dad, and she needed them.

'OK.' Olivia felt like she'd just told off Dillon, and the comparison scared her. There was another long silence between the two, David looking down at his hand on hers, and Olivia looking at the table edge. Her nerves were beginning to calm. She'd dodged the storm.

Eventually, David looked up.

'I know you're having an affair,' he said, calmly but with malice. A card played with the joy of winning rather than upset. 'You didn't visit Dad that day.' He withdrew his hand and tightened his tie around his neck.

'What do you mean?' Olivia asked, fear now seeping through every inch of her body; water in her eyes, hands trembling.

'That man, GI Joe, at the home. I'm not an idiot. That wasn't the first time I've seen you together.' He stood up to leave, as if he had somewhere important to be, as if his morning off had been a farce all along.

'David?' It was barely a whisper.

'Nothing,' he replied, shrugging his shoulders. 'Just, I'm watching everything, OK? That's not all I've seen either,' and with that, he left, gently closing the door behind him.

31

Enid held her sandwich loosely in one hand. The bottom slice of bread, along with some of the ham, hung down from the top slice and a small shred of lettuce, covered with warm mayonnaise, slid down onto her shoe. It felt most unpleasant, but she was too deep in thought to do anything about it. Kara and Duncan had helped her and Betty down to the bench and now the carers were standing next to the drive entrance, chatting. Duncan had mentioned on the way down that it might be the last trip to the bench for a while. Winter was coming and the air had grown colder. Enid and Betty were sitting next to each other, both wearing thick coats and wrapped in blankets. Betty had finished her sandwich earlier, albeit with some help. Neither of them chatted.

Frank and Evelyn often joined them on the bench, but Frank had barked all kinds of obscenities when Kara had asked if he'd wanted to come, so he'd remained inside. Evelyn always enjoyed the fresh air and the view, but Enid hadn't seen Evelyn around much lately.

Enid wasn't enjoying the view as she normally would. No one would have known it to look at her, but Enid was busy. Her mind was darting from one memory to the next. She felt like she was improving, she was remembering recent events and not just the old ones. Not the usual nostalgia, but useful information. Information she could use.

Somewhere nearby, close to where she was sitting that very moment, Roy would be in his new room, wondering where she was. The thought of him alone in an unfamiliar place tore at her heart. She was still furious at Barb for letting it happen, and at the carers where she lived for that matter. Everyone, it seemed, was conspiring against them.

A piece of ham dropped from the sandwich to join the lettuce and mayonnaise. She turned to see that Betty had dozed off, and then looked down at her sandwich. Crumbs from previous mouthfuls of sandwich were scattered, without obvious pattern, around her blouse and trousers. An unintentional low noise escaped her mouth as she tried to lean further forward to see the whereabouts of the lost ham.

'Bless,' she heard Kara say from over at the gate. 'They're both sleeping.'

Blast you, Enid thought. Blast you both and blast my daughter. She wanted to cry, and she would have, had it not been for the sound of a vehicle coming down the road. She made only the slightest movement of her neck to look. The road was empty, as it had been since she and Betty had sat down. A group of pigeons took off briefly from the pavement, and then lowered themselves back down to the exact spot where they had previously been. The motor grew louder as a single-decker bus slowly emerged from behind the wall at the end of the road.

Enid didn't move. She could watch the bus roll closer from where she was sitting, and she didn't want to draw attention from the carers. If they thought she was asleep, well, more fool them. The shape on the front of the bus looked familiar, but Enid couldn't be sure if it was the same as what she had drawn on the tissue, however long ago. She had studied that tissue, why couldn't she picture it now?

The buses that drove down the road next to Enid's home were few, and the number of buses that stopped at the bus stop next to the bench were even fewer. This bus stopped.

Enid thought of Roy. She knew that there was no way of her knowing which room he would be in, or which building, but she did know that Roy would be trying to reunite with her too, and logic stated that he would make his way home, so that was what she must do. She had daydreamed about finding herself on this bench alone, with a bus stationary next to her. She never thought she'd go through with it, but if she was ever to see Roy again, this might be her last chance. She looked at Betty. She may as well have been alone. She looked over to the carers. They were both holding mugs now. Enid could only see one of Duncan's arms, sticking out from the wall in animated conversation, facing away from the bench. Kara was watching him and laughing.

Enid gathered her bag from down by her feet, and very slowly she stood up. She watched as a young man stepped off the bus and walked past, ignoring her. The doors went to close, and Enid stopped, but then they opened again. Enid took three more steps forward as she heard the young man's voice talking to the carers. He must have come to visit someone.

'You gettin' on?' A strong Bristolian accent came from inside the bus. 'Need a hand?' Enid lowered her head, stepped through the door and nodded, looking around as if she was hiding, which of course, she was. 'Where you goin' then, m'darlin'?' Enid didn't answer. She lifted her bag to look for payment. Small bright stars danced before her eyes and her head felt light. She was out of her depth.

'You got a pass?' the driver asked, and again Enid nodded, as she fumbled some onions, her purse and someone else's watch out of her bag.

'Don't' worry 'bout it. I believe you.' The driver was speaking slowly and clearly, but still heavily accented. The words meant nothing. Enid looked up at him, sensing from his tone that something was expected of her. 'Don't worry 'bout it,' he repeated, pressing a button which pushed a long piece of paper out of a machine. 'Here's your ticket.' He passed Enid the paper, then put her purse, the onions and someone else's watch back into her bag, and closed the door.

Enid sat on the seat closest to her and looked out of the window. She couldn't see Kara or Duncan; presumably they were both next to the gate still. She watched a seagull land on the pavement next to a still-sleeping Betty, look at her with a tilted head and then edge closer to the bench. Ham, lettuce and mayonnaise, all sprawled among a bed of crumbs. The seagull snatched up the ham quickly, threw his head back and allowed the salty meat to fall down his throat as the bus pulled away.

PART TWO

THE NEST

32

The dining room was more crowded than usual. It seemed like most of the residents wanted to sit in the same place. Olivia looked around the room, confused. Something strange was happening. She'd passed a large gathering of carers and four police officers in reception, but no one had spoken to her except Duncan, who had said she could still visit Martin. She hadn't mentioned Enid this time; she needed to see Martin first, just in case. As ridiculous as it was, she needed the alibi. Duncan had hurried her in and ushered her over to Martin. There weren't any other visitors in the dining room.

'By yourself?' Martin asked.

'I'm afraid so.' She held onto the handles of her handbag, implying a fleeting visit, and looked closely at her father-in-law. There were similarities to David, but Martin's face was softer, and somehow gentler. Maybe it was in his expressions rather than his features.

'Where is,' Martin started, 'where is, oh fiddlesticks…' He looked to the ceiling and chuckled.

'David?'

'Yes. David. Where is David today?' Martin's eyes were glazing over, and his voice was even quieter than normal, distant. Olivia breathed in deeply.

'He's at work, Martin; it's a weekday.' Martin was no longer listening.

'My biggest regret,' he said, and then went as if to finish his sentence, but didn't.

'What's that, Martin?'

'I should have paid more attention. Always screaming.' Olivia didn't know if Martin was talking about himself, or David. 'We never did have a good... Oh, my biggest regret.' Olivia studied him.

'Your son loves you, Martin. God knows he has his issues, but his relationship with you is not one of them.' There was a smile somewhere behind Martin's eyes, hidden in the constant shaking that no one had really noticed starting, but was now one of his distinguishing features.

Olivia looked around the room again. Why was the dining room so full? The carers in reception had seemed somewhat on edge, flustered and worried. Duncan had rushed her in. There had been police.

'What's going on, Martin?' Olivia asked.

'Hmm?'

'This.' Olivia spun her index finger in a small circle to indicate their surroundings.

'Oh, nothing,' Martin replied. Olivia didn't know what to say. He must have noticed.

'Is Enid here?' she asked eventually.

'Hmm?'

'Enid?'

'No, no. No Enid.' Martin looked confused. 'I don't know an Enid.' He stared into Olivia's eyes, as if questioning her question. Then he tightened his lips and looked past her, indicating the end of a conversation.

'No, Martin. You do know an Enid. I don't know how well you know her, but she lives here, with you.'

'Hmm?' Martin looked back at Olivia, as if she'd only just arrived. 'Who's that?'

'Enid.'

'Enid lives with me? I don't think so, I…'

Olivia interrupted.

'She sits over there sometimes.' She pointed at the seat directly opposite Martin's. 'She always has her handbag with her, and she seems to be playing with a napkin most of the time.' Olivia waited for a response, and then she waited a little longer. She didn't mean to get frustrated with him.

'Don't worry Martin. I can ask one of the carers when I leave. They might know.' The door opened and Olivia glanced over. It was Duncan. He was looking stressed and not quite in control. The room behind the door seemed to have become even busier. Olivia shrank into her chair before looking back at Martin. 'It's you I came to see anyway,' she lied.

'Enid,' Martin said, his eyes suddenly full of life, 'with the napkins; pretty.' Olivia sat upright, alert again.

'That's right,' she said, wondering if Enid was indeed pretty. She supposed she was for her age.

'She's gone.'

Olivia felt like she'd been punched in the stomach. Enid was dead. It was true that she'd barely known Enid, but for some reason Enid had become Olivia's only remaining thread of hope. It was pathetic. Martin hadn't been acting himself lately either. His dementia was progressing. Soon Olivia would be completely alone with David.

'Such a kerfuffle,' Martin continued, and then he rolled his eyes. 'The police, the counting, like we're children.' He looked grumpy all of a sudden. 'We're not children,' he sulked. 'I'm not a child.'

Again, Olivia looked closely at her father-in-law. She couldn't recognise him. There wasn't even a shadow of the intelligent and thoughtful man she'd known for much of her life. There was very little left of the meaningful bond she felt they'd shared throughout her marriage to his son. She'd often thought that she was closer to Martin than David even. The bond must still be there of course, he was the same man – just a little older – but she couldn't see it any more, and she doubted Martin could. He was drifting away.

'You meant paramedics,' she corrected him. 'For Enid, I mean.' Martin looked indignant.

'I did not,' he replied. 'I meant what I meant. The police. We've had them all here, shouting all over the place. Disrupting the peace. The police have been.' He said the last sentence as if he were giving new information.

'The police?' Olivia asked. 'Do you mean the ones here now? They're not here for Enid though.' Martin was frowning at her. 'Are they?' she asked, a glimmer of hope for Enid. Maybe she was alive. 'Are they?'

'That's why we're all here, in this room.' He paused. 'Like children.' Another pause. 'In a school.'

'She's alive then – Enid?' Olivia asked bluntly, her mind in two places at once. Martin frowned, scoffed.

'I said she was alive,' he responded.

'So, is she here?' Olivia asked.

'Hmm?' Martin responded implying that he hadn't heard. Olivia looked back over to the door to reception, where carers panicked, and police loitered.

'Is she in some sort of trouble?' Olivia was so confused, and she wasn't sure Martin was the person to clear up facts.

Martin shrugged.

'I don't know where she's gone,' he said, and then he chuckled. 'I don't know if I'm coming or going half the time.'

As Olivia left, she saw that the worried carers in reception had been joined by a few managerial types dressed in suits, and the four police officers had split into pairs, talking to each suit in turn. Duncan stood by the exit rubbing his eyes. His large arms lowered to his sides revealing the stress in his face. Not a young man. Olivia guessed around her own age, maybe a little younger. Gym body but a face reflecting his profession: tired, but genuine; trustworthy.

'Is Enid around?' she asked him, innocently. One of his arms rose again and he rubbed his forehead with thick fingers, then straightened his face.

'She's disappeared,' he answered, before fumbling his words and looking panicked. 'Sorry. I don't know what I can and can't say. You're not related to Enid, are you?'

Olivia shook her head.

'I don't think I can tell give you any more information. I don't think I should've said that if I'm honest.' Martin had been right: whatever was going on here was related somehow to Enid.

'I understand,' Olivia said, reaching for the door, slightly taken aback.

Duncan sighed. 'Take a seat,' he gestured to the empty sofa, and Olivia did. 'I'll find out what I can tell you.'

Olivia was suddenly very aware of David. He wasn't there of course, but his voice echoed through her skull, each emotion she had felt that day coming with it. *I'm watching everything.* She didn't believe it, and so what if it was true? She was just sitting alone on a sofa in David's dad's home, and at least she had actually seen Martin this time. No, there was nothing to worry about.

She listened to the numerous conversations happening around her. She heard carers asking when people, presumably other carers, would be coming in for cover, and she heard someone talking about the steps down to the little cove, and how hard they were to navigate. Not everyone was speaking – some of the carers just stood about looking nervous. A woman in a suit leaned against the stair banisters biting her nails, several people were looking at their phones. Olivia noticed one of the police officers had started talking to one of the managerial types, near the reception desk. She leaned in.

'OK,' the police officer said. 'I'll need Enid's address.'

'Of course, it's…it's…' The woman scanned through an A4 hardback notebook with her finger before reading aloud. '35, Oaktree Avenue.'

'Thank you,' the officer replied, slowly writing down the address and then looking up. 'Have the family been informed?'

'We've called the daughter; she's on her way in now,' the woman confirmed.

'We have officers out looking for Enid, of course, but…'

Olivia sat back and took out her phone. She opened Google Maps. *35 Oaktree Avenue.*

Looking up, she saw Duncan walking briskly back to her. Thick arms, wide neck and a tight t-shirt. *That man, GI Joe, at the home.* David's voice haunted her. He had meant Duncan. She looked back down at her phone, gathered her bag, and stood up to leave. She reached for the door handle as fast as she could but was too late. Duncan's hand pulled the door inwards towards them both.

'You're off,' he said. 'I can't tell you anything about Enid, I'm afraid.'

'No, no, I understand.'

He was holding the door open for her but practically standing in the way, as though he didn't want her to leave.

'How are you doing?' he asked.

Olivia felt like pushing past him but didn't want to seem rude.

'I'm fine,' she said, then worried that she'd sounded short. 'I'm good, thank you.' Duncan's smile radiated genuine concern and kindness. He stepped back slightly, opening the door wider.

'Good.' His soft Scottish accent was in stark contrast with her rushed, spikey responses. 'Remember what I said; try not to take too much on.'

'Yep,' she said, walking through the door backwards, nodding. 'Thank you, thank you again, and I hope this all gets sorted.' She gestured around reception with her eyes.

Duncan sighed again. 'Aye,' he said. 'Look after yourself.' Olivia heard the door close as she turned to see David's car parked down the drive. The breath fell out of her, winded. Her feet walked almost of their own accord as she stumbled down the stepped pathway to the car. I was visiting Martin, she told herself. I was visiting Martin. She could see David through the driver's window. He was looking at her, grinning widely, the spider watching the fly.

'Are you visiting your dad?' she started to ask loudly as she came closer to the car, praying that he would be. Martin would be able to tell him that she'd just been there, with him, and then she would claim that Martin had simply forgotten her being there the first time, and this would be proof. But David gunned the engine and began to reverse the car.

'David?' she said, panic rising in her voice, as the car began to turn. 'David?' Her heart pounded through her chest, and she felt her skin clam up.

As David pulled away, she faced out towards the sea, gaining composure. Then she turned, and walked back to her own car, not looking up at the home. Not giving anything away.

Enid clutched tightly onto her bag. The bus was almost empty. On the other side of the aisle sat an elderly man, wearing a flat cap and glasses which were so big they covered his cheeks. Further back, a young woman with a pram sat, silently tapping her phone. No one talked.

Enid recognised the sounds that surrounded her; the struggle of the bus's heavy engine, the release of compressed air each time they stopped at a three-way junction. The patterns on the chairs were familiar too. Enid couldn't be sure, but she guessed that they hadn't been changed since long before her new life in the dementia home.

Through the window, she watched a world that she hadn't seen in a very long time pass by. Barb had driven her through these streets, from the home to the tearooms, from the tearooms to the home, but they hadn't meant anything to

Enid then. Today, she saw her whole life. The seafront pub that had served her favourite fish and chips, the bandstand that she and Roy had sat outside on deckchairs watching a local brass band, the crazy golf that Barb had loved as a child. Distinct, previously forgotten memories.

She had watched as Barb learnt to play tennis, and she saw herself on the court, picking up the balls that Barb missed. They were both decades younger, and the court they were playing on was now old and faded. The bus rolled past the model steam engine which still had bunting flying from the tops of its carriages, children waving to pedestrians, pedestrians waving back. There was Roy. Barb was sitting on his knee, waving. Enid lifted her hand up to the window to wave back as the train continued around the track and out of sight.

Another pub; family funerals; birthdays; days out with Donald; nights out with Roy. Houses of friends, houses of strangers, brick walls that Enid used to pass every day. She knew it all. It was all second nature. Grand Victorian buildings that she had never been in but had touched as she'd wandered past them as a young girl on her way to school.

She knew every exterior, every street, every piece of her life. There was the corner shop next to where she lived. She was nearly home.

Enid found herself crying. She saw everything.

Except, she didn't.

She couldn't see inside the buildings. She couldn't see any of the rooms, their interiors, their layouts. She couldn't see the pictures on the walls, and she couldn't see the people inhabiting them. Unless – as Enid hoped he would be – Roy was doing the same thing as she was, and making his way home, she knew that she couldn't see Roy.

33

'I REALLY DON'T THINK this is necessary, Roy,' Enid said, but Roy just held up the screwdriver in one hand, the bolt lock in the other, and raised an eyebrow.

'I've been meaning to do this for ages anyway,' he said. 'It's not just for Donald. I may as well do it now, while we've been talking about it.' He had calmed down now, and Enid had conceded that an extra lock wouldn't do any harm, though she also doubted it would make a dot of difference, and it definitely was for Donald.

After Roy had kissed Barb goodnight the previous evening, he'd asked Enid about the phone call. They'd been in their room, right next to Barb's, so they had to whisper. Enid had told him the truth; Barb had answered the phone, told her it had been Roy, and then, when Enid had taken the receiver from Barb, the phone had gone dead. Roy claimed to have no recollection of the phone call.

'Did I say anything?' he'd asked.

'I don't know,' Enid had replied. 'You must have said it was you, or Dad, or something, for her to know.' Roy had looked pensive while Enid finished putting the clean clothes away.

When they were downstairs, Enid had gone to turn the main light off and put the lamp on, ready for an evening of TV, but Roy had interrupted.

'I need to tell you something,' he'd said, clearly worried, worked up before he'd even begun. 'I saw Donald at the school gates.' Enid had just stared at him. 'And I think it must have been Donald on the phone with Barb.'

At first, Enid had been cross with Roy for not telling her straightaway, but Roy had said he hadn't wanted to worry her, and that he hadn't necessarily thought there was anything to be concerned about. They'd gone through the events of the phone call in detail together, and eventually both agreed that it had likely been Donald on the other end of the line.

Worry had grown into upset for Enid, and her upset had somehow morphed into anger for Roy. He'd had nowhere to aim his anger, so he'd paced the lounge, unsure how to deal with the frustration of not knowing how to protect his family. Like many men, Enid realised, Roy didn't always know how to express his more complex emotions. He had paced, and he had vented. Crucially, he had held it together, and eventually he had hugged Enid tightly, and apologised for not telling her about the school-gate incident sooner. She had assured him that there was nothing to worry about, and eventually Roy had conceded.

Late in the evening, they'd made the joint decision that Barb would miss the following day's school. It would be the weekend after that, and she'd be home anyway. They could deal with Monday when it came.

Roy grunted out words with each turn of the screwdriver. 'I...have to...put it up,' he said, 'if only...for...my own... sanity.' Enid agreed. 'Ugh, there you go,' he said, standing back from the porch door. 'Tomorrow, I'll look at alarms in the DIY shop. This is just an extra lock, for the inside of the porch. There's more to do, to protect you, and to protect Barb.' He picked up his toolbox and walked into the hall.

Enid leant on the kitchen side. Her husband had turned his anger into something productive. That is what made Roy the man he was, she thought.

34

The sight of her house brought tears to Enid's eyes. She sharply inhaled, pushed them away, and with great effort, stood up and into the corridor of the moving bus. The young mum who had been sitting behind her started organising her belongings in the pram. Enid felt her waiting patiently behind all the way to the front.

'Gettin' off?' the driver asked, slowing the bus.

'No, oh…um… No.'

'Do you need a hand?' the mum interjected, and Enid incorrectly refused, but then gratefully accepted. When they were both off the bus, the woman left.

The day was bright, though not sunny. Pale, white clouds threatened a miserable evening, not yet oppressive. The wind blew through Enid's hair, which was thinner than it once was but still permed and dyed to her style. She raised both hands to hover above her hair, not wanting it to lose its shape.

The road was familiar to her, wide and fast. A main road only in the context of the rest of the town, which mainly consisted of independent shops, cafés and residential cul-de-sacs. Enid and Roy had lived near there – very near there in fact – but she didn't know where exactly. The bus had driven away and Enid found herself alone. Occasionally, a car drove past, possibly speeding; it certainly felt like it. There were no other people around. Not for the first time that day, Enid had the odd sensation of knowing exactly where she was and being completely lost at the same time.

The cold seeped through the arthritis in her fingers and her hips ached. It dawned on her that, unless something were to click in her mind suddenly, she was now homeless.

A single drop of rain landed on her hand. Her old home was off this road somewhere, and the road only offered her two directions to choose from. Enid turned to her left. Rows of houses lined the main road on both sides, all a similar style: the practical cubes of the early fifties. They were all the same style as the house she had lived in with Roy in fact.

Enid slowly turned her whole body to look down the road, this time to her right. One side was lined with yet more houses – again, a call-back to a decade before Enid had Roy, when she'd been just a little girl. Smaller roads rooted between the gaps after the semi-detached ones. On the other side of the road, the long line of houses and smaller roads stopped, and a large, grassy field opened up. Enid had to make a decision, and with logic failing her, she found herself drawn to the grass. It felt natural to walk that way.

The rain grew heavier. She felt her hair blow behind her as she crossed the road. Every step was slow, but she was lucky, and no cars interrupted her as she passed the white line dividing the two sides. She looked both ways as she crossed, though she realised it was pointless. It wasn't as if she'd be able to dodge out of the way. Just as she had both feet on the pavement, a horn blasted loudly behind her, and a car sped past. Enid leant forward and held onto the flat wall in front of her to steady herself. She stood upright again, stared at the grass to her right, which had now become her one and only goal, turned, and took a step towards it.

Did she live near grass? Roy did like gardening, but Enid remembered a fair amount of that being inside a greenhouse.

When she reached the field, she felt her heart drop with sudden flooding emotion. Across the grass she saw a small playground, climbing frame, swings, a short fireman's pole and a metal slide. It was Barb's playground. Enid had walked to and from this park every day for years, once.

'Oh,' Enid said to the empty field. A seagull took flight from the worn patch of grass in front of the slide. Barb slid down to take the bird's place, a shadow of Enid's past, played out in front of her like a cruel mirage.

She realised that she would never see Barb again – not as the innocent child playing in the park, or as the wonderful caring woman that she had become. She would likely never see Roy again either. It was unlikely that he would be doing the same as she was – trying to find their old house in the rain – on the same day. His face always looked sympathetic now when she thought of him. Sympathetic, and old. There was a flash of a caravan, a memory of rain pounding on a roof, Roy going out in the wet, a holiday and then…violence?

'Are you alright?'

Enid jumped. She turned around to see a young boy,

possibly still in his teens, in a raincoat with the hood up. His hair was wet and flat against his pale forehead. 'Are you lost?' he said, and when Enid still didn't reply, he offered, 'Do you need help?'

'Oh... I... I'm not allowed out of here,' Enid eventually responded. The boy frowned, but not impolitely, and looked around him.

'Out of where?'

'Uh...Oh dear...Um...' Tears were rolling down Enid's cheeks, getting lost in the rain.

'Do you live near here?' he asked loudly.

Enid felt desperate for words.

'I can ring my mum if you like?' he offered, though looking a little helpless. 'She might be able to help.' He reached out to Enid gently with one of his hands and Enid flinched. She hissed at the boy, and he put both of his hands in the air. 'It's alright,' he told her, 'I won't touch you. I'm just trying to...' But before he'd finished his sentence, Enid had jolted her whole body towards him. One of her hands hit the boy's chest, and he jumped backwards.

'Hey,' he shouted, scared and retreating, 'I just wanted to help.' Feeling threatened, Enid lowered her head, fixed a hard stare on the boy's face and made a low growl.

'You're lucky I haven't called the police,' he said. 'You're mad.' He turned and ran, back towards the bus stop from which Enid had just walked. She was furious. How dare he call her mad? She was just doing what any mother would do; she was protecting her daughter. Barb was playing on the slide. Enid went to chase the boy, but he'd already gone.

She shuffled after him to warn any of his other potential victims, but she soon forgot about the boy, and her anger subsided. Everything hurt. The effort she had expended to get her to this place was now taking its toll on her spine and both her thighs. She couldn't move her fingers for the cold, but she could feel a bruise growing on one of her hands, though she didn't know why. Her legs continued slowly moving her down the familiar street, but her feet didn't leave the ground, and she didn't feel in control of them any more. She felt numb.

She watched as house after house slowly passed her by, each as recognisable as the last, yet each equally strange, and none of them offering any clues. A world she'd once known but could no longer navigate.

Then she saw the police car, the police officers, a woman and a man, walking into a door that Enid knew well. She had used that door during her best years.

A flash of red flew by inside the lounge window, from the television to the sofa. Enid recoiled and shrank her head down into her shoulders. She saw herself, inside a caravan, picking a plate up from the worktop and holding it high above her head. She remembered Roy opening the door and the plate coming down on him.

She raised her hand to her open mouth as she watched a fluorescent blue wing stretch out from behind the lounge curtains. She backed away, feeling winded. Pushing herself painfully into one of the bushes behind her, she wedged her body between the branches and a tanned wooden fence. The police were looking for her, and she had to hide. She remembered now. She had attacked Roy.

35

Olivia had driven only two roads from the dementia home before she pulled over and dropped her head on the steering wheel in frustration. She thought only silent expletives, unable to consider what had just happened with any focus or clarity. He'd driven away. He'd seen her, smiled menacingly, and then driven away. Was this what he wanted – for her to suffer ridiculous levels of fear, to be unsure of what would happen next? What would happen next, she wondered.

He'd not mentioned the first time she'd been to visit Enid since he'd threatened her in the kitchen. He seemed to enjoy creating the suspense and watching her worry, the power of holding the strings, some twisted keeper of her destiny. It was unlikely, then, that he would mention what had happened that day at home that night. There was no quiz night, and it was David's night to cook dinner, so she was doubtful that he'd drink more than a glass of wine. Not enough to alter his mood, or to throw him off his game. Once he'd physically punished her for that day, the game would be over. He'd want to cherish that power, so, Olivia thought, she had time.

She wondered whether he'd still be watching her now, and decided that no, he had what he needed. She was free for now. She sniffed, blinked her eyes dry and exhaled. Opening Google Maps, she found *35 Oaktree Avenue* still loaded on the screen. She paused before touching the blue Directions button and pulling away.

As she drove, Olivia found herself checking the mirrors excessively, paranoid about being followed. Rear view, wing, wing, over and over. She barely looked out of the windscreen, driving with the instinctive confidence that comes with never having been in an accident. There wasn't any sign of her being followed, but she breathed no sigh of relief, remaining vigilant.

She leant over to look out of the passenger window as she approached Oaktree Avenue. A police car was parked in the drive. She knew Enid wouldn't be there. If she was indeed trying to find her way home, she wouldn't attempt it with a police car in the drive. How intimidating. Olivia kept her foot pressed evenly on the clutch and drifted past the house, heading…well…home, she supposed.

Why had Enid run? Olivia remembered the joy in Enid's face when she'd told Olivia that Roy would be moving in. Surely this couldn't be about that. Maybe the reality of Roy hadn't been as good as the memory of him. Either way, Enid needed a friend, not a manhunt. Olivia was already in the black as far as David was concerned. Nothing she did now could make her own situation worse, so she resolved to return to the house later that evening.

As Barb left her parent's house, she almost turned the key to lock the door, forgetting that the police were still inside. She wasn't thinking straight – exhausted from emotion and stress. Being inside the almost-empty house had proved too much. She had grown up in that house, played in it, felt all the early emotions that children feel, and then used them to learn how to navigate life. She'd met Calvin before she'd moved out, she'd married him, and then, when her life compass had failed and she'd found herself divorced, she'd moved briefly back in with her parents, Alex in tow. Now, she realised, she was single-handedly responsible for moving both of her parents away from a building that she knew meant so much to her and to them. She'd had to put the house on the market to cover the costs of the care homes – not that it was selling. After she'd signed the paperwork, she'd cried.

She understood why her mum had escaped, but she couldn't escape the self-appointed blame for having moving her in the first place. What must her mum think of her now?

Barb had endured long conversations with the police already that day, and several of the carers. She had been angry with the home, she'd shouted at Kara, and then apologised. She'd cried in an office and drunk too much caffeine. Now all she was left with was guilt and exhaustion.

She knew that tomorrow she would have to call work and put in a request to take some time off – an offer that had been on the table for some time now. They must have noticed the stress in her eyes, the new wrinkles across her forehead and around her neck, her hair changing colour. The offer had been well meant – Barb knew that – and it had been communicated as a favour, compassionate leave, but it would be unpaid and now more than ever she needed the money. The house wasn't selling, and her parents' savings had nearly depleted. Presumably, it would be up to her to make up the difference. When her mum returned to the dementia home her parents would go into debt.

When her mum returned? Barb caught herself. *If* her mum returned. Before leaving, she'd asked one of the officers the likelihood of her mum being found, and instead of a direct answer, she'd been told that someone would visit the house during the night and then again in the morning. The house, she'd been told, was where they believed Enid would be trying to get to. But then, when she'd asked the officer how long someone her mum's age might be able to survive in this weather, she'd been told, simply, that they were hopeful that Enid would be inside. Barb couldn't bear the thought of her mum standing alone in the rain, cold and confused, but the image kept rearing its ugly head. In her mind, her mum was soaking and cowering, next to a grave. She wanted to go out and look for Enid, but there wasn't anywhere not already being searched.

On her way home, Barb wondered how she would tell Alex. She knew she would have to tell her at some point, but she worried she'd get the blame at a time when she needed support. Alex was with one of her friends that night though, and then sleeping at her dad's, so at least that nightmare could wait. Then a realisation flooded Barb with dread. How would she ever manage to tell Roy?

36

THERE WAS NO ONE TO HELP Enid escape the branches jabbing her ribs and the fence behind her, and there was nothing for her to hold on to to stop her from falling as she emerged, but she couldn't stand in the cold any longer. It was dark now, and although the rain had stopped, her clothes were wet through. She could feel the damp throbbing in her joints.

She had spent all afternoon watching her old house from behind the bush on the other side of the main road. She had watched police officers intermittently walk into her home and then leave. She had seen Barb going in, and then, sometime later, although she couldn't be sure how much time, she had watched Barb leave again too.

Enid had stared at the sign stuck into the lawn. Had it always been there? She couldn't read what it said, but there was a childlike picture of a house next to the words.

Knees bent, back curved, Enid attempted to steady herself. Small leaves were stuck to her face, along with clumps of her own hair. It could have been any time of night – early or late – Enid didn't know. The streetlights had come on some time before and the main road was quiet again. Slowly and painfully, Enid crossed the road to her house.

She couldn't go inside; she couldn't remember whether there was still an officer in there or not, but she needed warmth and she needed shelter. Her feet ached as they struggled the last few steps, through the side gate which had been left open, and towards the caravan.

The door was locked, and Enid smiled to herself. 'Roy,' she muttered, proud of him for remembering to lock it. She reached under the door, feeling like her spine might break from the pressure of her shoulders, and pulled out the key. She blew at the rust on the corner; a pointless habit, she knew. Rust didn't just blow away.

Inside, the caravan was cold, but Enid knew there were blankets somewhere. She started looking through the drawers and cabinets.

The cupboard below the sink: pans, washing-up liquid and dishcloths.

The cupboards above the sofa: mugs, plates and plastic cups.

The boxes below the sofa: bedding, sheets and pillows. What was she looking for again? No matter. These could keep her warm while she tried to remember. Enid placed as many of them as she could manage on top of her and sat, weighted down, on the sofa.

She noticed two pens and a pad of paper along the sofa, just out of reach. The paper was full of shapes that she couldn't decipher. She recognised them as writing though. It was her own, and it was Roy's, but she couldn't read the words. She stared hard at the top sheet.

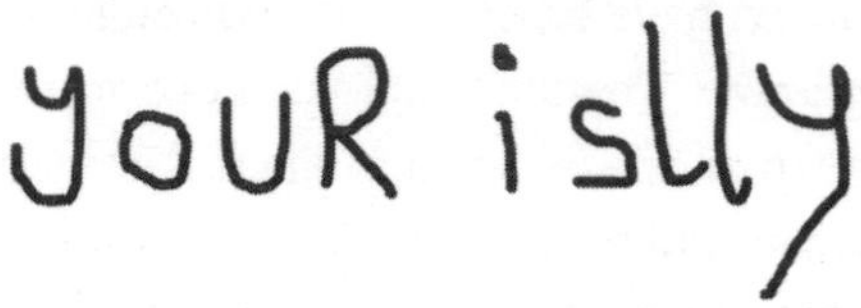

It meant nothing.

She remained awake, still, other than a shaking which she couldn't control, unable to relax. Occasionally, a car drove by and then the caravan would return once again to the night's silence. Enid didn't know whether she had warmed up or if she'd just become numb when the headlights of a car turned into her drive and flashed through the caravan window. Her eyes widened and her lips began to tremble. The headlights were turned off and Enid heard the sound of two car doors opening, shutting, then of two voices that she probably didn't know, or at least didn't recognise.

'One last check. I'm off at nine tonight. I've told the daughter to get some sleep. She's been out all evening, looking.'

'Doubt she will though.'

'No. Has anyone told the husband yet?'

'Roy. No, Sarge. Not us anyway.'

Enid smiled instinctively at the name, and then shrank into the sofa, remembering how she'd hurt her husband. How she'd forcefully brought the plate down onto his arm. He must have shown the police the bruise.

'I don't know how much he'll understand,' the voice outside continued. 'It's being left with the daughter I think.'

'You think?'

'It is being left with the daughter, Sarge.'

Footsteps.

Enid heard the familiar sound of her own front door being unlocked and pushed open. It echoed through her as she tried to understand the conversation she'd just heard. She needed to find Roy, to explain herself, to let him know that it had been an accident. She would never hurt him – not on purpose. He would help her, surely, he would. He always did.

The front door opened again. The same two sets of footsteps, but no talking this time. Car doors opening, shutting. An engine starting. Headlights flooded through the caravan window, lighting the room once more. The car backed out of the drive, and Enid watched as the shapes disappeared into the darkness.

37

Barb gazed at the glare from the television set. John Noakes, Peter Purves and Lesley Judd were sitting along the *Blue Peter* benches, each with a different pet; two cats and a dog. How she wanted a dog. The screen cut to John in the cockpit of an RAF aeroplane.

'Now, I'm not only a passenger here,' John said calmly to his audience, 'but I've been told I can co-pilot too.'

Barb jumped up from her knees closer to the television.

'Sit back down,' her dad hissed, flapping his hand up and down. He was standing in front of one of the open curtains, hidden from outside, but every so often peering out. Barb giggled and did as she was told, her eyes not leaving the screen. Her mum, sitting on the sofa behind Barb, audibly sighed.

'I couldn't see it yet, but already we'd begun to descend,' John narrated. 'I thought Jimmy would take the controls, but he said I could take the plane down, and land it on the tropical island.'

Barb's mouth widened. She'd imagined what it must be like to fly before, though in her dreams it was never in a plane; she'd had wings.

She had watched far more television than usual over the weekend. Neither her mum nor her dad had taken her to the play park as they normally would, and she hadn't been allowed to accompany Roy to the corner shop for his daily paper.

There was an unsettled feeling that had nestled itself deep inside the pit of her stomach, but it wasn't specific. Both her parents were doting on her more than they usually did, and the last two nights she'd heard them both waiting on the landing before she fell asleep, rather than heading downstairs to do whatever adults did after bedtime.

The previous day, she'd overheard them arguing when she'd been reading in her room. They didn't shout, and they weren't any louder than normal in fact, but Barb had picked up on the negative tones. She'd heard her dad tell her mum that they should call the police, but her mum had told him that they shouldn't, and that *he* was harmless.

Barb didn't know who *he* was.

Her mum had called her dad a stupid man, and he'd accused her mum of having a soft spot for *him*. *He* was a stupid man too, her mum had said, but just that, and nothing more. Barb had listened, but she had not understood.

After the argument, Barb had come downstairs to find them hugging in the kitchen. For the rest of the weekend, they'd been tender and considerate towards each other, regularly making sure the other was alright, and constantly declaring their love for each other. The effect on Barb was confusing.

A slight shift in the family dynamic, a six-year-old's entire life.

The television remained the same though: the programming schedule was unchanged and there was warmth in its glow. The television offered familiarity, and familiarity offered a perceived security.

'Well, we got down very safely,' John said through the microphone in his helmet, now grounded. 'How did I do?'

The RAF pilot confirmed that John had done very good, actually.

'He's out there,' Roy whispered.

'Get away from the curtain then,' Enid said. She hadn't been paying attention to *Blue Peter*. She'd been watching her husband nervously.

'You might think that, with grace and daring, I've just landed a four-engine, million-pound plane on a tiny island in the middle of the Indian ocean,' John interrupted, his helmet off and his voice louder, 'but in reality, I haven't been more than twelve feet off the ground.' He stepped out of a grey door and showed his audience the simulator he'd just 'landed'.

Barb felt her whole body drop. She was so disappointed. John Noakes had never flown, nor had he landed an aeroplane. She turned to look at her dad. Who was out there? Who was he talking about? Then she turned further to see her mum, now sitting up straight, worry in her eyes.

'Can I go outside to the birds?' Barb asked. Her dad walked away from the window and sat down next to the record player.

'Oh, Barb,' he said, his eyebrows tense and concerned. 'Not now.'

Barb huffed. It wasn't fair. She had only seen the birds once over the weekend and she was worried that she would miss the chicks fledging the nest. Fledging was her new word.

'But I want to see the fledging of the nest,' she said, still unsure if she was using the word correctly.

'Will you take her?' Enid pleaded with Roy. 'She can't go out by herself, but she's OK with you.' Barb frowned at her mum, but she didn't think to ask what she'd meant. She had been accompanied by her dad the last time she'd seen the blackbirds too. He had insisted, though Barb hadn't thought to question it then either.

Roy stood back up as *Blue Peter* ended and Enid changed the channel. The screen cut to an eagle soaring across an open field, with spectators lined up along the hedgerow, watching. Then a straight-faced man appeared. He wore a thick rainbow-striped jumper, and he had a parrot on his shoulder. The parrot eyed him.

'Join us at Birdland,' the man said, 'for hundreds of spectacular displays.' The parrot pecked the man's ear. This man had become something of a celebrity in the household. Each time he came on the screen, Barb would jump up and down, and ask her parents if they could all go to Birdland. Repeatedly, she'd been told that, yes, soon they could go. But over the last couple of days the excitement seemed to have dwindled.

'Maybe, soon,' her dad had answered the previous day before bath time, but with no real excitement in his voice.

'I don't know,' her mum had said just that very morning. 'We'll see.' Barb had sensed an increasing lack of conviction.

The screen filled with a logo, followed by the directions needed to visit Birdland.

'Please can we go to Birdland?' Barb asked, choosing not to jump this time; a genuine question demanding a genuine answer. Her mum shot her a look, but it was her dad who replied.

'No,' he said. 'I'm sorry, and I think we're going to have to take you out of school for a couple of days.' Barb tightened her face. The answer had been so unexpected that she couldn't reply. She needed time to unravel it, to understand.

'He'll leave soon,' her mum said quietly. 'He'll get bored soon. He always gets bored.' Barb felt the comfort of her mum's warm familiar smile. 'We will go to Birdland,' Enid told her definitively. 'Not now, but soon.'

That night, Barb woke from sleep to hear loud whispers next door, in her parents' room. She picked up her teddy, placed its bare arm in her mouth and sucked. Her parents were always telling her not to put it in her mouth as it could damage the old toy, but they couldn't see her now and there was something about the feel of the material that she found comforting. After a while, the stuffing grew damp, and Barb started sucking her own saliva back into her mouth. She shuffled her legs to the side of the bed and sleepily walked to her bedroom door, where she could hear the whispering more clearly.

'No,' she heard her mum saying sharply, scolding Roy. 'We need to let her do things; she needs to go outside.' Barb was vaguely aware that her mum was talking about her. She hadn't been to school so far that week, and she'd been accompanied by either her mum or dad every time she'd asked to play in the garden. Neither parent had properly discussed what was going on with her, but of course she had noticed. More than anything, Barb missed watching her birds and she was worried that she'd miss the chicks leaving the nest.

'I'm keeping her safe,' her dad retorted in a whisper louder than his actual voice. He was cross, which was something Barb wasn't used to, but even she could recognise the fear behind his anger. 'If we called the police…' he started.

'And what would they do?' her mum interrupted. 'It would just wind him up, and then what?' Roy didn't reply, and for a few seconds Barb found herself standing in the night's silence, with only the glow from her nightlight for comfort. Her mum sighed.

'I found her pretending to be at school yesterday. She'd put her bear on the sofa and was sitting in front of it on the floor. The bear was a teacher.' Barb heard her dad mumble something, defeated. 'She was pretending to be herself, Roy. No child should have to do that.'

Barb felt the guilt softly working its way through her stomach. She crept back to her bedroom and slid her feet into her slippers. She pulled her teddy out of her mouth and hugged it tightly on the way down the stairs. She wanted to see her chicks, to talk to them, to confide in them, to share her sadness.

She slid the patio doors open slowly, so as not to alert her parents. It wasn't until she turned, about to shut the door, that Barb noticed the shape darting across the lawn towards the nest in the weeds. The shape noticed her too and took a sharp right-angle to the side of the garden, behind the greenhouse, through the grapevine and out through a gap in the fence.

A fox.

Barb gripped her teddy tight, and she screamed, frozen to the spot.

38

When Olivia opened the door, with the two children in tow, she found David already at home. She could hear the cooker fan on its highest setting and the windows had steamed up. David cooked once a week – always a slight variation of the same curry. Over-fried vegetables in too much oil with sauce poured on at the highest temperature. She used to be grateful that he took on this weekly task, but now she just dreaded him being home.

Dillon threw himself onto the sofa and reached for the remote. Oona pulled her trains out of the toy box. Olivia didn't greet David on entering the kitchen; she wouldn't know what to say. It would ultimately be up to him how he decided to approach, or not approach, the incident at the home earlier.

'Alright, kids,' he called through to the lounge.

'Right, Dad,' came Dillon's reply. Nothing from Oona.

'Don't get too comfortable, I'm dishing up in a minute.' He pushed past Olivia holding a pan of boiling rice before emptying the contents into a colander in the sink.

'Can I help?' Olivia asked, sitting at the table to get out of his way.

'Hm?' David asked. He turned to look at her, eyes hard. 'Well, as you're already sitting down, no. No, you just relax.' There was no point in arguing. Even if David did intend to discuss what had happened earlier in the day, she knew he would never do it in front of the children.

'David,' she said, finding her window of opportunity between him dishing up and Dillon and Oona coming in.

'Hm?' he asked again, the noise short and lacking emotion, yet somehow swollen with power.

'I bumped into Susan earlier.'

'Hm,' David replied, looking at the plates as he spooned rice onto them from the pan.

'I've agreed to go for a drink with her.' Olivia pulled out her phone and scrolled, 'tonight.' She hoped that this would be hard for David to argue with. She'd been complaining that she didn't have friends for a while now. He always told her that she should get back in touch with the old group, knowing full well that she would be too embarrassed to. He never fully understood what had happened with her and her friends, he'd told her, but Olivia knew that they both understood, fully.

She braced herself for a spiteful comment, but none came.

'Kids,' David called, and Dillon walked in, complaining that he wanted to finish the programme. Olivia took the opportunity to fetch Oona. She'd done it; she'd dropped the lie. David hadn't agreed as such, but he hadn't disagreed. Had the children not been in the next room, she had no doubt that he would have hit the roof. She knew that he would check up on her alibi too, which meant that she actually would have to speak to Susan. The thought was daunting, and yet dizzying at the same time.

She didn't talk over dinner. David asked Dillon questions about school, and he pulled silly faces at Oona, making her giggle. Olivia tried to refuse the children pudding, as it was bath and bedtime, but David insisted.

'We're in no rush,' he'd said, pulling crumble out of the freezer and then cooking it in the oven rather than the microwave, much to Dillon's amusement. Olivia ran a shallow bath as the others ate, fetching both children as soon as David had fed the last painfully slow spoonful to Oona. As she lathered Oona's hair, she was relieved to hear his office door shut.

After their bath, both children went to hug their dad goodnight, Olivia waiting for them outside the office. When they came out, she placed Oona in her cot and then tucked Dillon into bed. There was one thing she needed to know before leaving for Enid's house. Halfway through reading with Dillon, she paused.

'Have you ever been scared of Daddy?'

Dillon laughed. 'Scared of Daddy? No, don't be silly, Mummy.'

Olivia felt a wave of relief, tension easing somewhat in her shoulders. Thank god. He saved his venom for her. The children were perfectly safe. How about Mummy?' she asked, normalising the question. This pushed Dillon's giggling to another level, so she kept reading until he was asleep. She kissed him and then Oona, who had already fallen asleep.

David appeared as she was putting on her coat.

'Where are you really going?' he asked, apparently hurt.

'I'm seeing Susan,' Olivia replied, pulling her second arm through the sleeve, ready to make an exit. David wasn't angry though. He wore the expression of an abandoned puppy.

'How long has it been going on?' he asked. Olivia leant in and kissed his unmoving lips.

'You really don't have anything to worry about,' she told him, forcing compassion into her voice. 'I'm not seeing anyone. I promise, there's nothing between me and that carer from the home. I barely remember his name. I'm seeing Susan, rekindling an old friendship, like you always tell me I should.'

Olivia wasn't sure what game he was playing as she pulled out of the drive, but he stood in the doorway and watched her leave, arms slumped by his side, face like a smacked arse.

There were no cars parked in Enid's drive. No one answered the door when Olivia rang the doorbell, and when she'd tried the handle, she found it locked. The house was in a quiet street, visible from the main road, so she waited until she couldn't hear any cars before side-stepping along the thin concrete to peer through the window. Using what little light seeped through from the patio doors at the back, she saw that Enid's living room appeared empty.

Olivia's heart dropped. She had hoped so much that Enid would be there, though she was unsure why. Now she would have to call Susan, create an alibi, then make an excuse for having to do so. This whole pointless night would have consequences with David too, even if he believed the alibi. She wanted to cry.

With no real expectation, she walked around to the side

of the house, through an open wooden gate and alongside a caravan to check the side door. That too was locked, so she opened a smaller gate through to the garden. The lawn was overgrown, and the potted plants had seen better days, but it was September, and it was obvious that the garden had once been loved. Enid wasn't there.

Olivia turned to leave. She was about to walk back to her car, to sit for an hour or so before driving home, when she noticed a key hanging from the caravan door.

She leant forward and peered through the plastic tinted window. Again, it was dark, but there was no mistaking the outline of someone on the sofa. Olivia felt breath catch in her throat. As the room came into focus, the dark shape turned into Enid, and she wasn't moving. Olivia tapped on the window, and whispered Enid's name. When she didn't move, Olivia hit the window harder. This time, Enid breathed heavily before opening her eyes, only slightly.

'Ugh...' Enid's voice was low, the sound of someone who hadn't spoken in a long time. She tried to clear her throat with a cough and only produced air. 'Uh,' and then another, more successful cough. 'Yes,' she called, not looking at Olivia, lifting up the pillowcases and sheets that lay across her lap, and then laying them back down again in the same place. 'Yes?'

Olivia walked around to the door and slowly opened it.

'Hello,' she whispered, peering into the caravan.

'Uh,' Enid said again.

'Enid, can I come in?'

Enid nodded, looking around the room, as if trying to place herself. Olivia stepped inside, leaving the door ajar. She wanted Enid to feel safe with her.

'Uh,' Enid stammered, looking at the small sink next to

Olivia. 'Uh, holi. Um. Holiday.'

'No, Enid. You're not on holiday, but you are in your caravan.'

Olivia watched as Enid pieced together her memory. Enid reached out and touched Olivia's hair, which was damp and tangled from the rain. She breathed deeply, and let out a disappointed, slightly panicked 'oh'.

'Are you OK?' Olivia asked, and Enid nodded. She didn't look scared any more but held an expression of sorrow and of regret. 'Are you cold?' Enid nodded again.

'No,' she said.

Gently, Olivia closed the door and sat on the sofa next to Enid. There wasn't much space between Enid and the pad of paper, which Olivia didn't want to move, and despite Enid's effort to shuffle, she found that her shoulder touched Enid's.

'Oh, you are cold, Enid. You're freezing.' Enid looked at her sadly.

'Uh… I… Well.' Olivia put her arm around Enid's back and pulled her in tightly. To her surprise, Enid leant into her, and Olivia felt a warmth that she herself hadn't felt in a long time.

'We need to get you back home,' Olivia said quietly. She could feel Enid shaking against her shoulder. 'There's not any rush though.'

'No,' Enid said.

'No,' Olivia repeated. 'OK.' Neither spoke for a while. Olivia wasn't going to make Enid go back; it wasn't her place. 'Why did you leave?' she asked, voice still hushed.

'Uh, well…' Enid shifted in her seat. 'I think…Roy, I hurt. You know, hurt him.' Olivia stared ahead, her eyes narrowing. She didn't believe that Enid could hurt anyone.

'Did he move in with you, back at the home?' Olivia felt

Enid shake her head gently against her side. 'No,' Olivia said, beginning to understand. 'You haven't seen Roy then, for…' The sentence trailed off. 'Enid,' she turned to face her, lifting her gently as she did, 'do you want to find Roy?'

'Oh yes,' Enid gushed. She bit the side of her bottom lip and raised her eyebrows, a young girl in love.

Olivia made a hasty decision, but in her heart, she knew it was right. 'I'll try and help you find Roy.' She spoke slowly, taking her time to make sure that Enid understood. Enid touched her own chest with her fingertips. 'Enid, I'm Olivia. We've met before. I don't think that you would have hurt Roy. I won't take you back to the home – not yet.' This wasn't a purely selfless act, Olivia realised. She didn't want to go home either. 'Does Roy live here?' she asked, and again Enid shook her head.

'Uh, oh.' Enid looked at her own lap as if to compose herself and then looked back at Olivia. 'Um, uh, new, um… home,' she said. 'New home.' Olivia gave the faintest of nods, before wrapping the sheets resting on Enid's lap around her shoulders.

'You're freezing,' she said, thinking fast. 'Do you mind if I find a way into your house? I might have to break in.' Enid didn't answer, but her eyes seemed to smile. 'Alright then, I'll be back in a minute.' At the door, Olivia smiled at Enid and said, 'Don't go anywhere.' She was relieved to see Enid smile back, recognising the joke.

Back outside, Olivia held onto the side door handle to Enid's house and shoved her shoulder into it, but it didn't budge. She placed her hands onto the kitchen window from the garden and shook, but of course it didn't move. She didn't know the first thing about breaking and entering. When she pulled at the handle on the sliding patio door though, there was a jolt. A small movement. Just a suggestion of possibility. She tried again, and managed to move the whole door, just enough for a slither of an opening. It wasn't locked. She held onto the handle with both hands and pulled back, her entire bodyweight behind her. The movement was rusty, but she was in.

'Alright Enid, I've managed to find a way in. One of your patio doors was unlocked.' Enid raised a hand and opened her mouth. After a moment, she closed it again.

'There's a knack,' she said, and despite the situation, Olivia laughed. She held on to both of Enid's hands and helped her to her feet. Enid didn't resist, and the two women left the caravan face to face, Olivia backwards and Enid forwards.

The small police station up the hill only opened in the daytime. Olivia figured they would probably have someone there overnight, just to pick up phone calls from the family, in case of developments, but they wouldn't be back to check Enid's house until the force was back on shift. That gave Enid and Olivia roughly until eight. They'd be safe in the house until then.

Once Enid was inside, Olivia went back out to fetch the bedding from the caravan.

'I need to make a couple of phone calls,' she told Enid, as she struggled to turn on the electric fire in the lounge. 'But I promise,' she grunted as she forced the dial round, 'I'm not ringing the home.' She felt the warmth of the fire on her face as it came to life. 'There,' she said to Enid. 'You warm up.'

Enid pulled the duvet up to her chest and took a deep breath in. The house was dustier than she'd remembered, and the smell wasn't quite right. Gone were the days of biscuits and tea, of Roy in the garden walking freshly cut grass into the house. Most of Enid's possessions had been removed too, with the exception of the furniture and a few pictures. Slowly, it appeared, her old life was physically disappearing from the earth.

When they'd come inside, she had allowed Olivia to lift her feet onto the sofa, and she had watched as Olivia had put a cover expertly over the caravan's duvet. Now, Enid was lying horizontal, snuggled up with the fire on in her own lounge. She could feel her body coming back to life, the warmth seeping in through her skin into her bones.

Olivia was on the phone in the hall. She hadn't closed the door fully behind her, and Enid was glad. It was nice to feel company, to have movement elsewhere in the house.

'We've just got so much to talk about, I'm going to stay over at Susan's.' Enid could hear the words, but she didn't pay much attention. It wasn't any of her business. Then Olivia snapped. 'Stop,' she said abruptly, and Enid started to pay more attention. 'Stop it. Stop.' She was almost shouting. 'David, no. You're being paranoid.' Enid clutched the duvet, and for a second, she thought she could hear the telly behind her. *The finest exotic birds in the world.* She heard the flapping of large wings taking off, felt the tip of one in her hair as it flew past, and then, just as quickly, it stopped.

'Look, I'll be back in the morning. I love you. Please don't worry.' Olivia's voice was calming, placating. 'No, I do love you,' she said, before taking the phone away from her ear and looking at the screen.

Enid had recognised Olivia in the caravan, but only as a familiar face. She didn't know how she knew her, only that she did know her. Olivia hadn't taken Enid back to the home and she'd offered to help find Roy, so Enid had trusted her, known that she was on Enid's side. But now she saw it – the car outside, the violence, the made-up eyes. She saw David's smirking face.

She watched Olivia lift the phone once more.

'Hiya,' she said, tone once again changed, this time a forced nonchalance. 'Yeah, long time. Very long time. How are you?' Olivia started pacing up and down Enid's hall as the person on the other end spoke. 'I have a huge favour to ask,' Enid heard before Olivia turned and walked away towards the kitchen. Enid overheard her say, 'Vouch for me. No, no, I'm not in any trouble,' as Olivia turned and headed back towards the front door, then turned again. This time she stopped walking next to the kitchen, and Enid found it hard to hear anything. When she did finally resume pacing, all Enid got was, 'yes, we should actually meet for a drink soon – I'd like that.' Then there was a lot of thanking before a quick goodbye. Olivia came back into the lounge.

Enid wanted to tell Olivia that she understood what she was doing, that everything would be well in time, that time is in fact the greatest healer as well as a perceived enemy. But she couldn't. There was too much she wanted to say to Olivia. She wanted to tell her that she was proud of her, but she only ever had the capacity for a few words at a time, and so, with wet eyes, she just nodded.

39

Enid woke up groggy, her body even heavier than usual. She used to lie in bed in the dementia home and imagine walking through her old house, back when coming home had felt like an impossibility, when Enid had been certain that she would never see her old walls again. She used to walk through each room, remembering only certain flashes of décor and moments of her life, but clinging onto those details like they were the only pieces of her left.

Now, sitting on the sofa in her own lounge, her and Roy's lounge, she felt more lost than ever. Had she remembered it wrong? Had she never hung pictures on the walls? Where were the small china pots which she had been sure she'd kept on the mantelpiece?

It had taken her a long time to sit upright from her position on the sofa. Olivia was sleeping on the floor below her, and it had been hard not to wake her. Enid wanted to be alone. It was still dark outside, and she needed some time.

She had recognised Olivia just a few minutes after she'd woken up. A small fraction of a lost reality, curled up on the floor. Olivia was a reminder that Enid had lived in a different house to this one before today. She also remembered that Olivia was in danger, though she couldn't remember what the danger was.

Light from the street outside seeped in through a crack in the curtains, just enough to navigate the room. The silence of night in Enid's own road was familiar. She stood up quietly and slowly, steadying herself by holding on to the shelf next to her to stop from falling. Didn't there used to be a record player on that shelf, along with pictures of a man whose name she could no longer recall? Avoiding the sleeping body on the floor, Enid edged her way past the nest of tables and towards the hall.

She held on to the door handle and looked back at Olivia. She looked so peaceful now, but soon it would be morning. Enid went out into the hall and closed the door behind her.

'Roy,' she hissed up the stairs. The hall was darker than the lounge, but she could still see the walls, the stairs, and the path to the kitchen. An old classic teddy sat underneath a wicker chair on the corner at the top of the stairs, before the landing. One lopsided eye, one withered arm from where Barb had sucked at it, bare patches all over its body. Enid saw herself in a different house holding on to that same teddy, a little girl finding comfort in softness, and then she saw Barb, just three, sitting on her knees in front of the chair, leaning forward and talking to the bear about an imaginary trip to the beach. Barb faded. The bear remained.

'Roy,' Enid hissed again. If he was up there, he would be

asleep, and Enid would have to shout louder. Best to check downstairs first, she thought.

She looked down at the table next to her. The phone was missing, if she was right in thinking that there had ever been one there. No phone books, no contact sheets or old notes left by her or Roy, but the table itself was familiar. The scratches on one of the legs from when Barb, as a toddler, had scraped keys across the varnish; the circle of faded paint where a plant pot had once sat.

The coat rack was where it had always been, and Enid recognised it instantly, but that wasn't quite right either. Tall, wooden, majestic…bare. There were no coats, there was no shoehorn leaning against the bottom. No shoes.

Enid looked up. The picture that she and Roy had been given on their wedding day still hung on the wall opposite the stairs. Intentionally or not, she had looked at this picture at least once, nearly every day for the majority of her adult life. She knew the intricacies of every brushstroke, each stretch of blue that had a wisp of white in it indicating the crash of sea on the shore. She reached out and touched it. She felt the bumps of the windows painted onto the small beach huts, and the raised brail of the sand. It was exactly as it always had been.

She walked through the hall, past the stairs, and into the kitchen.

'Ken,' she whispered, 'Ken.' Enid looked into the corner of the kitchen where Ken's bed should be. The tiles on the floor were bare and Enid became overwhelmed by emotion as she relived the sadness that she had felt when Ken had died. Briefly, all the other dogs that Enid and Roy had loved flashed in front of her and then disappeared. The kitchen had never felt so empty.

'Roy,' Enid called a little louder than before, more distressed this time. She needed comforting. In the past, when Roy couldn't sleep, he would sometimes come downstairs and make himself a cup of tea, but the kettle had disappeared. Perhaps he had taken it upstairs. Enid looked around her. The kitchen was unused. Other than the boiler that rested in the corner, the surfaces were clear, and the shelves were empty. There weren't even any mugs.

Enid almost fell from the kitchen into the largest room of the house, back where she'd started, in the dining room which faced into the lounge. She and Roy had their wedding day picture taken against the window in this room, with the garden behind them – Roy's pride and joy. Enid looked out of the double doors; the garden was overgrown now. It was dark though; it was still night; Roy could deal with that in the morning.

'Roy,' she tried again. She was shaking. 'Roy,' shouting now. Her head nodded frantically. Roy's chair was in the lounge and the sofa was in the same place as it had always been, but Roy wasn't on either.

Through the tears in her eyes, Enid saw that the mantelpiece was empty. There was no wedding picture. Had there been a wedding? Was this even their house?

'Roy,' she tried to scream, but her voice cracked, and it came out whispered. 'Roy?' She felt as if she had died.

Then she heard her name.

'Enid?' It wasn't Roy's voice, but it sounded familiar, nonetheless. She felt hands on both of her shoulders, and she burst into pained tears as the hands pulled her back into an embrace. It was her future, her present. It was all she had now. It was Olivia.

Enid turned and sobbed into Olivia's hair as her life caught up with her. This wasn't her home – not any more. Roy didn't live there, and neither did she. There were shadows of their lives together; the sofa, the painting in the hall, the tread on the carpet where they had once walked, where they had once lived, but those shadows were fading. One day, Enid realised, somebody else would live there and the house that she knew with Roy, and with Barb, would slowly disappear.

Just like Roy had, and just as she expected to do herself.

40

Enid pulled a face when she took her first sip of tea. It was different to the tea she had become used to in the dementia home, but she forced a smile for Olivia before putting the cup down.

'I couldn't find milk,' Olivia explained, 'and the water was boiled in a pan from the back of one of your cupboards. When the shops open, I can get some milk and better bags.' Enid raised her hand and shook her head.

'No. Oh, uh, no.' Her head continued to shake after she'd finished speaking, just to make sure that Olivia had understood that she was grateful, both for the tea, and for the company. Slowly, Enid picked up her mug again. If nothing else, she could appreciate the warmth.

The sun had risen but it was still very early, and it was blocked by a sheet of husky grey clouds. Olivia leant forward and rested her elbows on her knees. 'This might surprise you Enid, but I'm hiding too.'

Enid let out a small laugh, but then looked at Olivia apologetically. Enid knew that Olivia was hiding.

'Well, yes,' she said. 'You...you... Well. You know, you...' Olivia looked at Enid with wide surprised eyes, before straightening her face.

'Yes, Enid. Of course. Sorry, you're not stupid. Of course, you know.'

'No. I, Uh,' Enid tried. She only knew that Olivia was hiding, she didn't know the whole story. She suspected certain parts, but she didn't know. 'I don't, you know... I, uh. Not. I don't.'

'It's fine, Enid. Really. Of course, you know. It's why you told me about your first husband, back in the home.'

Enid didn't remember telling Olivia about Donald and she couldn't be sure of what had and hadn't been said. Instinctively, she reached up to touch the skin above her right eyebrow.

Olivia looked thoughtful. 'I knew,' she said quietly, 'that you knew.'

Enid gave a small smile. She didn't know – not really – but she was glad that Olivia was with her now, and that she was safe in this moment.

'I'm so sorry, Enid. This isn't your problem, it's just...no. This isn't your problem.'

Enid searched for the right words, and somehow felt less pressure to find them than normal.

'I...uh. Oh, here.' Enid said. Olivia didn't reply. 'Here,' Enid repeated, and Olivia nodded.

'Yes,' she said, gratefully. 'Thank you.'

There was a pause in which Enid felt completely comfortable. More comfortable than she'd remembered feeling in a long time, though Olivia may not have been feeling the same.

'Right,' Olivia said, snapping out of the moment. 'The police will be here at some point today, to look for you.'

Enid felt an involuntary noise escape her lips.

'No,' Olivia comforted her matter-of-factly. 'We're going to move back to the caravan, just until we've worked out what to do.'

Enid shook her head, quickly and resolutely. She remembered the cold, the sheets and the pillowcases that had barely covered her, the fear she had felt when someone had tapped on the window outside. She didn't try to remember who had been tapping. She remembered the darkness, and she remembered a fraction of her past: the rain; a holiday; a plate landing on Roy's arm. Her own hands on the plate.

'No, no. No.' Enid was firm.

'Not the caravan then. We don't have to hide in the caravan if you don't want to.' Enid looked straight ahead resolutely, staring at nothing, angrily. 'Enid, let me be clear about this: you don't have to do anything if you don't want to.'

Enid felt her face soften. She thought for a few seconds, before looking at Olivia and pointing out to the garden.

'They'll see us in the garden,' Olivia said. She didn't sound annoyed, even though Enid realised herself that her suggestion had been stupid. She was just passing on information. Enid sighed and attempted to stand up, and Olivia jumped to help her. Slowly they made their way to the rusty sliding doors at the back of the dining room. Olivia forced them open, and they walked out into the garden.

Enid gazed up at the windows that overlooked the garden and wondered who lived in them now. She prayed there would be no one peering out. They walked past the weeds, overgrown and spreading across the patio. They walked through the gate.

'Uh…so…we could, you know.' Enid stopped and gestured towards a single garage, part-hidden behind the parked caravan. 'Uh…it was, Donald's. You know... Donald. He used to tinker.'

Olivia looked at Enid.

'Roy's?' she asked, and Enid nodded, feeling awful.

'It's perfect, Enid,' Olivia said. 'Can we get in?' She opened the garage door. It looked stiff, but it was unlocked, and with enough effort she managed to pull it open. Inside was almost bare; Roy's worktop with the hall carpet wedged between it and the wall, their old wine buckets, a barbeque standing next to some old rags, four stacked plastic garden chairs and a small electric heater. Olivia plugged the heater in. 'Shall we sit?' she asked, closing the door behind them.

Enid stared at the wine buckets. She thought about the summers she'd spent with Roy, sifting through the grapes, pulling out the rotten ones. She remembered the fun they'd had crushing the grapes together, although she couldn't recall the actual process – just fragments and still images. The buckets were stained in all the same places. She noticed the same stains every summer.

'This is nice,' Olivia stated, helping Enid down onto one of the cushion-covered coated plastic garden chairs. 'Can I ask, why not the caravan?'

Enid remembered the plate, felt her insides turn upside down. She hated herself when she thought about what she had done to Roy in that caravan.

'It's where I…uh. Oh, where I.' Enid looked at the ring on her finger. She saw tiny pieces of sticky toffee pudding stuck to it and she tasted the bad stew. Then she looked again around the garage – Roy's garage. It was practically empty, almost unrecognisable. She remembered Roy; he was thirty; he was fifty. He was standing by the pier, and he was throwing Barb into the air. He was kissing her. He was on one knee. He was in the lounge playing *Countdown* as an old man and he was at the printers asking Enid out every day as a younger one. He was learning to change nappies despite his friends mocking him, and eventually, he was perfecting it. He was in their home, and he was in the garage. He was bruised, in the caravan outside. 'It's where I, um, where I hurt him,' she said.

'Oh Enid,' Olivia sighed.

Enid closed her eyes. 'I love Roy. I…uh…' She let out a frustrated groan, and then opened her eyes again. 'I love him.' Olivia's phone started to ring, but she carried on looking at Enid with soft, caring eyes.

'I know you do, Enid.'

The sound of the phone filled the silence between them before Olivia slowly asked Enid if she could check who it was. Enid knew that she was Olivia's priority, and she felt grateful, if a little undeserving of the attention, but Olivia was much younger than she was, and she had her own problems. Enid nodded, and Olivia took her phone out and looked at the screen.

'Hiya Susan.' There was the tone that Enid had heard last night again. An attempt at a relaxed demeanour, shrouded with a nervous energy. Olivia stood up and paced the garage. 'Slow down, slow down. He's been where?' Enid listened intently, though she didn't have one iota of the context. 'David's been *there*? Fuck. Fuck. Fuck.' She looked at Enid. 'Sorry.' Enid didn't mind. 'What did you tell him? Fuck. Where is he now? Fuck.' Olivia's pacing quickened as she listened to the person on the other end of the phone. She started biting her thumbnail. 'Thanks, Susan. He's fine. Honestly, don't worry. No, please don't worry. It's fine. I'll call you later, OK?' She looked once more at the screen, before looking back at Enid. 'Sorry, Enid. Sorry.' She sat back down on the plastic chair next to Enid. 'We need to find Roy.'

41

Olivia still hadn't opened her messages app, but she could read the latest from the lock-screen.

Don't listen to your answer phone. Sorry for texts earlier. I just miss you and want you to come home pls. Love you. xxx

She didn't even want to think about the earlier messages. They would be vile. There was no way David would be able to find her here though, and while she hated that he'd been to Susan's, it meant that the children were at nursery and school. Olivia knew now that she would never return home. She had limited time and relative safety with Enid. She would collect Dillon and Oona before the end of the school day and go… where would they go? Somewhere safe. Maybe Susan's? Maybe even Enid would come.

She opened the browser and searched for a list of all the care homes in the area. There were twenty-six. Enid looked at the screen, though Olivia doubted that it would mean much to her.

'So,' Olivia began, trying to think of a way to narrow the search. 'Enid, do you know if Roy has dementia?' There were only two homes dedicated to dementia, and Olivia knew that Roy wasn't in one of them.

Enid looked at Olivia. She hadn't understood the question.

'Uh…' she said.

'Dementia,' Olivia repeated patiently. 'Does Roy ever forget things?'

Enid thought for a second. 'Oh no,' she said happily, shaking her head. 'No, he's very good, you know.'

Olivia looked hard at the list of care homes on her phone. Down to twenty-four. If she had been the person looking for a place for Roy to live, she would probably have tried to place him as close to Enid as possible. There were three care homes near Enid's. Summer Lane, Elm View and The Hawthorns.

'Do you remember the last time you saw Roy?' she asked.

Enid was concentrating, looking hard at Olivia. She looked like she wanted to help but didn't know how to.

'Uh…' she said. 'Um…well, you know.' Olivia gave an encouraging nod, but Enid just looked apologetic.

'That's alright, Enid,' Olivia said softly. 'I wonder if he's even in a home yet. He could be in a hospital.'

'Oh no,' Enid said again. 'He's very, uh. You know.' She bounced her arms up and down in front of her. 'You know.'

'Healthy?' Olivia offered, and Enid nodded. 'I know,' she said, 'but he doesn't live here any more. I'm trying to work out where he might be.' Olivia tapped the screen quickly with both thumbs and Enid watched, fascinated. 'There are only two hospitals that he could be in. I can ring them both.' It occurred to her that Roy might not be in hospital, or at any of the care homes. Would she tell Martin if someone close to him had died? Not these days. Probably not. It would just be too much for him.

The phone rang seconds before Olivia had a chance to call the first hospital. She almost declined the call, but saw it was the nursery.

'Hello?'

'Hi, is that Olivia, Oona's mum?'

'Speaking.'

'I'm just ringing to let you know that Oona has a bit of a temperature,' the woman on the other end of the phone said. The implication that the child should be taken home from nursery was evident in her tone. Ordinarily this would be a frustrating phone call to receive, the rest of the day's plans ruined.

'I can pick her up right away' Olivia said, thinking fast. 'Give me five minutes.' She ended the call. 'I have to pick up my daughter,' she told Enid. 'She's only two and I don't want nursery to call David.'

'Oh, you must,' Enid said dramatically and sincerely. 'You must.' Then she scrunched up her face and held clenched fists up in front of her. 'Little, tiny…oh, you know.' Olivia wondered whose daughter Enid must be thinking of.

'Can I bring her back here?' Olivia asked. Enid nodded, looking bewildered and confused, but appreciative of a plan. 'I will come back, Enid, and when I do, I will look for Roy with you.' Enid didn't reply. 'I promise not to tell anyone' – Olivia paused for a moment to emphasise the point – '*anyone*, where you are. I need you to stay in the garage though, Enid. I won't be long, but I need you to stay in the garage, in case the police come when I'm gone.'

Enid nodded. She looked very serious, processing.

'Alright,' Olivia said, picking her bag up. 'I'll be back in ten minutes.' She lifted the garage door cautiously. No one was outside. 'Love you,' she said as she lowered the door back to the ground.

Enid's skin felt a little prickly from the portable electric heater. It seemed to turn itself on and off of its own accord. It was off now. She tried to relax in the garden chair, but couldn't help wondering where Olivia had gone. Looking around the garage, she saw her wine buckets against the wall. She wondered how Roy's grapes were getting on that year. Maybe they could have a barbeque with Barb's family later in the summer if the weather kept up.

It took a while to stand, but she wanted to check in Roy's worktop drawers. The surface was usually full of gizmos and gadgets – things she never understood – but today it was clear. She was always on at Roy to tidy the garage, but it wasn't like him to actually do it. She wondered if he'd just pushed everything into the drawers. She smiled at the thought of him doing that – he wouldn't be trying to deceive her; that really was Roy's idea of tidying.

But the drawers were almost empty. Just a shoe-polish-stained cloth, firelighters, metal tongs, a few loose wires, some matches. But mostly, Roy had done a good job. Enid was proud of him.

She picked up the firelighters and matches. She should start the barbeque up, she decided, ready for when he came back. White dust from old charcoal flew up when she lifted the barbeque lid, making her cough. How long had it been, she wondered? They were well overdue one.

It was usually Roy who would get the barbeque going, but Enid had watched him enough times to know how. She emptied the box of firelighters onto the wire rack and picked one of the larger ones to hold. But then, how would she light a match with a firelighter in one hand? How did Roy do it? She placed the firelighters onto one of Roy's rags on the floor and then retrieved a match from the box. The match snapped when she went to light it. The arthritis in her knuckles made it difficult to grip just one match at a time, but she persevered the second, third and fourth time, snapping each match on the box with the wrong amount of force. When the match fizzled and then caught alight on the fifth go, Enid hadn't been expecting it. She stepped back, dropping the box and the lit match on the floor. Cowering behind her own hands not to look, she whimpered.

When she found the courage to lower her fingers and look down at the floor, she saw that the match had gone out, but the firelighter was blazing, and the flames had already spread to the old rags.

When Olivia arrived at the nursery, Oona was propped up against Lena, one of the staff members. Her face looked pale, and she was curled up under a blanket.

'Poor sausage,' Lena cooed. 'She was feeling fine this morning.'

Olivia sat down on the floor next to them and held her daughter tightly. It had only been one night, but the guilt flowed painfully through her body and the softness of her daughter's voice brought on tears.

'Mumma.'

'Mummy's here,' she said, sniffing. 'I've missed you so much.'

Lena looked confused and a little uncomfortable.

'I'm glad you answered,' she said. 'We rang a couple of times, but it went straight to answerphone. We rang her dad as well, but no luck.' Olivia stared at Lena through tired, wet eyes. 'Don't worry. We rang again after you'd answered to let him know that you were coming and that he didn't need to worry.'

'Thank you,' Olivia said, full of breath, unable to voice the words properly. She quickly picked up Oona. 'Have you got her bag?'

'I'll be back in a minute.' Lena headed towards the cloakroom and, as soon as she was out of sight, Olivia hurried with Oona into the corridor.

It only took a few minutes to drive to Dillon's school. As she crossed the car park, Olivia could see the school secretary at the window. Mrs Gray's office faced the staff car park and the main pedestrian entrance to the school. Olivia forced a smile and gave her a wave. Was she walking too fast? Could the secretary sense that something was wrong? Had she sensed something when Olivia had called her from the car? She made an effort to slow down before she reached the school entrance. David would be on his way to the nursery now, and then, presumably, he'd also come to the school. She hurried into the building and knocked on the office door.

'Come in,' the secretary offered from inside. Olivia had

never been overly familiar with the school staff. She'd seen other mums stop and chat with various teachers – Mrs Gray or Mr Alvarez, the headteacher – but Olivia preferred to keep relationships strictly business. In truth, contact with members of staff scared her. They had a duty to report concerning behaviour, and Olivia suspected that she, with her regular body aches and frequent heavy make-up, may well fall into that category.

'Morning,' she said, walking into the office. She tried to sound as light as possible. 'I'm here to pick up…'

'Yes, yes, I know. It was me you spoke to on the phone.'

'Ah, yes.' Olivia patted Oona's bum in her arms. The child had already fallen asleep, just walking in from the car.

'Wait here, I'll go and collect him,' Mrs Gray said, leaving the office. 'Please, call me Carolyn though. You don't have to be lumbered in with the children.' Olivia knew that the secretary was being friendly, but she felt as if she was in trouble.

She looked around the office. Filing cabinets, a desk with a computer, a pinboard on the wall, a crocodile clip holding a picture of three children, presumably Carolyn's. The big window that faced out to the front of the school had smudges across it left-over from the cleaner.

'No, no, no,' Olivia muttered to herself as she watched David's car roar through the school gates towards the staff car park. She ducked behind the desk, patting Oona's bum to keep her asleep, as the door behind her opened.

'Here we go,' the secretary paused. 'Why are you under the desk?' She touched her desk with both hands next to where Olivia was crouched and leaned forward to peer out of the window. 'Is everything alright?' Dillon was walking into the office, but Olivia didn't have a choice.

'That's my husband,' she said, looking at Carolyn. 'Please,' she heard herself begging and she hated herself for it, 'please, can you get rid of him?' She'd never been so aware of her own words. Oona was asleep, but Dillon must be listening, and he was definitely old enough to sense her fear.

Carolyn pressed one button on her phone.

'Can you come out to reception please?' She hung up and left the office, turning back to Olivia as she did. 'We'll ask him to leave.' Olivia was surprised to see that Dillon had crouched down next to her, and she pulled him in close. Surely, he wouldn't be hiding from his dad.

She cursed herself for not taking the children out to the parent car park where she had parked, around the back of the school. They could have driven to Enid's to hide. It was too late now though. David would be close to reception, if not inside it, and there was only one door to the office.

Olivia doubted she'd physically be able to stand because of her fear, even if she had to. Her face was wet now from Dillon's tears, wiped over her cheeks with his hair. He was hugging his mum tightly. Poor thing; he must be shaken from the commotion. How could he possibly understand what was going on? He loved David.

Olivia lowered her arm from around his shoulder and rubbed his side in an attempt to comfort him. Dillon flinched and inhaled sharply as if in pain. Olivia kissed his forehead. When she went to lift his top to see what had hurt him, Dillon pulled it down.

'Please,' she said, and after a moment, he let go. Olivia let out a sharp, high-pitched noise as she saw the long bruise down her son's abdomen. She pulled his head into the crevice between her chin and breast and whispered meaningless comforting words.

Outside the door, Olivia heard her husband's voice.

'I'm here to pick up my son,' he said, strict and in charge.

'Hi, Mr…sorry, you're Dillon's dad. We haven't spoken much before, have we? I'm Mr Alvarez, the head.'

'Is he here?'

There was a moment's silence before Mr Alvarez replied.

'Dillon? Yes. He's at school. Sorry, I'm sure I can help. Do you mind me asking why you need to pick him up?'

'I don't need to give a reason to pick up my own son,' David said. 'I'm his dad.' His tone was harsh, but he sounded in control of himself. He was in public.

'I'm sorry,' the head said calmly. 'Of course, you're his dad. I understand, but I'm afraid I do need to ask the reason why you want to take him out of school early.'

David answered quickly. 'Personal reasons.'

'Oh, I hope everything is alright?' asked Mr Alvarez, solemnly.

'Yes, of course everything's alright,' David barked back. It seemed the calmer Mr Alvarez was, the closer David came to losing his temper. 'Now, please, where is my son?'

Tears flowed freely down Olivia's cheeks. She could hear every word that was said outside the office door, and so could Dillon. She cried for her son. This was never meant to be their family. Her children shouldn't have to hide from their father. She couldn't get the image of Dillon's bruise out of her head. Perhaps it had happened in the playground. Not in a million years had she thought David could hurt the children.

'I'm sorry, of course,' Mr Alvarez was saying. 'We're used to speaking with his mum, Olivia.'

'Liv, yeah. She's at home. She's expecting us any minute.

She'll be furious if I come home without him.' David was on the border of shouting now.

'Please, sorry, I am going to have to ask why…'

'I'm not telling you fucking why,' David exploded. 'Get my fucking son, now.'

Olivia flinched, holding on tighter to her son's head, pushing him tightly against her. She had heard David lose his temper before, over and over again, in the day and at night, drunk, and sober, but never in a public place, never in a school – in his own children's school. Any doubts that she may have had about Dillon's bruise faded.

'Now,' David barked again. A moment passed before Mr Alvarez responded.

'If you're going to shout and swear, you'll have to leave,' he said, still calm. 'This is a school.'

'I'm not going anywhere without my son.' David was quieter, but his voice was still full of malice.

'I will call the police.'

David didn't reply straightaway. Presumably he was weighing up how real Mr Alvarez's threat was. Olivia felt Oona's head arch back. She was waking up. Olivia prayed her daughter wouldn't make a noise. She made an 'O' shape with her lips, afraid to make the actual noise to shh. She patted her daughter's bum through the sling, and jigged her body up and down.

Oona let out a huge cry. She was ill. It was inevitable. Olivia stood up and bounced quickly around the office, her tears dripping onto the toddler's head.

'Shh…shh,' she said rhythmically, unsteadily.

'Mum,' Dillon hissed at her, urging her to keep quiet. There was a loud banging on the outside of the office wall.

'That was Dillon,' David shouted from the other side. 'Is she in there?' He spat out the word 'she' like Olivia was some disgusting object. The door burst open, and David stood in the doorway glaring at the three of them.

Olivia watched as Mr Alvarez pushed past David and stood in front of him.

'I will call the police, make no mistake,' he said, 'unless you leave, that is. Now.'

'Alright,' David shot back. 'I'll leave, but she's a liar.' He pointed two fingers over the head's shoulders at Olivia. 'She spews shit.' Both Oona and Dillon cried harder now. Olivia carried on bouncing her daughter. Her lip was shaking, and she got the feeling that her whole body would join in if she were to stop bouncing. 'I'll be outside when you're ready,' David said, before backing out of the office.

'I'm sorry,' Olivia heard him saying to Carolyn in the reception hall, 'you really can't listen to her though. I'm sorry to say it, I am, but she's sick. My wife really is ill.' When Carolyn came back into the office, Olivia noticed that she too was shaking, and had turned paler than she had been when Olivia had first turned up.

'Are you OK?' Carolyn asked her.

'Thank you,' she said, unable to convey just how much she meant it. Mr Alvarez was watching out of the office window. Olivia couldn't bring herself to look, but she knew that David would be out there.

'You can stay here as long as you want,' he offered. 'Mrs Gray won't mind.' Carolyn nodded, agreeing. 'Did you drive?'

'Yep,' Olivia replied, feeling stupid. Even now, after this, nothing was going to happen. She was being sent home.

'There's a different way out to the parents' car park,' he

said. 'Whenever you're ready, if you want, I can escort you to your car and he won't know you're leaving.' He came away from the window and looked directly at Olivia. 'You can call the school anytime – or the police. I can call the police now for you if you want me to. I would be very happy to do that.' He seemed to emphasise the word 'very,' which made Olivia feel a little safer. She was about to take him up on his offer when he asked her if she and the children felt safe going home, or if they had somewhere safe to stay.

'Yes,' she answered, tightly. 'Yes, we do.'

She needed to get back to Enid.

Enid squeezed her eyes tight. She pressed her back against the garage wall, feeling the sharp of the bare bricks through her clothes. Her lips were constantly moving, uttering noises rather than words.

The fire on the rags hadn't gone out. As far as Enid could tell, it should have by now. The flames should have died out and faded into the hard concrete floor, but instead they were strong, lighting up the underside of the barbeque. She should have waited for Roy to come home, but she couldn't even remember where he had gone, let alone when he would be back.

She took a few anxious steps toward the burning rags. How did one put out a fire without a tap? She could feel the heat against her legs now, her chin warming as she came closer. She coughed at the smell of smoke as, with difficulty, she lifted her right foot and, balancing on her left, she kicked at one of the blazing rags. Feeling unsteady, as though she might lose her balance, she dropped her foot onto the flames, and let out a silent but agonising scream. She pulled herself back away from the fire, her face tight with pain, her foot burning from the heat, though not, thankfully, in flames.

Once she had recovered herself, allowing time to fade the pain, she looked back at the flames. She couldn't stamp them out. She lifted her arm, expecting to a see watch. When, oh when, would Roy return?

She scanned the room, unwilling to give up yet. She wanted Roy to come home, but she didn't want him to see her in this state, to see quite how badly she'd failed. Over by Roy's worktop – the old hall carpet. Enid remembered having it changed, it must have been years ago now. One of those items that never make it to the tip and instead become just another piece of furniture, a job for another day.

She shuffled over to the worktop, each step feeling like the skin was peeling from her foot. The carpet wouldn't budge, the worktop was pressed too close to the material. Enid held on to the desk, placing her fingers on the underside, next to the legs, in the absence of an ability to grip. She let out a grunt as her whole body jolted right, the worktop legs digging into her fingers and thumb as she did. The pain was excruciating, but the worktop moved. Only a jot, but it moved. She made the same movement again, immediately, and the worktop moved again. The roll of carpet was free.

Enid pulled it down to the ground and shuffled it towards the fire with her feet, eventually finding it easier to unravel the roll across the floor. It wasn't her shade of pink at all.

Her hands hurt, more than ever before. Her right foot felt ablaze with fire, and her back felt scratched from the wall. When she stooped to unroll the carpet over the lit rags, her hips and waist called out to her to stop, but she wouldn't. She pushed the carpet with all the upper body strength she could muster. The force sent her tumbling forward onto the rags, with only the carpet separating her chest and arms from the fire. She could feel the heat seep through the material and into the skin on her arm. She couldn't move. Her eyes clamped tight in agony and the muscles in her neck tensed to the point of shaking.

She didn't know how long she lay like that before she opened her eyes, but when she did, although the pain remained, the fire had gone out. Shakily, she pulled her hand across the carpet up to her face and grimaced at the deep burn in her forearm.

42

The garage was dark. The bulb had gone out and Enid had gone from burning – quite literally – to freezing. Her forearm was numb except for when she touched it, something she'd stopped doing very quickly. It had taken an age to stand again. She'd rolled onto her back and shuffled her head sideways onto the remaining rolled section of the carpet so that she was propped up against it. From that vantage point, she had examined the damage to her chest and stomach. Not much, the carpet must have extinguished the fire underneath her. It had been her loose arm which had suffered. That and her foot, though she couldn't work out for the life of her how she could have burnt her foot now. Eventually, she used her elbows against the rolled carpet to push herself into a sitting position, and from there managed to stand, with help from the worktop. More than once she was concerned that the whole top would fall and crush her.

When would Roy be home? It was a strange thing about Roy. She knew that he wouldn't scold her for starting the fire but congratulate her on putting it out.

There was a sliver of light from under the garage door, allowing through what little light was left. Enid wondered how to turn the heater on, though didn't trust herself to manage it, or even try. No matter, she thought. Roy, or one of the carers, would be in to help her soon; they could turn it on. If not, there was always that other woman, the one with the bruises on her face. Enid wondered where she had gone. Roy would be helping her with whatever she was doing, probably.

She needed the toilet.

'Uh…oh. Hello,' she called, but no one replied. 'Hello?' She looked around the room for her personal alarm. There was normally a button near her wasn't there? It must be hidden in the dark somewhere, hanging on a wall. The toilet can't be far away.

'Hello,' she said, much quieter than before. She wasn't sure who she was calling for any more; there didn't seem to be anyone around. She shuffled towards the sliver of light on the floor and felt the wall above it. It was rough, cold metal, and it moved. She kicked at the bottom of the door, a shot of pain racing from her toe up to her thigh. The door moved out, but only slightly, and in at the top, again only slightly. Then it closed. She tried again, still feeling the cold metal with her hands out in front. There was a handle. Enid pushed the bottom of the door with her foot, holding her breath before doing so, bracing for the pain. She pulled at the handle. The door jolted, stiff at first, and then took on a life of its own, swinging up. Dim sunlight flooded the garage. It was still daytime. Enid stood, looking at the back of the caravan. The curtains were pulled shut; not quite right.

'Uh…Roy?' She peered behind her back into the garage, noting the carpet that Roy had left out haphazardly on the floor. She'd be the one to tidy that up, no doubt.

Moments went past. Enid listened to the sky, to the occasional car that drove down the road on the other side of the caravan.

Best bring the milk inside.

She shuffled round to the front door and looked down at the step. It was bare. There was no milk, no newspaper, no doormat even.

Enid tutted to herself. Where was her head? They must not deliver today. She chuckled to herself. You're going mad, she thought.

The door was locked. Enid looked down at her body for a pocket, for her keys. Her clothes were filthy, there was a hole in her sleeve and pieces of the material were sticking to raw skin. Her hands were wrinkled. When had she grown so old? When she got inside, she would change. She knocked on the door.

'Roy?'

He wouldn't mind how she looked – he would love her anyway; Enid knew that. But she would change for herself; it's nice to look nice. She knocked again.

She went to call his name again but decided against it. There was nothing. Either he wasn't in, or he couldn't hear her. Her feet clung to the path as she shuffled back to the side of the house. She was limping with every other step, a deep scratching pain seemed to cut through her skin and into the flesh, though she didn't know why. Age, she supposed. She tapped on the kitchen window. 'Roy?' It was empty. No people, few appliances. Unlived in. A flash of regret, nostalgia, loss.

Maybe he's in the garden, Enid thought, and she pushed the gate open to look.

'Oh,' the noise fell out of her.

The length of the grass, it was spilling over onto the path. The neighbour's tree hadn't been cut back. The greenhouse looked empty of both Roy and his tomatoes; each pane of cloudy glass covered with spider webs. The grapevine which grew along the side had gone.

She inched her way along the house wall and over a clump of weeds, trying to make sense of the garden. She tried the double doors at the back of her dining room, more panicked than before, and found that, to her surprise, she could open them with only a little force. Someone – Roy perhaps – must have loosened them.

'I…um…oh, Roy,' she said again when she was inside, much quieter than before. 'I was…uh, shouting, you know.' Enid looked around the bare room. 'Stuck out...stuck out…' She didn't try to finish the sentence. The house appeared unlived in, but she knew it wasn't. It was her house; their house. Roy's and Barb's. The woman with bruises on her face.

Enid remembered the night before. She and that woman had slept there, without Roy, without Barb, downstairs. Enid pictured Olivia's face – a memory returning – but it wasn't bruised this time. She remembered Olivia's pain, and it ran deeper than her face.

Enid held on to the bare dining-room table.

'Oh, Roy,' she said again, but this time she didn't expect an answer.

43

'No, Dad, she's left the home, where she lives. She's left.' Barb paused again, waiting for a response or an answer. Roy watched her and sucked his lower lip.

'How's Alex?' he asked.

'I'm talking about Mum,' Barb shouted.

'Good, good.'

She looked around her dad's room. God, it was drab. Dated, yellow pastel woodchip wallpaper covered all four walls, three of them with a purple and gold stripy border stretched across them. The fourth – the wall next to Roy's bed – had pictures of birds stuck on it, faded, and cut out with scissors. Barb wouldn't be surprised to find they were stuck on with Pritt Stick, though she didn't want to check.

Roy was sitting on the large padded chair in the middle of the room. She felt small next to him, on the grey plastic chair which was always kept against the wall next to the door for visitors. They must never expect more than one.

'And Calvin?' Roy asked.

Barb felt winded. She went to repeat the same thing about her mum, but then stopped. 'I don't know,' she answered honestly. 'He doesn't really tell me anything any more – not unless it's about Alex.'

'Good,' Roy sniffed. 'Good, good.'

Barb felt her heart drop. He didn't remember. He thought that after this, she'd go back to Calvin and Alex, together as one family in their old home. But his mind was healthy, wasn't it? It was his body that was failing him. That's what they'd all said. She went to correct him but thought better of it.

'The police say they're doing everything they can, and I'm going to go home soon, in case Mum turns up there.' Roy watched her, blank. 'In case Enid turns up,' Barb shouted again, slowly. 'She's left the home – missing.' Roy smiled, his face radiating a moment of joy.

'Enid,' he said. 'Good, good. Send her my love.'

'She's missing, Dad,' Barb told him, not raising her voice this time. 'I don't know if I'll be able to.' She knew he couldn't hear her, and she was grateful. She'd stopped trying. He looked content, despite his surroundings. She was telling him out of a sense of duty; he wouldn't be able to help. If he heard her, and if he understood, she would still have to leave him here by himself, alone, in case her mum found her way back. She stood and threw her arms around his shoulders, as she always did when she was leaving.

'I've got to go, Dad.'

Roy patted her arm, by way of a hug. 'Right, well,' he said.

'I love you,' Barb said.

'Love you,' Roy said.

'Love you,' Barb shouted, in case he hadn't heard her the first time.

There was still a clock in Enid's lounge, painted faux-gold, but it didn't tick, and the hands no longer turned. She watched it anyway. She wondered what time it was, how long she'd been sitting on the sofa, how long she'd been alone. The lounge was dark from the overcast sky, but night hadn't fallen yet. It could have been morning even. She stared hard at the broken clock and tried to decipher it, to measure the length of her loneliness. She knew there would have been a time when she could have glanced fleetingly at the same clock, gaining everything she needed to know from it in a moment.

Her eyes drooped down from the clock to the fireplace and time stopped mattering. It had never mattered in fact – as if Enid had never looked at the clock, as if she had never seen it. Her head lolled to the side, then jolted back up.

'Oh…um,' then silence again. Enid knew she was waiting, but she didn't know what for any more. It wasn't Roy.

She felt the arm of her sofa with her forefinger and started to pick at the cotton halfway along the ridge. Then she stroked it. Ken had bitten the sofa's arm when he was a puppy. Enid and Roy were going to fix the damage, but when Ken started lying on the same part of the sofa to sleep, they decided to leave it. It was Ken's spot. By the time he had lived his life, neither Enid nor Roy noticed the damage on the arm any more. It wasn't worth fixing.

Enid tried to pull at the material around the hole, but her fingers were too swollen from all the activity, too numb and arthritic to feel where the cotton ended and the exposed padding began. She could see Ken now. She watched him as a puppy, pulling at her shoelaces and scrabbling at the wallpaper. She saw him lying in his bed in the corner of the kitchen and she saw an old dog, problems with his ears, lying contentedly in front of the fire. She stood in the room at the vet's. She watched as Roy tried, but failed, to hold back his tears, attempting to be strong for her sake. He was always such a softie. Now, back on her old sofa, Enid knew that Ken had died. She wasn't sad; it had happened a long time ago. The feeling of knowledge was calming, and slowly, painlessly, her solitude allowed her to watch the other pieces of her life fall back together.

Enid didn't live in this house any more – she knew that, and she shouldn't be sitting on this sofa. She pictured her room in the dementia home, seeing it clearly; she saw Kara helping her to dress in the mornings, to get clean and to eat. She liked Kara's face. She was always smiling, and always chatting. Enid noticed that her trousers were wet, but she didn't move, and she wasn't uncomfortable. She knew the reason behind the wet, but it didn't matter. She remembered the people who visited her in the dementia home: Barb, Alex, Roy. She felt lucky, and she felt loved. It had been her choice to leave the dementia home, to run away.

She felt her own disease, she saw her mistakes and reflected on the anger which grew so quickly inside her these days. She was grateful for the love that she'd continued to receive throughout her body's decline, and her mind's decline. That must have been hard for them. She remembered the love she'd lost when Roy had stopped visiting, her own despair, and the feeling of abandonment. She knew now that Roy must be in a care home – otherwise he would be sitting on this sofa with her, in their old lounge. Roy would always choose to be with her when he could be. She knew.

Enid couldn't picture Roy's new room though. She couldn't see his new bed, the building, or even the street. She didn't know who Roy would be living with, whether they would be nice to him or not, what the carers would look like, or *be* like. She didn't know anything about his new home in fact, but she did know, with a clarity that she hadn't felt in a long time, that she had never visited Roy there, and she knew that she had lost him.

She thought about Olivia. She saw her sitting in the home with David, opposite Martin in the tearooms along the seafront. She saw her in the supermarket, and she felt her presence in her room back at the home. She saw her lying on the floor, in Enid and Roy's lounge, by Enid's own feet. She felt the aches in Olivia's shoulder, the bruises around her eyes, on her cheeks. Olivia had seemed so worried, so anxious, but she had also been somehow stronger in Enid's own house. Enid looked at the hole in the sofa, under her own aging fingers, and she felt the emptiness of the room.

'I need you to stay in the garage, Enid. I won't be long, but I need you to stay in the garage.' Olivia's words played over in Enid's ears. She remembered the expression on Olivia's face – so stern. She was in the wrong place. Olivia would be looking for her in the garage. She could picture the walk from the house to the garage, but only how it used to be, when she and Roy were younger, little Barb sitting on the patio, watching the weeds. There was a dark patch in her memory, but there was light in that darkness. She wondered how many days she must have lost sitting in the dementia home, days that hadn't mattered and hadn't been missed.

The familiar pain seeped through her bones as she held on to the sofa and hoisted her body just above the cushions. The numb ache in her fingers, the pressure she felt on the palms of her hands, the weight on her toes, that deep scratching into the soles of her feet. She blew air from her mouth and frowned as she held the position, not standing, not quite sitting, the tight skin around her forearm stretching.

She pushed herself further up and balanced on her feet, swaying slightly as she often did. She looked ahead of her, through the lounge and into the dining room – bare, hardly recognisable.

'Ken,' she called, hearing the panic in her voice. 'Ken.' He needed feeding. Enid couldn't remember the last time she had put food down for him. 'Oh, uh,' Enid looked around the room. Flashes of Olivia asleep on the lounge floor, of Roy passing Barb her breakfast, of Donald next to the clock. A bird clawing at the caged lounge window, breaking the glass, flying away. Red, blue and yellow, shrinking slowly into the distance, disappearing in the sky.

Then, nothing. An empty room.

Enid tried to step forward, but she couldn't move. Her feet were detached from the rest of her body, the room lost focus and the fireplace started to spin. She attempted to raise her arms up for balance, but only one moved, and not far enough for her to see it.

As she fell, Enid watched everything she knew leave her. The tiny pieces that had made up her life flew around the room, distancing themselves from her body. She watched as Ken disappeared: he jumped excitably, and then he didn't matter any more; he didn't exist. Donald smiled, dimples on both cheeks. He winked before he faded, the bad times behind him, behind Enid. He was gone. He had never been. Enid saw Roy, younger than he was now, and she saw Barb, at every age; a baby asleep, a teenager offering glimpses of remaining dependency, a toddler getting up again after falling, and as a mum herself, looking after Alex. She saw Alex, saw herself tucking Alex up in bed, holding her when she had fallen out with her mum. Roy coming in from the garden, green hands, a loose vest. Barb in her pyjamas, clinging on to Enid's own teddy. Roy and Barb were together; everyday silent conversation. Roy bent to kiss his daughter's hair, a daily occurrence. The images were leaving, fading in front of Enid's eyes. She held onto them as tightly as she could, called out, desperate to keep her family with her. The lounge darkened, Roy faded, Barb shrank, nothing was in focus. A blur, and by the time Enid hit the floor, they were gone.

PART THREE

SCATTERED DEBRIS

44

THE LITTLE BROWN BLACKBIRD had watched with pride at each attempt her chicks had made to fledge. The last had almost been successful. Had the nest have been built higher, like their previous homes, the chicks might well have taken flight before hitting the ground. She looked down the lawn. She knew that the next time she flew to collect food for her latest little ones, it might be the last.

The garden was alive that day: two squirrels were perched on top of the greenhouse; butterflies weaved patterns around the grapevines and seagulls flew high above, barely moving in the wind. One of the squirrels darted from the glass roof to a branch and then back again. The second copied it. The first ran to the other end of the roof and placed a foot onto the grapevine. It was too flimsy to climb. The second almost crashed into the back of the first, stopping just short, shaking its head and rubbing its nose to compose itself. The bird watched this flirtatious game of chase play out, each squirrel never stepping more than a few metres away from the other.

She could see the man who lived in the house behind her nest. He was digging, down at the other end of the garden. He grunted and breathed heavily. Occasionally, he'd push his spade into the mud with one foot, step back and sigh, before wiping his forehead with the back of his hand. The bird watched as the man slowly and painfully removed a large bush from the soil to the sound of a small portable radio.

The squirrels balanced on the fence behind the greenhouse, both looking down into the neighbouring garden. The first hopped down and into the next garden along. The second followed.

The portable radio crackled, and the man grunted louder as the remaining pieces of the bush pulled a shower of soil out onto the lawn. Only the previous night, the bird had watched a fox spring from the same bush. Its departure would be welcome.

Enid was sitting on her knees in the lounge, leaning forward. She'd retrieved the A to Z from the car and spread it out in front of her. She placed her finger on the Clevedon motorway junction and moved it north.

Barb hadn't been to school for nearly a week now. Daily walks along the beach were becoming repetitive and the games that Enid and Roy had created inside the house were wearing thin. Enid knew that Barb was aware of how closely she was being guarded. The poor mite was missing the independence that she'd unknowingly gained over the past six years, and

Enid felt bad for stealing it away from her.

It was no good. She'd traced her finger halfway up the M5, but she couldn't remember which junction they'd need to take. Birdland wasn't visible on the map, which, to be fair, Roy had bought several years ago.

In the background, the television played quietly. Enid wasn't watching. She was hoping for the Birdland advert to come on to give her a clue as to the directions. Barb deserved a day out, and hopefully some fun might relieve Roy of some stress too.

Enid knew that he was right – Donald was stalking them. They'd seen him walking outside their house every day that week, more than once. He wasn't making any effort to hide it, and he never looked completely sober. At first Enid had told herself that it was just a coincidence, but she knew she was being naïve. He'd been outside the school gates. Enid could handle Donald stalking her, but she wasn't his quarry. He was interested in Barb.

Roy suggested every day that they call the police, but Enid didn't see how it could help. As far as she could tell, Donald hadn't broken any laws – not yet at least. But she also knew Donald was a weak man. She hoped he would stop soon, and until then, she would rise above it, but if he didn't, she would threaten him. She would threaten to tell his new woman what he'd been up to, maybe even threaten to make up some of the details. Then he would leave her family alone, Enid was sure.

She heard Barb bounce down the stairs two at a time. Without turning, she said her daughter's name.

'Where's Daddy?' Barb asked, sounding confused. She'd been playing by herself for over an hour. A rare occurrence, and one which Enid had made good use of. The washing-up was done, and there was a chicken in the oven.

'He's in the garden,' Enid replied. 'He's making space for a new flower bed.' She turned to look at her daughter. 'Barb?' She looked around to see that Barb was already in the dining room, on her way out into the garden. Barb stopped to look back at her mum.

'I'm going to see the birds,' she said.

Enid smiled at her. She hadn't told her about Birdland yet. 'Why do you like birds so much, Barb?' she asked, and Barb shrugged.

'I like the little ones,' she said, 'but they can't fly, and I would like to fly.'

'Some little ones can fly,' Enid said. 'The grown-up ones.'

Barb laughed.

'The little ones that can fly are insects, Mummy,' she said, before hopping outside and onto the patio.

The brown bird flew from her nest, aware that her two chicks were watching her, learning from her movements. She took the now well-known route over the side gate and down the drive, past the open side door, over the second gate and out into the front garden.

Pink and purple flowers stood in the soil which separated the grass from the drive. In the far corner, a young tree was taking its time to grow. It was in the slightly barer grass beneath the tree where the bird would find the best worms. The chicks had healthy and demanding appetites these days. She spent her time searching for the fattest worms she could find.

With her beak full, she made her way back to the nest, over the first gate and into the drive. She perched on the car roof as the gate behind her rattled, and then opened. A man staggered up the drive, red-faced and clumsy, and balanced himself on the bonnet of the car. Startled by the sudden movement beneath her feet, the bird flew up onto the garage roof.

Sensing danger, she turned. From the new vantage point, she saw the man stumble into the house through the side door, falling into a string of fake colourful birds with bells at the bottom. He clung onto the bells to silence them. There was a determination to his movements, but his balance was off. He shushed the fake birds and then ran a hand through his slick back hair, brushing it over to one side as he did.

The bird turned and flew from the garage roof and down to the nest. She saw the little girl hopping out of the glass doors and taking her usual position on the chair at the end of the patio. The two chicks lifted their heads high and opened their beaks. Her partner stood guard on the nest's wall, and the bird dropped her gathering of worms – some moving, some still – on the floor for the feast.

45

Olivia was driving fast, checking her mirrors obsessively as she did. She couldn't see David's car, but knew he'd be likely to follow, especially now that she had the kids.

She lifted her head and looked at her son in the rear-view mirror. He was looking down.

'Where did you get the bruise?' she asked. She already knew the answer, but still she dreaded hearing the words from Dillon's own mouth.

The lights in front turned red. Olivia hit the brakes suddenly, and then turned to glance out of the back window, before looking directly at her son, who hadn't replied. He avoided her gaze, stared down into his lap.

'We're going to a friend of mine's house,' she said. 'You might have seen her before, at Grandad's place. She doesn't live there any more. I'm helping her.'

Dillon carried on looking down at his legs.

Olivia tightened her lips and looked back at the road. She should never have left them with David; she must have known what he was capable of. How could she have been so stupid? This wasn't David's fault; it was hers.

She checked her side mirror. There was no sign of David's car, but the route was obscured, and they both knew Clevedon so well. He could easily be one, maybe two, streets away and completely unseen. She pulled her phone out of her pocket and dialled 999 as the lights turned to green.

'Emergency, which service?' The voice bellowed through the car speakers, though she wished it hadn't. What else must poor Dillon and Oona endure? She could see the day being replayed in their nightmares later.

'Police, please.' As she waited for the call to connect, Olivia looked behind her to the backseat again. Dillon's cheeks were wet, and he was touching his abdomen with his left hand. He was sitting on his right.

'OK, darling' she whispered, as the lights changed to green. 'OK. I know.'

'Police, what's your emergency?'

'I have information on a missing person,' Olivia stated, sorry to be breaking her promise to Enid. 'I don't know her second name, but Enid. I know where Enid is.'

Olivia could see the caravan beyond the gate as she drove past Enid's house. There was no sign of any police cars out front. She parked at the other end of the road, praying that Enid was alright.

'So, we're like spies,' she told Dillon, spinning in her chair, trying to boost morale. 'I think there's someone living in that garage over there. We need to be really quiet and super-quick.' She spoke in the superhero voice which she had used with him when he had been a couple of years younger.

'But why is your friend in the garage?' he asked. 'Is she a spy too?' Olivia was happy to see him cheered up a little, even if just through distraction. He seemed to accept the game.

'She is a spy,' Olivia said, her eyes widening, full of fake conspiracy, 'and she might not even be in the garage. We might need to find her.' Dillon smiled weakly, and Olivia smiled back. 'Come on,' she said, getting out of the car and placing Oona back in her sling. She was still a little clammy. She opened the door for Dillon, and they walked hand in hand back down the road towards Enid's.

'Keep walking,' Olivia whispered loudly as they reached the drive, not looking down at her son. He jumped, giggled, and followed his mum past Enid's house. 'Ready?' she asked. Dillon nodded. 'Turn.' When they reached the drive, Olivia bent down and whispered loudly. 'Go, go, go!' It was hard to keep up the façade, but it was necessary for Dillon. Olivia followed behind and through the gate, not looking back when she heard a car turning into Enid's road behind them.

Dillon walked in short, fast steps beside the caravan and Olivia found herself chasing after him as if he were running away from her.

'Get down,' she whispered. Dillon lay on his front, and she knelt beside him, cradling Oona's head as she did. She tilted her head down and peered under the caravan.

'Shit,' she exclaimed. The garage door was open.

'Mum.'

'Sorry, darling.' She stood and looked around the drive. 'Enid,' she hissed, and Dillon copied. She stepped backwards into the garage and turned. The barbeque was open and there was a half-rolled carpet spread across the floor with... Fuck. With burn marks through it. There was a faint smell of burning, old and distant. A bonfire long extinguished.

Enid had left. Presumably she'd been found by someone. The police perhaps. Thank God they'd come before the fire had grown out of control, she thought, holding herself responsible for leaving Enid in the first place.

She walked up to the back window of the caravan and raised herself up onto her toes. The curtain was still closed. They needed to hide somewhere.

'Enid,' Olivia hissed through the plastic window. As suspected, the caravan was silent. Behind her, Olivia heard her son's footsteps, in a rush and then stopping. Fast and then still.

'Shh,' he said. Olivia turned to see her boy, index finger up to his mouth, his eyes urging his mum to be quiet. His back was pressed against the side of the house.

'Sorry,' she mouthed. He nodded to his mum and slowly peered around the back gate into the garden.

She heard footsteps, slow and precise, outside the gate. Too loud to be on the road.

'Clear,' Dillon whispered, and Olivia nodded. He was still engrossed in the game, and apparently hadn't noticed the colour draining from his mum's face, or the worry that must be showing in her eyes. He hadn't seen that she was shaking.

She followed his beckoning hand into the garden and pushed her back against the brick wall next to him, praying the footsteps would be those of police boots rather than David's.

She paused; listened. The only sound was of her own heavy breathing.

'OK. Those doors.' She gestured towards the double patio doors into Enid's dining room, sure she hadn't left them open.

'We can get in,' Dillon's face lit up with excitement. He stretched out both arms and scaled the wall towards the doors before crouching down and walking SAS-style into Enid's dining room.

'Hello?' Olivia whispered, following her son, who had slowed dramatically since entering the house, apparently losing his nerve. She took a cautious step further into the dining room, patting Oona's back as she did, soothing only herself, as Oona was still sleeping. Dillon retreated from the table back to his mum and held tightly onto her leg. The change in mood was startling.

Olivia looked to her right; the kitchen was empty. It wasn't until she turned back to face the lounge that she noticed the body lying on the floor, just visible behind the dining-room table.

'Enid!' Olivia knocked into one of the chairs in her rush to Enid's side. Oona's head jolted with the movement, and she started to wake. 'Enid,' Olivia said again, this time an attempt at a firm, calming voice, letting Enid know that she was there. It came out quivering and tearful. She knelt beside Enid with Dillon still clinging to her clothes. He was looking back out to the garden, and Olivia couldn't blame him. Was Enid breathing? Panicked, she clumsily felt around Enid's neck with her thumb and forefinger.

'Mum,' Dillon said.

'She'll be alright,' Olivia tried to reassure him, knowing how futile her effort was. She could barely see through the mist in her eyes and her voice would be a scream if any real sound could escape. Her panic would be Dillon's, and Oona's fevered waking cry was almost lost in her ears.

'Mum?' Dillon repeated, increasingly scared.

'Enid, can you hear me?' Olivia choked out. 'We're going to find Roy, we are. Enid, can you hear me?' Enid didn't move, and Olivia's fingers were too shaky to find any pulse in Enid's neck. The old woman's body was sprawled the entire width of the living-room floor, facing out into the hall. There was no way Olivia would be able to move her, and hadn't she called the police to come? Olivia's breathing quickened and her vision narrowed. She could barely hear Oona, now screaming on her chest.

'Mum!' Dillon was shouting now: 'Mum!' Olivia looked behind her. Through the tears obscuring her eyes, she could just about make out the dark figure standing in the patio doorway.

'Where is he?' David asked.

46

As the police had suggested, Barb had waited at home on the off-chance that Enid might try to find her daughter's home. It was harder than it should have been, passive rather than active. Barb found herself sitting when action was needed. There was a consensus that Enid would be more than a little distressed by now; she was about to enter her second night alone – that was, if she'd survived the first. When Barb had asked, hopefully, whether her mum might be with someone who could be looking after her, she had been told that few people would be willing take in a confused elderly woman without the intention of ringing the police. The police had no leads.

Barb's fingernails were bitten down to the quicks, but she continued to gnaw on the skin around them. Her phone was on the kitchen table, near enough to hear it ring, but not close enough to stare at. She'd watched it enough over the past twenty-four hours. How many times had she checked the volume? The radio played the same song. Barb had never before realised how many times each song got repeated in one day on the same station. Everything the presenter said felt so trivial: traffic news; shout-outs; a charity podcast they wanted their listeners to download. It felt like the same pointless information, and then over again.

Barb kept picturing Enid outside, scared, sitting on a bench alone in the rain. She could see the struggle her mum would face trying to talk to strangers. She found it hard to remember words, and Barb knew that she'd fail under pressure. Some people were so rude, too.

She had pushed back the other images. Thoughts of her mum's wet, frail body lying in the woods, alive, dead, unable to move.

If the police were right, then Enid would have spent last night outside by herself. Barb couldn't imagine she'd have managed to create shelter or find warmth, and she was old, her bones brittle.

'Mum,' Alex's voice called through from the porch. Shit. Barb hadn't expected Alex yet. She'd been at Calvin's the previous night and wouldn't normally turn up at Barb's until the end of the school day.

'Hiya,' she called back, checking the date on her phone. It was a Friday. Alex had a free afternoon period before her last lesson.

Barb hadn't slept at all the previous night; she had come downstairs at two in the morning, made herself a cup of tea and stood at the front door, looking out, hopeful. She must have been standing there for a long time because it started to rain and stopped again, more than once. Occasionally, she had quietly talked into the darkness to her mum, though she knew that she was being ridiculous.

Now she looked like shit.

'You not at work?' Alex asked, throwing her schoolbag onto the kitchen side.

'Not today,' Barb replied. She didn't say why, and Alex wouldn't ask. She'd been signed off with stress a few times recently and Alex wouldn't want the awkward conversation. 'Let me get you something.'

Barb busied herself with bread and cheese, and they ate together. After her failings at telling her dad about Enid earlier that afternoon, Barb decided not to tell Alex; not now. It couldn't help, and it would ruin her last lesson. She would tell her later that night.

They talked about one of Alex's schoolfriends and a programme that Calvin had been watching which Alex thought looked good. Alex never spoke about her own life, but Barb learnt about her daughter though their conversations about other people. Today the chat was stilted. It was clear that Alex wanted to leave, presumably sensing Barb's unease, lack of sleep and desperation. Barb found herself quick to irritation and then quick to feel the guilt afterwards. She offered her daughter a lift to school, but the offer was rejected.

'I'll pick you up later then,' she said, to no response.

'See you later, Mum. Thanks for the food.' Barb watched her daughter sling her bag over her shoulder and head back to school.

'See you later,' she called. 'Love you.' She heard Alex echo the words back at her as the door closed. A wave of relief and gratitude that Alex, her own little baby girl, was still OK washed over Barb, before a tidal wave of guilt for her own mother swallowed it.

She walked to the front door again and leant on the frame, rubbing her eyes, which stung from a lack of sleep. It felt as if someone had pushed them through to the back of their sockets. Her head throbbed. Barb knew that if her mum wasn't found before nightfall, she would be found dead. Any remaining glimmer of hope, no matter how small, was quickly fading. She would do anything for her Alex, and experience had taught her that her mum would do anything for her.

She reached into her pocket and pulled out her car keys. Stay at home, she thought, echoing the police's advice. As if her mum might still turn up at the front door by that point.

47

Olivia rose to her feet, protecting both Dillon and Enid with her body; a wall between them and David, though they were least likely to suffer at his hands. Dillon clung tightly to her clothes, and she rested her hand on his head.

'She needs to go to a hospital,' Olivia stated flatly, her breath almost as loud as her words. David didn't even look down, showing no concern for the body on the floor. Olivia couldn't be sure he'd noticed Enid. He didn't speak or look at Dillon. His glare was fixed on Olivia. Not the toddler on her chest; her alone. And his face was dark with rage.

She was scared, but Olivia knew that anything he did now could not be kept quiet. There could be no more secrets. Mrs Gray and Mr Alvarez had seen how he was at the school. His own children were in the room with him now. Any wrong move and he could lose them forever.

But he was shaking. Olivia could see the veins in his forehead, his bald scalp red from front to back. The lenses of his glasses were practically steamed.

'Where is he?' David asked again.

'Who?' Olivia replied, as calm and as steady as possible.

'The man with my *fucking* children in his house.' He was shouting.

'Your *fucking* children?' Olivia spat back at him. 'Your children with the bruises you mean? Your children who you hurt last night? They're not *your* fucking children, David. They're children.'

David marched towards her, the devil's fury in his eyes, and Olivia heard Dillon wail by her leg. She raised her arms and batted them frantically in front of her, knowing it was pointless. He grabbed her by the hair and yanked. She fell to the floor, forcing her body sideways to protect Oona from the impact.

'Whose house is this?' David screamed, and then he laughed. 'I don't know why I'm asking,' he sneered. 'I already know who lives here. Come on…' Olivia felt his hand grab her hair again, his fingertips gouging into her scalp before he clenched his fist, and she was dragged back to her feet. 'Let's find him, shall we? Ask him why he's got my children in *his* house.'

Olivia wailed in protest, but she couldn't form any words through the fear. David dragged her through Enid's dining room by her hair, knocking her hip on the corner of the table as he stormed into the kitchen. Behind them, Dillon was sobbing, begging, pulling at his mother's trousers; a tug of war with his dad. A war which he was losing.

'A hospital,' Olivia managed to get out in between lost

breaths, but David didn't hear her through his own outbursts. He yanked her head up and down as he walked, her vision a slideshow; Dillon, carpet, Dillon, carpet. She did everything she could to cradle Oona, to keep her from falling out of the sling. She held onto the back of her daughter's head with her hand, but the jolting movement of her husband's grip meant that she just kept letting go, and then hitting her daughter as she tried to put her hand back.

'A hospital,' she said louder, high-pitched and barely coherent. They were the only words she could think of; the only words she could say in the panic, though they had lost meaning. Were they for Enid, for Oona, for herself?

'Oh yes,' David screamed back at her, tearing at her hair and yanking her through the hallway door. 'Oh yes, come on then. Where is he? We need to tell him about his cunt mother.'

Dillon was holding onto the door jamb with one hand and Olivia's trouser leg with the other. Olivia felt the tug as he was forced to let go of the frame to keep hold of her. She was bent double when she felt David's grip loosen, and she stumbled back into her son. Realising that she was free from David's grip, she wrapped both her arms tightly around Dillon, pushing his head close to her and his now purple-faced and screaming little sister.

She could only hear the three of them: Oona's short angry cries, in time with the convulsions she could feel pounding into her chest; Dillon wailing for his mum, sobbing like he needed to empty his entire body of the pain; and her own high-pitched, recovering wails between breaths. David wasn't shouting, and he wasn't looking at them.

Behind him, through the glazed panel, she saw the outline of a person approaching the front door. Whoever it was cupped their hands to the frosted glass and peered in.

'It's the police,' she whispered at her husband, with all the venom she could muster. David turned and looked down at the kitchen floor, where his family was huddled. Olivia watched as the anger in his eyes was replaced by panic.

'Don't fucking tell them anything,' he muttered, low and quiet. 'I've got the best lawyers; you'll be mincemeat.' Then he ducked low, bringing his face close to hers. She saw almost cartoon-like remorse in his eyes. 'I loved you,' he said, sincerely, pathetically, as if she'd hurt him, as if *he* were the victim. He looked like he might have more to say, but the sound of a key turning in the door behind him forced him to stop. He stood up and jolted into the dining room, almost tripping over his son, and then he fled out of the patio door.

Olivia pushed her face even tighter against the back of Dillon's head. He was looking down, the top of his skull pressed hard against her chest. David had barely acknowledged him – his own son. He had been completely deranged, un-attached from what was happening. Maybe he found it easier to ignore his children. Maybe to look at them would have softened him. Olivia was glad he hadn't.

'Hello,' a woman's voice came from the hall. She sounded assertive but worried, completely unthreatening. Olivia didn't answer, but Oona continued to scream, and she and Dillon were making enough noise themselves. Footsteps stopped in the kitchen doorway. 'Who the hell are you?' the woman asked. The words were an accusation, but the tone was full of compassion.

Olivia couldn't bring herself to reply. Her attention, her full focus, had to be on soothing her children. She managed to lift one of her hands to gesture the woman towards the lounge where Enid's body lay.

'It's OK, baby. Baby, baby,' she lulled to both her children, knowing that no explanatory words could help now. 'It's OK now,' she repeated, as blue lights flashed silently through the open door.

48

OUTSIDE WAS DARK, but Roy knew that didn't necessarily mean it was late. He was still in his chair. No one had yet lifted him into bed. He wasn't sure if he'd eaten yet.

Barb sometimes visited when it was dark outside. Maybe she'd be on her way. Mind you, sometimes she visited in daylight too, and Roy couldn't remember if she'd already been that day. He was sure Enid hadn't been though. In fact, he felt sure beyond doubt that Enid had never visited his new room. Of course, she wouldn't be able to make it alone, but couldn't Barb bring her, or take Roy to Enid's place of residence? But she hadn't. He would bring it up with her when she next came.

Roy could picture his Enid though, and he did, often, as she appeared in an old photograph that they'd kept in an oval frame. Her skin smooth and pale, her large eyes gazing back over her shoulder. She wore a big grey hat. He remembered that hat. How old had she been then? He could picture her later in life too of course, but this was as she was when they'd first courted, and he knew it was how Enid pictured herself.

How he longed to see her. Every cup of tea a carer bought made him wish he could do the same again for Enid. The familiarity of such a small gesture with his lover felt so distant now.

Roy lifted his forearms up from the arms of his chair, and they hovered just above, in the air. He wondered how long it had been since he'd moved, since he'd put any strain on these muscles. The small movement felt like his arms had woken from a long and deep sleep. He placed his hands on both arms of the chair and applied a little pressure. He hadn't tried to stand unaided in some time, but if no one was going to bring his Enid to him, he would jolly well have to take matters into his own hands.

He felt the weight of his body, first in his elbows, then shooting up his upper arm, until a sharp pain in his shoulders forced him to drop his wide frame back down onto the cushion. The impact was minimal, he hadn't managed to lift himself far, but he had to sit for a while for the pain in his shoulders to subside.

'Dinner,' a voice shouted from the door. A woman walked in and placed a plate on the table in front of him. Roy looked down at it. Beef, potatoes, carrots and broccoli. Lovely.

He rubbed his left shoulder and slowly rotated his right, stretching the joint. The woman knelt in front of him and looked directly into Roy's eyes. Roy looked back; it would be rude not to.

'You've not been trying to get up again, have you?' she asked slowly and, Roy presumed, loudly.

'Mm?' Roy answered. 'No, no.' Because, he hadn't. Had he? What need would there be to do so? He had everything he needed right here; beef – and he loved beef. 'Thank you,' he said with a gentle nod, before picking up his cutlery.

49

Barb looked at her reflection briefly in the rear-view mirror. She was tired, worried and exhausted, her skin patchy from stress. Her mum had clearly suffered. Enid had a dark bruise around one of her eyes which continued across her cheek down to her neck. She had second degree burns on her arms, first degree burns on her feet. One of the doctors at the hospital had told Barb that Enid was suffering mild hypothermia too. Had she spent the previous night outside, it would surely have been worse. Barb knew what 'worse' meant. It wasn't clear yet what Enid had been doing the night before, but Barb must have someone to thank for her mum's survival.

Once she had been told that Enid was stable – unconscious, but stable – Barb had driven back to the house. She had told Alex about Enid's disappearance, explained why she'd been short-tempered earlier that day and attempted to justify the decision not to tell Alex about Enid sooner. She didn't mention the family she'd found crying on Enid's kitchen floor – wouldn't know how to. She didn't understand herself. The woman had been familiar, as had the children in fact, but Barb couldn't place them. Alex had been at first concerned for her mum, then tearful for her nan, and then, finally, cross again with her mum. Barb couldn't blame her.

Now, back in the car, she wondered how she would ever tell Roy. Of course, it had crossed her mind not to tell him at all, especially after her last attempt. His hearing was going, and Barb now had her suspicions about his memory, but after seeing how upset Alex had been at her brief deception, she knew that it was the right thing to do.

She thought of Calvin, back when it had been good between them, before the affair. What she wouldn't give to have him with her now, just for some company, a sounding board, support, a shoulder. Without Calvin beside her, Barb realised that all she wanted – all she needed in fact – was her mum.

Back at the hospital, Barb strode purposefully to the ward. The relief of knowing her mum was safe was enough, and she felt no need to rush, Enid would be asleep regardless, but it seemed important to look rushed for some reason.

Enid had been put in a ward with four beds, two empty and one surrounded by a blue curtain. Her bed was the closest to the window. Barb stopped in her tracks. The woman from the kitchen was sitting by Enid's bed. Her oldest child, the boy, was on one of the empty beds behind her reading a book, with his little sister asleep next to him, a sheet folded for a pillow under her head. Barb watched the woman examine Enid's face. Perhaps the bruise around her eye. Perhaps the purple on her cheek. She was touching her own forehead. Could she be looking at Enid's scar?

The woman turned and saw Barb, then stood up to leave, looking both apologetic and worried, but Barb shook her head and told her to stay. It still wasn't clear to Barb what had gone on here, but this woman wasn't a threat. She had the feeling that she had a lot to thank her for in fact.

Olivia sat silently opposite Enid's daughter. She had introduced herself awkwardly, and then the children. Barb had introduced herself and then they'd both just watched Enid without saying anything. Dillon asked Olivia if he could use her phone to watch cartoons and she told him that he could.

There was a police officer outside the room. She'd already given a statement and been told that David was being held for questioning after they'd found him packing a suitcase at home. Of course, there would be more to follow – further questions, maybe a court case, she didn't know – but she felt safe within the hospital walls. The sterile bedside equipment, the plastic tray tables, the hard laminate floor. Olivia felt safer than she had in months, maybe years.

Enid was stretched the length of the bed, her head heavy on the pillow. The bruise had turned from purple to black, but still she looked peaceful. Her body and expression relaxed and at ease. Her breathing was heavy, but it was also slow and steady. Her arms lay on the bed either side of her, palms facing down, touching the sheets. Her clothes had been loosened and she was covered up to her torso with a sheet and blanket.

Dillon looked up from the phone.

'Mum, where's the toilet?'

Olivia glanced around. The sign for the toilets was outside the ward, pointing down the corridor. Oona lay peacefully on the empty bed next to Enid's. 'Can you hold it, for your sister?' she asked, and Dillon shook his head, no.

She couldn't let him go alone – not after what he'd been through. He wouldn't leave the room without her, she was sure. Olivia looked again at her daughter, sleeping peacefully, having just had her second dose of infant paracetamol from one of the nurses, and then she looked up at Barb.

'Can you,' she wasn't sure how to ask, 'watch my…' Barbara smiled an agreement. 'She's asleep,' Olivia said apologetically.

'Of course,' Barb said quietly. 'Anything.'

50

Enid looked at the clock on the fireplace, and then at the television. The adverts would be on soon. She had continued scanning the A to Z, but she couldn't find Birdland anywhere, and it wasn't listed in the appendix. She heard the side door open. The bells on the end of the string of birds jangled, and then stopped abruptly.

'Roy,' she called, 'Barb's just gone outside, can you go back out?' Roy didn't reply. Enid heard him walk through the kitchen and into the hall. 'Roy,' she called again, still looking at the television and waiting for the adverts, 'go and see Barb. She's outside, love.' Enid heard the heavy breathing in the lounge doorway before she heard the voice.

'Enid, love,' Donald said, his voice heavy with alcohol. Enid turned and froze. She watched him lean on the door frame.

'Get out,' Enid said quietly. 'Get out.'

Donald looked at her confused, like he couldn't understand why she would make such a request. 'She left me,' he said, walking into the room and sitting on Enid's sofa next to the record player. Tom Jones winked at him from the shelves.

'You're drunk,' Enid said flatly. 'Roy is outside.' She went to shout, but Donald cut her off.

'Our daughter's outside too,' he said, and Enid recoiled, disgusted.

'She's not your daughter,' she said, and Donald shrugged.

'Maybe,' he said. The clock ticked. Donald sat forward. Enid could smell him. 'But maybe she is, Enid, and look,' he shuffled uncomfortably, 'I'm single now.' He closed his mouth, pressing his lips together tight to stifle wind.

Enid watched his chest rise and fall.

'So, she left you,' she said. 'Can you blame her?' Enid remembered the nights she'd spent alone, wondering where Donald was. Worse, she remembered the nights he'd come home. There had been something about Enid that made him angry. It didn't seem to matter what she did, or what she said. He'd hated her.

'Come on,' Donald said, smirking, 'when we were good, we were good.' His eyebrows raised in a way that made Enid feel sick.

'You're drunk,' she said coldly, her eyes narrow, focusing on him as if he were a bomb, and she was waiting for the explosion.

'Give me another go, eh?' he laughed. 'We could be a proper family now: me, you and the kid. Everything we ever wanted.'

The television screen to the left of him cut from eagle to owl, from hawk to buzzard, and Enid noticed a familiar middle-aged straight-faced man in a thick rainbow-striped jumper looking directly at the camera.

A parrot stood on his shoulder, eyeing him.

Roy stood back and admired the hole he'd made in the soil. There was some levelling to be done, but he was satisfied with the lack of remaining roots. The full bush lay behind him, a scattering of mud browning the lawn around the leaves. Roy pictured pristine rows of white and pink flowers, and smiled. When they were in bloom, Enid would be able to see them from the kitchen window. The garden was his gift to her.

'Barb,' he called up the lawn to his daughter. She was sitting on the front edge of a patio chair, watching the nest in the weeds. It was an image Roy was used to seeing. She hadn't heard him over the portable radio, so he made his way up the lawn. She turned when she saw him.

'Daddy,' she said, excitement in her voice.

'Barb, love,' Roy replied. 'Shall we go inside? Get a sandwich?' He walked around the back of his daughter, placing one hand on her head and the other on the patio door, ready to open it.

'No, Daddy, it's happening. They're leaving the nest.' Roy let go of the patio door. He looked down at Barb, pulled out another patio chair from under the table and sat down next to her.

'Are they now?' he asked, looking towards the nest in the weeds. Sure enough, one of the chicks was perched on the side of the nest. The other was behind, watching with both parents. Roy watched the chick move from one foot to the next and then back again. It looked up into the sky, and then across the garden. It looked up towards the garage roof. For several minutes in fact, the chick prepared itself. Roy marvelled at this unique moment, a milestone in the chick's life, and indeed in the lives of the older birds. The delicate wings stretching as the bird prepared for independence. The simplicity of the moment and yet the complexity of everything that had led to it. Nature, family and life, all contained on top of a single patio slab. Then, in a fraction of a second, the chick darted into the air. The flurry of feathers and the batting of wings was instant, and then it took off. Only one chick remained in the nest.

Roy looked up at the garage roof where the little bird had landed. It didn't look back to the nest. Instead, it faced down the drive, flapped once more, and then it was gone, a new life cycle beginning.

Roy looked at his young daughter and smiled. She had waited for this moment, and he was glad that he'd been able to share it with her. Barb was still looking at the nest, and Roy followed her gaze. There were only two birds left. The two adults. The male, his orange and black eyes gazing blankly out of the nest and down the lawn, and his smaller brown mate, hopping up and down, side to side.

'They both left,' Barb said. Roy smiled at her. The second chick must have fledged when the first was on the garage. Barb's voice was quiet, and Roy sensed a hint of sadness in it. He put his arm around her. 'Will they come back?' Barb asked. Roy shook his head, looking back at the nest.

'Probably not,' he told her. They continued sitting together as the air grew cold. The two remaining birds moved closer to each other, and then one flew away. The last brood of the season.

Enid stood up in the middle of the lounge, full of suppressed rage. The A to Z scrunched under her toes. She looked at her ex-husband slumped on the sofa. He was smaller than she remembered.

'Barb is not your daughter,' she spat, quietly and clearly. Beside her, on the TV screen, the parrot leaned in closer to the presenter's head.

'Join us at Birdland, for hundreds of spectacular displays,' the man said. The parrot pecked his ear.

'Barb is kind and caring,' Enid whispered. 'She notices people around her. She notices animals. She cares about them. She feels love, has empathy. She could never be your daughter.' She stepped forward, towards Donald, looming over him. 'And I could *never* be your wife.'

The man on the television looked back at the parrot.

'Did you try for a baby again?' Enid asked, coldly. Donald didn't reply. His eyes were weathered, unfocused and...was that fear? 'You did,' she said, seeing the answer written in his face. 'And nothing, I suppose. Did you blame her for that too? Like you blamed me for all those years.' A sadness washed over her, and the spite and anger left her voice. 'I'm glad she's left you, Donald,' she told him. 'She deserves better.'

Neither of them spoke.

'...and the finest exotic birds in the world.' The parrot on the television extended her neck, put her head to one side and picked at the presenter's hair with her beak. 'Like this fine beauty here.' The presenter leaned away from the bird.

Enid remembered the night that Donald had come home drunk, smelling as he did now. She had cowered from him then, scared of what he might do. She had been desperate for his affection.

'Barb doesn't know you,' Enid said, eyeing the parrot on the screen. For a second she saw flashes of red, blue and yellow, a macaw spreading its wings, shaking its head, and smashing through Enid's own lounge window. Enid paused, gathering herself. She wasn't going to miss this chance. She'd waited an hour for this sodding advert.

'Stay there,' she said quietly, raising one finger to Donald. She knelt on the floor and picked the pencil up from the carpet. She looked away from Donald, holding her hand up to him once again. She turned the pages of the A to Z and found the inside front cover. Plain white card. Then she looked up at the television.

The screen filled with a logo, followed by the directions needed to visit Birdland. Enid squinted her eyes, and then looked back to the blank page.

'Junction 14,' she said, as she wrote it. When she looked up, Donald was stumbling to his feet, holding on to the sofa arm for balance. Slowly, drunkenly, he stumbled towards the hallway, banging his shoulder on the door frame as he left.

Enid just watched and shook her head.

Roy slid open the patio door. He felt Barb dart past as she ran straight through the dining room and into the lounge to see Enid.

'Mum,' he heard his daughter shout excitedly as he followed her into the house. 'The chicks have done fledging, they've done their fledging, Mum.'

'They've fledged,' Enid corrected her. 'They've fledged the nest.'

'Yes, but Mum,' Barb continued, 'you're not listening; they did it. They've gone.'

'Oh Barb,' Enid smiled. 'I'm so glad you saw it.' She was holding one of the sofa's cushion covers in her hand, and Roy nodded questioningly towards it. Enid tilted her head at him. 'When was the last time we properly cleaned the sofa?' she asked.

She was good, was Enid; she thought about the things Roy never would.

'It really was something,' Roy told his wife. 'Those chicks. Such strength in something so fragile, and just like that, they've gone.'

'Just like that,' Barb repeated sadly, 'they've gone.' She looked close to tears. Roy knelt close to her and went to say something, but Enid interrupted.

'It's OK, Barb,' she said, breaking into a wide smile, 'because me, you, and your dad can see more birds – when we go to Birdland!' Barb's face instantly lit up, Roy saw her eyes fill with excitement before she started to dance around the living room. He frowned at his wife above their dancing daughter. They couldn't go to Birdland – not now, not with Donald outside their house, watching them every day. Enid pulled him close and kissed him.

'It's fine,' she told him. 'Honestly, it's fine,' and with these simple words, Roy knew that it was.

51

Enid lay motionless on the hospital bed with her eyes closed. She wasn't sure if she could move; she hadn't tried, and she didn't want to.

'She's been showing all the right signs,' a voice said. It sounded distant, soft, but also authoritative. Someone assured. Enid couldn't guess how old they were. In fact, she couldn't recall any numbers at all. 'We'll keep her in obs,' the voice continued, 'but it is just a case of waiting now.'

There was a pause and Enid felt someone holding onto her forearm. Not Roy. She knew the feel of his fingers.

She tried to open her eyes, to see who it was, and where she was. She didn't know what she was expecting to see, couldn't remember falling asleep. She couldn't remember where she lived in fact, but she could remember who she lived with. The same man she'd lived with for most of her life. Her Roy.

But her eyes didn't open. They didn't even twitch. The voice spoke again, this time much louder. It took Enid by surprise, but still, she didn't move.

'It's nice to meet you, finally.' It was almost a shout. 'A pleasure,' and then, louder again. 'A pleasure.' Although the words were loud, they weren't unfriendly.

Enid heard a distant low grunt.

'I'll be back soon,' the voice said, quiet again.

'Thank you so much,' another voice said. Enid knew this voice. It was her daughter's. Always busy. Barb had such a fast-paced life, but there was a subdued sadness that Enid couldn't quite put her finger on. It was Barb alright, but as a child, needing her mum.

Enid wanted to say her daughter's name, to offer comfort for whatever was wrong. She wanted to ask for Roy, but her mouth didn't move.

'Thank you,' a third voice said. Enid began to lose track of the noises, of the voices surrounding her, and then they all stopped, and she was engulfed in the silence.

Enid saw nothing but darkness, heard nothing but a ringing in one of her ears. She felt empty. She felt the loneliness down to her bones.

Slowly, other noises came into focus again. A few shuffles. Clatter from a different room. Pages turning somewhere. Enid's face felt numb, and her arms and feet began to sting. She felt sure that she was positioned flat on her back with her arms by her sides, arranged like a corpse. It was not comfortable.

Enid's mind screamed. She screamed for help. Then she screamed for Roy.

Her lips moved. She had heard her own voice, she had felt it – just a whimper. Another hand, this time on her leg. It was heavy and clumsy, painful on her skin, but her heart jumped; that was Roy's hand.

'Lover,' a new voice, low and more stifled than she'd expected – more air – but it was Roy. The accent, the flow, the familiarity of those two syllables. Enid made another noise; just air escaping her lips, and she opened both eyes.

'Mum?'

'Enid?'

Enid tried to reply. Her mouth was moving better now, but the words weren't forming. She managed a loud groan, then breathed deeply, trying to suck in saliva that wasn't there. Her mouth was so dry.

'Don't worry, Mum, you're alright.'

'Look who it is,' another woman said. Enid's eyes scanned the room, face tense, her body motionless: a bed, a screen with a continuously moving line across it, an unrecognisable woman, Barb, some children. On the windowsill Enid saw a macaw, a bright beacon against the grey sky outside. She heard a loud caw, and then a scream which quickly soothed to a calm clucking. Enid watched the bird soar through the glass and away, up into the sky. Finally, right at the bottom of her bed, Enid saw Roy.

PART FOUR

TWIGS AND WEEDS II

52

Roy's wheelchair was lowered out of the back of the minibus, and he found himself perched on a steep hill overlooking the sea. He hadn't been expecting to go anywhere today, and he couldn't remember anyone telling him that he would, but he was appreciative of the trip anyway. It was good to feel the sun on his skin, the glare of summer on his face. He wondered if he'd ever been taken anywhere else since he'd moved into the home, but there was nothing that he could recall.

He'd been taken somewhere picturesque – there was no doubt about that. The line of trees that stretched along the road, just before the sea's horizon, felt familiar. There was something second nature to the shape of the landscape and Roy knew that were he able to see far enough, there would be a pier jetting out into the sea, hiding his own life's memories in its cracks.

Barb leant in front of his view and started to say something, but Roy couldn't decipher what.

'Mmm? Yes yes, very good,' he replied, pretty sure that the response had been appropriate. Barb stood again and Roy felt a jolt as someone released the brakes on his wheelchair. Another jolt, as someone grabbed the wheelchair handles and then, slowly, Roy was turned away from the sea to face uphill.

An old Victorian building loomed above, and Roy found his eyes instinctively drawn to the lower right side of it. His eyes wouldn't allow him to make out any details past the bush partially obscuring the building, but he knew that if they would, he would see a window, and occasionally, just occasionally, he might even be able to make out the wispy grey curls of his wife.

The door in front of him opened, and a short, dark-haired woman walked out, leading a young boy by the hand. With her other arm, she was cradling a fresh-faced toddler against her chest. Blonde curls bounced across the toddler's pale features as the woman walked. Then, on seeing him and Barb, the woman stopped. Roy didn't know her, but she seemed to know him, or maybe Barb.

'Enid said it was today,' she shouted, and although Roy thought he'd heard, he found himself suspicious. He often misheard things these days.

'Yes, yes, very good,' he replied.

'I didn't want to assume,' the woman said as she lifted her head up to look at Barb, behind him. Then, as she and Barb engaged in conversation, Roy found himself lost in his own thoughts. She couldn't have said Enid. He had just been picturing his wife in the window, he must have misheard, a mere daydream seeping into reality.

The woman turned around and Roy saw that the door had opened again. There was a man in a knitted jumper and dark tinted glasses walking out. He was holding onto someone else, steadying them by their arm. A thin, frail body stepped slowly out of the door, looking down, watching her step.

And then she looked up. It was Enid.

53

'PHONE FOR YOU, ENID.' Olivia listened to Kara pass Enid the phone. It was always hard to know when to speak next. Enid gave no clue as to when she was holding the phone to her ear, as if she suspected a cold caller to be on the other end.

'Hello, Enid?' There was no response. Olivia could hear Enid stuttering something, to Kara presumably, but not into the phone. 'Enid?'

'Uh…um…' There was a long silence. 'Uh…hello?'

'Hi, Enid, it's Olivia. How are you?' She spoke slowly. Another silence.

'Oh…um…good. Yes…good. Thank you. And um. How are…uh...uh…oh. Oh, you know.'

'I'm good, thank you, Enid. It's lovely to hear your voice.'

Enid laughed. 'Silly,' she said. Olivia smiled, though she knew Enid couldn't see. It was silly, but it was true.

'And how's Roy?'

'Oh,' Enid said. Olivia could picture Enid now, scrunching her face and lifting her shoulders happily. 'He's lovely. Just so… oh…you know. So…' and then Enid sighed.

'I know,' Olivia said. 'Is he with you now?' There was a long silence before Enid answered.

'Um…oh.' She didn't know what she'd been asked. 'Well anyway,' she said, as if she were about to hang up.

'Is Roy with you now?' Olivia asked again. She heard Enid fumble for the right words.

'Now?' Enid asked. 'Roy? Um…yes.'

'Good.'

'Silly question,' Enid laughed, as though Olivia had been testing her. 'He's always here,' she said, as though he always had been.

54

Olivia stood outside the building, waiting with everyone else for the car to arrive. She wore a black dress and tights, black boots, her big dark green coat with the fluffy hood, black gloves and a black bobble hat. Her face was pale from the cold, and she could feel the air on her legs through her tights. The square building behind her looked bleak; glass doors, large windows, wooden beams across the front.

On the road nearby, a group of seagulls took turns to break from the pack, unsuccessfully searching for crumbs near the doors. Beyond them, the long road led down the hill to some large black iron gates. Olivia watched the gates, if just for a point of focus.

It felt strange not to have Dillon or Oona with her. The three of them were staying at an old friend's house down in Devon. Normally, when they weren't at their new school or nursery,

Dillon and Oona would be with Olivia, either in the house or at the nearby park. She'd made progress over the past seven months and was beginning to trust her own judgement again. She hadn't told anyone other than the friend-cum-housemate that she would be away, and she certainly trusted her – owed her even – but still, Olivia found herself looking at her phone repeatedly; it would be nice to have an update.

She looked around the patio. It wasn't crowded. One of the seagulls was edging closer to the paving below her feet. It bobbed its head, and then edged away again. A few people stood in a small circle talking. Someone laughed quietly, but the general mood was appropriately solemn.

Olivia had spoken to Barb briefly, and said hello to Alex, Enid's granddaughter. Barb was looking good in suit jacket and trousers, with a grey shirt. Since Olivia had moved, she and Barb had spoken a few times on the phone, mostly about the funeral. Barb knew that Olivia had kept in touch with Enid, and she'd seemed grateful to her for that. In a bid to convince Olivia to come that day, Barb had said that she could use some support since Calvin, her ex-husband, wouldn't be there. However, now that the day had arrived, Olivia didn't feel comfortable taking up Barb's time. It was her mother's funeral. Barb should be with her family.

She felt self-conscious standing alone – a little scared even. Seven months since their separation and David was still awaiting trial, still working, still living in the house that the four of them had once shared. He had no reason to turn up today, she realised, other than to see if she would be there, but she wouldn't put that past him. He didn't know where she lived now, and he hadn't seen his children since the week after his arrest, when he'd shown himself up again, this time in front of the children's social worker.

Olivia had considered wearing a dark veil, something to hide behind, but she'd decided against it. She'd thought of Enid and of Donald, and what Enid must have gone through in the separation, in the marriage even: that scar. She'd thought of the strength that Enid had shown, in her later years, searching for her Roy, and she'd thought of everything that Enid had done for her, in simply reaching out, noticing her. No, Olivia didn't want to wear a veil. She was being strong – for Enid.

'Hi,' the man beside her said, his expression flat, unhappy but friendly. 'I don't think we've met. I'm Neil.' Olivia smiled at him in the subdued way that is expected at funerals. 'How did you know…' He didn't finish the question, and instead gestured at the building.

'I…' Olivia started, and then thought for a second, 'I'm a friend.' Neil nodded. 'You?'

'Neighbour,' Neil said. 'Lovely neighbours, they were,' he continued, 'I do miss them.'

Olivia smiled, tight-lipped and apologetic. 'I'm sorry,' she said.

'The new lot are nice though,' Neil said. 'Nice couple; young daughter.'

They both stood for a few seconds. Neil looked at his shoes, so Olivia looked back down the road, at the gate. She heard him kick the ground, shocking a venturing seagull back onto the road.

A long, black car drove slowly around the corner and through the gates. Olivia could see the top of the coffin in the back. As the door of the funeral home opened, the seagulls took to the sky in unison. A few settled on the ground again, presumably having seen crumbs from the air, but as the hearse drove closer, they all flew behind the building towards the beach.

'If people can take their seats now,' a man's voice came from the doorway behind Olivia.

As she turned, she caught sight of the last of the birds disappearing behind the building. She held onto her clutch bag and began to well up. She looked down to hide her face and scolded herself. Who was she to cry? She was surrounded by Enid's family, and by her close friends, but she would miss the phone calls with Enid, and the support that Enid had given her. There had been a time when Olivia had needed Enid.

She felt a hand on her shoulder.

'It's OK,' Barb whispered. 'I know, but it is OK.' Olivia sniffed and looked up. Barb was holding herself well – for Alex perhaps. When tears started rolling down Olivia's cheeks, she felt even more guilty. She thought about the last conversation she'd had with Enid, only two weeks before.

Barb squeezed Olivia's shoulder and hugged her. 'Come and sit with us,' she said, 'please.' Olivia nodded, and together they walked inside; Barb, Alex and Olivia.

Beside them, Kara pushed Roy.

'Tea, please,' Roy said, knowing the answer without hearing the question.

He watched as Duncan asked Evelyn the same. Evelyn nodded, more than she normally did. Then it was Betty's turn. Betty didn't reply, because Betty never did.

No.5 The Beach was quiet today, and as Duncan went to the counter Roy found himself lost in memories. He was aware that he was losing large portions of the day, and that he wouldn't remember what he'd had for breakfast even before the plate was taken away, but also, he knew that he did remember the important things. It had been in this café that he and Enid had shared their first date. He had told Enid's mother that she had raised a wonderful daughter in here, on that very day, and he'd been welcomed into the family. His life had changed that day.

It had also been in this café where he and Enid had shared their last date. Two cups of tea and a shared slice of Victoria Sponge. Roy remembered that too.

He remembered the important things.

Duncan returned to the table, saying something in his soft Scottish accent but Roy couldn't hear exactly what. He placed a cup of tea in front of Roy, and two coffees – one for Evelyn and the other for Betty.

'Thank you,' Roy nodded.

He looked out of the window at the pavement where a bag of crisps had been dropped. He tutted, looking at Evelyn for agreement. Evelyn sighed loudly, before clearing her throat. She didn't say anything.

When he looked back out, the crisp packet was being blown along by the wind, scraping the pavement each time it landed.

A young mum pushed a toddler past the café, along the seafront. In the car park, a woman wrapped in gloves, scarf and hat held onto her elderly father's elbow as she helped him slowly into the passenger side of her car, and a teenager rolled down the hill past the pier on a skateboard, hood up, headphones in.

Roy watched as a flock of seagulls descended from behind No.5 The Beach and onto the pavement in front of the window. Two birds took it in turns to peck at the remaining crisps, flicking the foil packet further into the sky with each peck. When the flurry was over, the packet floated back down. The rest of the gulls spread out across the road, searching for a stray crisp which they might have missed.

Over at the parking bay, the woman closed the passenger door gently. She walked around to the other side of the car, removing her gloves, her scarf and her hat. When she was in the driver's seat, she slammed the door and started the engine.

Once again, the birds flew away.

THE REAL NANNY ENID

In many ways, this book is a tribute to my Nanny Enid, my mum's mum, and my Grandad Les' wife. The real Nanny Enid spent the last two and a half years of her life living at Osborne House in Clevedon, a residential home specifically designed for the comfort of people with dementia. She did try to escape (regularly), but she didn't manage it. The real Nanny Enid seemed very happy at Osborne House and, over time, she comfortably referred to it as home. Nanny Enid moved to Osborne House about three months after Grandad Les moved into a different care home. Their needs were different, so they couldn't live together. There was something, while unavoidable, incredibly tragic about that.

I was thirty-two when Nanny Enid died and, unsurprisingly, I'd known her all my life. I'm glad that my now five-year-old son had the chance to meet her, and likewise, she, him.

I watched as my nan's dementia slowly took over; it made her scared, angry and confused. She sometimes attacked her carers and there were times when she clearly felt imprisoned, both in the care home and in hospital. Let's be fair to Nan here; in a very real way, she was.

The one thing I noticed throughout the last few years of her life, was that Nanny Enid never lost her identity. She found it hard to speak and would stutter and stammer her way through seemingly nonsensical sentences, but if you made a rude joke, she'd still fall over laughing. My Nanny Enid was funny, and terribly, terribly rude.

I was lucky enough to grow up with five grandparents – that's one more than most people in my generation; Nanny Enid, Grandad Les, Nanny Eve (who pops up in this book), Grandad Roy (but not the Roy in this book, just to make things confusing) and Grandad John. The real Nanny Enid did get divorced from my Grandad John, though (and I can't stress this enough) my Grandad John was nothing like Donald in this book. Nanny Enid then married my Grandad Les. The various illnesses that my grandparents eventually suffered from, including dementia, cancer, a heart-attack and general old age (Grandad Les lived to be over a hundred), never defined them as people. It saddened me to think that people who didn't know them might see them as being just another elderly person. No elderly person is just another elderly person.

I'd like to think that the Enid in this book isn't just the Nanny Enid I knew over the last few years of her life – the one with dementia – but also the one I knew for the other twenty-nine years of my life. I'd like to think that Enid comes across as the same Nanny Enid who threw her knickers at the TV when Tom Jones came on, and who made her own wine every year with her husband, both getting absolutely hammered on it afterwards. The same Nanny Enid who threw a Christmas party in the garden every summer because 'it's nice to have a reason to get the family together'. The family-oriented Nanny Enid who always had time for everyone and who was never afraid to express how much she loved us, every time we saw her. Every single time. Sometimes as a kid, being told how loved I was felt a tad too much, and it was a little embarrassing, but in retrospect, that was my failing.

To clarify, other than Enid and Evelyn, none of the characters in this book are based on anyone in my family. Barb is not based on my own mum, although I hope that Barb shows a similar strength. Nanny Enid didn't work at a printing press (though her second husband did). She was the secretary at the department of architecture at Bristol University. Evelyn, as I've already mentioned, is based on my Nanny Eve. I don't know why I decided to put Nanny Eve in the same care home as Nanny Enid, other than, perhaps, to give her some familiar company (they used to do crosswords together).

My mum took the real Nanny Enid to see Grandad Les regularly, and I know that Nanny Enid looked forward to those days. She'd talk about them every time I saw her. When they were together, they found it difficult to communicate, but they'd happily sit in each other's quiet company.

Nanny Enid died on 25 July 2018 and every year since, members of my family have taken it in turns to hold a summer Christmas dinner in her memory.

ACKNOWLEDGEMENTS

You write acknowledgements before a book comes out, and then when it does, you find a whole new bunch of people who support it. *Tiny Pieces of Enid* is my second novel, so first I'm going to thank everyone who helped make *We Are Animals* a success after it was published. Thanks to the independent bookshops for stocking *We Are Animals*, for championing it, and for being so welcoming and kind when I've popped in for a visit. Thanks to the book bloggers and readers who shared it, book box businesses for choosing it, book clubs for reading it, libraries for loaning it, my dad for leaving it on a cruise ship, and then whoever it was who picked it up afterwards, because books are for sharing. Thank you, Waterstones, for stocking an unknown debut from an independent publisher (that's cool, man, very cool). Thanks to all the authors, literary festivals, radio stations, magazines and newspapers which featured *We*

Are Animals. I'm sure I've missed a million people here, but to anyone who helped with *We Are Animals* after publication, thank you.

So, now to *Tiny Pieces of Enid*.

The dedication at the front of this book is to my mum and Nanny Enid. This book is full of my nan's life, and my mum's experiences of my nan's life, so thank you, Mum, for both allowing me to write the book, and for helping every step of the way.

My wife, Gemma, has read *Tiny Pieces of Enid* about five times. I'd like to say she did that because it's just *that* good, but it was the opposite, and then she helped, and now it's better. Thank you, Gemma, for that, but also for everything else you do. Thanks to my son, Indy, because, although he is yet to read anything I've written (or indeed, anything anyone has written), he does actively encourage me and get excited by the number of identical bookmarks we have in the house. He's even written his own book with stickers and felt tips, which is just, so cool. Thank you, Indy, for being the awesome son that you are.

A huge thank you to Jane Harris, my editor, without whom *Tiny Pieces of Enid* would quite literally have been a different story. I also want to thank everyone at Eye and Lightning Books, in particular Dan, Simon and Clio for your continuing support and belief, and to Nell Wood for creating one of the most beautiful covers I've ever seen.

I've had a lot of help writing *Tiny Pieces of Enid*. I'm lucky to have had so many friends read, make suggestions and tell me what was working and what wasn't. Gemma Tordoff (friend *and* wife – get in), Hannah and Harry Parkin, Mum, Dad, John Howell, Paula Ewins, Katie Ewins, Gaye Giles, Holly Pothecary and my auntie Helen were all early readers and offered both help and support. I'm also part of a Facebook group consisting of authors first published in the 2020 lockdown, which meant I was lucky enough to have a hive mind of writers sharing ideas and helping with certain chapters. Thanks guys, your help was invaluable.

This book took a lot of research, mainly around dementia, domestic abuse and the habits of various birds. My sister Katie helped by checking how true to dementia the writing was, Jenny Tabley helped me to understand the likely movements of the police, and Alice (Bookologist), helped with a million obscure facts about parrots.

Thanks to my dog, Luther, for resting his head on my lap while I was writing, and to Bert, my cat, for walking along the keyboard. If you've noticed any typos while reading, that was him.

Finally, I'm sure I've missed people in this, but a general thank you to all my friends and family for being the fantastic people you are.

If you have enjoyed *Tiny Pieces of Enid*, do please help us spread the word – by putting a review online; by posting something on social media; or in the old-fashioned way by simply telling your friends or family about it.

Book publishing is a very competitive business these days, in a saturated market, and small independent publishers such as ourselves are often crowded out by the big houses. Support from readers like you can make all the difference to a book's success.

Many thanks.

Dan Hiscocks
Publisher
Eye Books

By the same author

We Are Animals

A cow looks out to sea, dreaming of a life that involves grass.

Jan is also looking out to sea. He's in Goa, dreaming of the thief who stole his heart (and his passport) forty-six years ago. Back then, fate kept bringing them together, but lately it seems to have given up.

Jan has not. In his long search he has travelled the world, tangling with murderers and pick-pockets and accidentally holding a whole Russian town at imaginary gunpoint. Now he thinks if he just waits and does nothing, fate may find it easier to reunite them – if only he can shake off an annoying teenager who won't go away. But then, perhaps an annoying teenager is exactly what Jan needs to help him find his old flame?

Featuring a menagerie of creatures, each with its own story to tell, *We Are Animals* is a comic Homeric odyssey with shades of Jonas Jonasson's Hundred-Year-Old Man. A quirky, heart-warming tale of lost love, unlikely friendships and the mysteries of fate, it moves and delights in equal measure.

Ewins' adventurous tale elegantly combines elements of romance, thriller and comedy while exploring long-lost loves and moving friendships
Woman's Own

A humorous read, packed with colourful characters and imagery
Buzz Magazine

A heartwarming tale of lost love and unlikely friendships, featuring a menagerie of animals who each have their story to tell
Waitrose Weekend

A feel-good story about how sometimes the best thing to do is just have faith that everything will work out in the end.
Popsugar

If you are seeking support for dealing with dementia, visit alzheimers.org.uk or dementiauk.org.

The following organisations offer support for those suffering from domestic abuse:

womensaid.org.uk (women)
refuge.org.uk (women)
mensadviceline.org.uk (men)
galop.org.uk (LGBT)